When the street was again safe, Mom and I moved forward. Her mood restored itself, and she was once again humming while I struggled with the two bags of Chinese food. I think we were about a block away from home when Mom suddenly stopped. I had to walk another ten feet forward before I realized that I'd just left her behind, and my wrists throbbed. Irritated, I stopped and turned.

"Mom? What's up?" I said.

Mom didn't answer right away. She just stood there, quiet, as if she were listening for something that only she could hear. She looked up, sweeping her gaze along the top of the grungy apartment building across the street from where we stood. I stared at it, frowning. I didn't see anything unusual there. It was typical lower-middle-class housing, with decaying bricks and some broken windows, the lights all yellow and murky. Nothing looked suspicious on rooftops anywhere, either.

"Mom!" I called. "Come on, these things are heavy! And I'm starving!"

She didn't seem to hear me still, but after several more seconds of standing, listening, and searching, she finally sighed and walked toward me.

"I'm sorry, honey," she replied, taking one of the bags from my hold and gently guiding me back home with a strangely firm hold around my free arm.

"What's wrong? Did you hear something?" I asked.

"Hmm? Oh, no. It was nothing. I thought I saw something move up there, but it was just my imagination." She ended that with a small laugh that sounded a little tight and forced, but I didn't push things. We just fell silent for the rest of the way, and once we crossed the threshold, I suddenly realized that I was panting and a little sweaty.

GLBT YA Books from Prizm

Banshee by Hayden Thorne
Changing Jamie by Dakota Chase
City/Country by Nicky Gray
Comfort Me by Louis Flint Ceci
Curse of Arachnaman by Hayden Thorne
A Field Guide to Assassins of Muromachi Street
by Tamara Sheehan
Heart Sense by KL Richardsson
Heart Song by KL Richardsson
I Kiss Girls by Gina Harris
Icarus in Flight by Hayden Thorne
Josef Jaeger by Jere' M. Fishback
Masks: Evolution by Hayden Thorne
Masks: Ordinary Champions by Hayden Thorne
Masks: Rise of Heroes by Hayden Thorne
The Mediocre Assassin's Handbook by Tamara Sheehan
The Next Competitor by K. P. Kincaid
Repeating History: The Eye of Ra by Dakota Chase
Staged Life by Lija O'Brien
The Suicide Year by Lena Prodan
The Tenth Man by Tamara Sheehan
The Twilight Gods by Hayden Thorne
The Water Seekers by Michelle Rode
Without Sin by J. Tomas
The World's a Stage by Gail Sterling

Curse of Arachnaman
Hayden Thorne

Illustrations by Pluto

Prizm Books
a subsidiary of Torquere Press, Inc.

Curse of Arachnaman

Curse of Arachnaman
PRIZM
An imprint of Torquere Press, Inc.
PO Box 2545
Round Rock, TX 78680
Copyright 2010 © by Hayden Thorne
Cover illustration by Pluto
Published with permission
ISBN: 978-1-61040-005-3
www.prizmbooks.com
www.torquerepress.com

www.prizmbooks.com

Dedication:

For John and Brent, a couple of seriously righteous
dudes

Curse of Arachnaman
Hayden Thorne

Illustrations by Pluto

Curse of Arachnaman

Chapter 1

I got you now, you vile fiend! Take that!" came the enraged shout. The voice, clear and young and vibrant, echoed through the dingy tunnels. A series of little popping sounds followed, like balloons exploding. Actually, they *were* balloons popping.

"Vile fiend?"

"I know. I amaze myself sometimes. Oh, oops. Sorry. My bad."

"That helium monster was mine!"

"Sorry. I got carried away."

I sighed and shifted my weight because both of my arms had fallen asleep. It was uncomfortable as hell, lying on that cold floor, tied up and stretched out over old rail tracks. Or, rather, broken concrete bearing marks where old rail tracks used to be. At least the surface wasn't too bad against my body.

What was worse was that my glasses kept inching down my nose because of the fact that, hello, I was lying on my side, completely helpless. The old subway tunnels were cold, with chilly blasts coming in through cracks and wherever else they managed to squeeze through. What sucked even more was that every once in a while, I'd get a whiff of something like Eau de Sewer, which made my stomach turn. I hoped that one of the superheroes would get to me soon before I threw up. That would be a real mess, seeing as how I was also gagged and couldn't manage anything more than a whimpering little "mmphrgh" every ten seconds. Oh, yeah, did I mention that I was also tied up? Like, both hands bound behind my back and both feet practically fused at the ankles?

Did I also mention that I had only about three minutes left before the train would come around to run me over because, well, trains always threaten innocent kidnap victims of big, bad supervillains? I said "three minutes" because that was what the battered old alarm clock pretty much showed me the last time I looked at it as it stood a couple of feet away from my head.

Charming.

Another series of popping sounds broke through the hollow calm of the tunnels.

"Aha! I got you now, you—"

"Stop. You already said that."

"Help me out here. I'm running out of virtuous things to say."

"Just yell and sound really pissed off. That's enough."

"Magnifiman always has the cool lines. I think we should come up with our own."

I strained my eyes to catch the time. Did it say

two minutes now? Jeebus. What a craptastic time for my glasses to shift and force me to use my one-step-up-from-blindness eyesight to check how much in danger I really was.

"Mmphrgh! Mmphrghghhhh!" I squirmed in my bonds and tried to make as much noise as possible—as much noise as one could manage, anyway, with nothing but clothing against concrete to go by. If I'd had a titanium skull, I'd have started whacking my head against the ground to gain someone's attention, but I wasn't that lucky in my gene pool, so...

"Ha! Take that! And that! And that! Want more? Do you? Fine! Eat this! And this! And this!"

"Mine!"

"Mine! Ha!"

"Whoa, did you just try to singe my boobs?"

"Sorry, Freddie. You were in the way. Mine!"

It sounded like a Chinese New Year parade somewhere in the subway tunnels. All I could hear was a really fast succession of pops, sort of like firecrackers. The superheroes were mad as hell. They finally kicked up their game. It was about damn time, too.

"Where is he? Do you see him?" The voices were much louder now. I could even hear distinct movement, but I still couldn't figure out where because the acoustics were pretty weird down there. If anything, they sounded a little creepy, being disembodied voices that seemed to come from everywhere and nowhere.

"No. Maybe he's in here."

"How much time do we have?"

I glanced at the clock. By that time, my glasses had completely fallen off my face and lain there, one temple crushed under the weight of my head. Great. I was dead.

Brrrrriiiinnnngggggggg! The clock rattled from the force of its alarm. It was one of those cartoon clocks with the dorky happy face that jumped and danced around as it rang, and you squealed and threw soggy cereal at the TV while soaking your diapers. Yeah, like that. It was also so old and sad that I actually pinched my eyes shut and shrank away from it because I figured that it was *this* close to exploding from all that force.

"There! He's there!"

"Damn! We're too late!"

I rolled my eyes. The clock continued to ring, and it was driving me nuts. I squirmed to see if I could use my nose to nudge my glasses back on, but all I could manage to do was to dislodge them some more so that they lay tilted, with the free temple raised, and my right eye barely peeking through what bit of prescription lens it could get nearest to. I felt like a total loser dork.

Within seconds, one of the tunnels at the other side of the old platform came alive with three superheroes. There was first a series of loud pops that seemed to follow the tunnel's length because the noise grew louder. I flinched when the tunnel's mouth vomited torn rubber as the last collections of balloons exploded in the heroes' wake. In flew Miss Pyro, Calais, and Spirit Wire, bits of balloon carcasses floating and swirling around them like colorful rubber confetti. They spotted me lying helpless on the railway tracks. Then again, only a blind man would've missed me. A blind man who was also deaf, that is.

"Who's gonna save him?" Spirit Wire asked.

"Pfft. Why even ask?" Miss Pyro snorted. She gave Calais a nudge. I think. It was a little hard trying to catch details with eyesight that had long since gone to hell. "Go on, boyfriend."

Calais took all of a fraction of a second—I've yet to learn how to gauge his speed—to appear beside me, taking the alarm clock and shutting it down. Then he worked on my bonds, leaving my gag for last because he wanted to sneak in a kiss. Which he did. Too bad I was too annoyed and cramped to respond, so I just made like a limp doll that made a face at him while he got all Romeo on me.

"Hey, is this what they call the gay agenda?" Spirit Wire called. "Gay boys indoctrinating two innocent, über-straight girls with dirty same-sex kissing?"

"What, are you feeling a little gay yet? No? Okay, let me kiss him some more and see what happens," Calais yelled back. I thought I heard Miss Pyro snort and giggle.

When Calais pulled away, I fumbled for my glasses and put them back on. "I'd have been dead by the time you got to me, you know." I grunted as I pushed myself up to a sitting position. "You guys are thirty seconds late or something. You wouldn't have seen anything left of me by the time you got here. Blood and guts and severed body parts all over? That'd be me." Story of my life, really.

"Sorry," Calais said, grimacing as he sat back on his heels and rubbed the back of his neck. "We kind of got tangled up in balloons back there. I mean, literally. The Sentries doubled the obstacle course, and they actually made helium monsters that were a real bitch to destroy."

"Really? From what I heard, you were all going back and forth over cool, superhero things to say when you beat the crap out of a thug. Whatever happened to just blowing them away first and then impressing them with kickass sayings afterward? You know, like, destroy first, ask questions later?"

He jerked his head in the girls' direction. "Talk to them about it. I've always been cool with just a shout or a scream."

"Sorry, Eric," Spirit Wire said, waving at me and flashing me a sheepish little grin. "I guess I got carried away."

"No kidding," I grumbled, taking Calais' hand as he stood up and helped me to my feet. "Where's Freddie?"

All three superheroes fell silent for a moment and exchanged looks. Did they just misplace one of their own? I blinked. "You *lost* him? What happened? Did he turn himself into a brick wall or something? I hope he didn't transform into a helium monster that you just shot at back there, or you'd have a lot of explaining to do to the Sentries." Besides, he was still working on turning himself into Joshua Bell because he found out about my fanboy infatuation with the man, and I'd be damned if I were to let the other heroes accidentally kill off Freddie without him getting around to achieving that first.

Miss Pyro spun around and looked back in the direction of the tunnel through which they'd just come, resting her hands on her hips as she stared. "Hey, Freddie? Is that you?" she called out.

"Yeah, it's me. Hold on. I'm coming," Freddie yelled back, his voice echoing. Actually, it wasn't his real voice, but we all knew that it was him. He was in disguise, so he really sounded like, well, whatever his disguise happened to be. From where I stood, I guessed that he'd turned himself into a woman. I wasn't exactly sure why he'd choose to be a woman in the face of extreme violence and bloody murder, but I guessed that he must've decided to be a warrior princess or queen or something. A really butt-kicking female, that is.

Soon we heard footsteps, which grew louder and louder. Then Freddie appeared from the shadows in full disguise.

"Sorry, man, I panicked and shifted to the wrong mask and, uh, I kinda got stuck. Don't worry, I'm working my way out of it," he said with a sheepish little chuckle as he stood before us all as Elvira, Mistress of the Dark.

We all gaped at him. Spirit Wire was the first one to find her voice. "Dude. How do you expect to fight an army of killing machines as Elvira? Scratch their eyes out with your nails?" She paused. "Hey, are those press-ons? They look pretty cool."

Elvira-Freddie cleared her throat. Better to stick to the gender of the disguise and avoid letting the confusion mess me up any more than it already had. "I was practicing speed-masking. You know, switching disguises pretty fast? I've been getting better at it, but I think I switched too fast, too many times. I was doing pretty good as Lara Croft, but Miss Pyro tried to burn my boobs, so I tried to change fast to something else, and..." She shrugged and pointed at herself. "I guess if we were still fighting helium monsters out there, the chances of my boobs getting roasted by fireballs would've been higher with this disguise." She glanced down to stare at her chest.

"You short-circuited? Sort of like a computer freezing up when you open and close too many browser windows or something?" I asked. Calais turned to me.

"How old is your computer?" he asked. He looked genuinely surprised behind his half-mask. I narrowed my eyes at him.

"Not everyone can afford state-of-the-art technology, you know. Okay, the point is that you guys let me die, hypothetically and all that," I said, turning back to them. "I heard you getting all worked up over catchphrases and all those things, while I lay there, all tied up and drooling behind my gag, breathing in sewer air and praying like hell that no mutant rats came out of their hidey-holes to eat me alive."

"We were slowed down," Calais admitted, glancing at the others. "We really need to work more on speed and efficiency when it comes to search and rescue missions."

I raised my hand. "Question—can I be paid for my services as fake innocent victim? It's not that easy getting all tied up and left on dirty concrete, waiting for superheroes to come around and pretend like they're rescuing me."

"Oh, think of it as your contribution to the greater good of Vintage City, Eric," Miss Pyro chirped, flashing me a perky smile. "You know that we still need to work on our skills even after we advance in our powers."

"Yeah, but...." I sighed and turned to stare helplessly at Calais, who gave me *that look*. I really can't describe it beyond "smoldering." It was this hot, sexy stare that you can only achieve when wearing a superhero's half-mask. God*damn,* I wanted to do him right then and there. "Never mind. Feel free to tie me up and abuse me whenever you need to."

"Cool. Thanks, Eric. You're a real sport."

I looked back at Miss Pyro. "Real sport, my ass. I was talking to Calais about getting tied up and abused. As for being everyone's practice victim, I demand a written contract with all kinds of clauses that make sure I'm taken care of. I mean, can I at least have some kind of cushion to lie down on? And why do I have to be tied up and gagged every time?"

"Because I enjoy doing it," Calais murmured, his smile kooky and lopsided. Oh, *baby*.

My face warmed up. "Dayum. Dress the guy in super-tight spandex, and he morphs from sweet geek to animalistic sex machine. Okay, you're forgiven."

Spirit Wire clucked. "Man, you're sure bitchy for an innocent victim."

Everyone fell silent when a deep, familiar, very masculine voice spoke from out of the blue. "All right, everyone. That was pretty bad. You're letting yourselves get distracted by trivial things and the fact that this is only a search-and-rescue practice mission. When we regroup tonight, we'll have to go over details with Dr. Dibbs before we head on out to the mean streets of Vintage," Magnifiman declared. His speech was fluid, his manner confident. He was simply Mr. Perfect, which I really didn't want to say in front of Calais because of the usual brotherly dynamics between them when in superhero mode. Heaven knew, Calais already put up with so much stuff about his older brother's intimidating list of virtues everywhere he turned.

"Does that mean that we have to get together an hour early?" Miss Pyro asked.

"Yes, Miss Pyro. It's necessary to clear things up before tackling our next mission. Are there any other questions?"

I cleared my throat. "Yeah," I replied, raising my voice. "Can I get paid for being the repeat victim in these practice runs? It's not easy, you know, getting tied up or stuffed inside something, while everyone figures out what catchphrases to use when destroying people."

I stared at the old speakers that were mounted against one of the half-crumbling walls. The Sentries had set up several of those things up and down the subway tunnels for these practice missions, and Magnifiman and Dr. Dibbs always used them to communicate their observations of everyone's performance. There were cameras set up, too, that monitored the heroes' progress, and I'm sure that behind the scenes, all kinds of fancy gizmos and gadgets were all at Magnifiman's disposal. I was never shown what went on behind the scenes, naturally, seeing as how it was all, you know, classified information and stuff like that.

For a few seconds, Magnifiman was quiet. "Okay, are there any other questions?" he asked.

I sighed, my shoulders drooping. "I'll have to take this up with my union," I said. Of course, I just needed to form one.

"Very well, then. We'll meet at the usual powwow time and place later. Oh, and Calais? Mom wants to know what you want for dinner, so be sure to give her a call ASAP. Magnifiman, over and out." Then the speakers went dead.

Mom. Magnifiman said "Mom." Well, wasn't that just the cutest thing *ever*? I glanced at Calais and grinned. He pointedly ignored me as he squared his shoulders back, lifting his chin, and pretty much did all he could to look extremely blasé and macho about it. Yeah, every once in a while, there'd be this little slip between the two brothers about family-related matters, which always embarrassed Calais. It was sort of like when you showed up at your kid's school with a big, pink bouffant because you'd had an accident with your hair color the night before. Calais' level of embarrassment tended to be somewhere in that part of the Teenage Humiliation Spectrum. So no matter what he did, putting on a show of manly indifference, the blush that always crept up from his neck onto his face always took the wind out of his sails. I guess it didn't help during that moment that everyone else was grinning at him.

"Okay, everyone, you heard the man," Spirit Wire said, finally. "Let's go and get ready for today's powwow." She paused when her stomach let out this gurgling, bubbling sound. "Well, not until after we grab a bite to eat. I'm starving."

"I haven't had pizza in a while," Freddie, who'd transformed into Oscar the Grouch, said. He glanced down at his green, stumpy, shag carpet-like furry body, clucking and shaking his head. "Oh, Christ..."

"I'm game," Miss Pyro chirped. "We can go to my favorite unpopular pizzeria. It's not too far from here. We can all walk there. I promise, it's not froufrou."

It was agreed, and so the little gang of superheroes changed back into their "normal" forms. Incidentally, it was always a good thing to be in the company of only one superhero during the transformation process because each of them had his or her own "poof-voila!" method, and when they all changed at the same time? It was like total brain meltdown. In fact, I'd call that my own personal psychedelic moment without the drugs.

I had to pinch my eyes shut while flailing and crying out because Miss Pyro exploded in a blinding burst of fire, Calais melted into a pillar of swirling, twisting haze, Spirit Wire literally flickered black and white, sort of like a TV screen going crazy, and Freddie—who continued to escape Bambi Bailey's notice, so he still didn't have a superhero alias; he was the lucky one, I guess—"melted" from one form to another. Weird, but his transformation had evolved, from what I saw. Before, when the Trill was still alive, he just vanished behind a burst of white light, but I guess that with his powers gathering strength and complexity, his transformation method also morphed along with his, well, powers of morphing.

So imagine being in the middle of all those transformations. If I first thought that being the sole victim for their heroic practice sessions entitled me to monetary compensation, getting all blinded and brain-damaged from Simultaneous Heroic Combustion pretty much secured my eligibility. I mean, seriously, how many other regular people out there had to be subjected to that, once, twice a week? Zero. I counted. *Zero.*

Within seconds the air cleared, and it was safe for me to open my eyes again. Sure enough, instead of four impressive and dangerous superheroes standing around me, there were four teenagers in urban gear all straightening their clothes and patting their hair and all that. Calais was Peter. Miss Pyro was Wade. Spirit Wire was Althea. Freddie was, uh, Freddie. They exchanged relieved grins, with Wade turning around and waving at us to follow her.

"Oh, you guys are gonna like the deep dish pizza," she said, adjusting her bag over her shoulder. "It's totally awesome."

Peter held my hand as we followed them out of the crumbling underground subway. As we walked through one tunnel after another, our voices echoing up and down the damaged area, I noticed the remains of balloons littering nearly entire platforms and train tracks. The Sentries were expected to come around later to clean up the place and then secure it from accidental visitors outside. These tunnels used to be the Trill's fake hideout. Now the heroes used them for practice, and the area was completely blocked from the rest of Vintage City.

See, in my world of unexpected superheroes and supervillains, we never had the benefit of high-tech headquarters, hideouts, and training whachamacallits that you always see in superhero comic books. Hell, no. We had to use what was there, namely, Vintage City's crumbling urban landscape. I guess we should've been grateful because being forced to make do pretty much taught everyone to be good in improvisation. I mean, seriously, helium monsters to whack at for practice rescue missions? Who'da thunk?

Anyway, the heroes had a small collection of "practice areas" all over. There were a couple of abandoned warehouses near the city's southern border that they'd taken over with the mayor's permission. There was this old, old, run-down apartment building that was *this* close to being condemned. Yeah, they got permission to use that, too. Of course, the kicker was that with me being their prized "victim," I'd be bound and gagged and left helpless in some choice spot somewhere in these hulking safety hazards. Half the time, I just wondered when the roof would cave in on me as I lay there, completely immobilized, while they all fought their way through all kinds of obstacle courses set up by the Sentries.

It's good to be appreciated, ain't it? By the way, my

family knew that I'd agreed to help with superhero practice missions. What they didn't know was in what capacity. I figured it was best to shut up about it for now before Mom and Dad freaked out and tossed me into a seminary.

Chapter 2

I guess the only consolation I got after these superhero practice missions was the fact that Peter
always took me home after a meal either together
or with the group. Sometimes he went in with me,
and we made pretty good use of what little time we
had left together by playing video games in the living
room and/or with me pulling him down for a tor-
rid makeout session on the couch. Yeah, we could've
moved on to my room, but that would mean running up to the attic, and, really, would anyone expect
horny toad teenage boys to delay gratification?

We'd been caught a couple of times already, after
the fact. It was a good thing that the front door was
locked and was also hard to open, so that we'd have
some warning when big sis, Liz, would fight with
her house keys and try to break the door down by
throwing her weight against it. Unfortunately, during
those two times, we'd gotten a little too tangled
up, so that we nearly broke furniture scrambling

to button up and make ourselves look decent. Of course, when Liz saw us as she made her way toward the kitchen, we were both disheveled, beet-red, shirt buttons poking out of the wrong buttonholes, and grinning stupidly at her.

"Uh-huh," she said.

"Hi Liz! You're home!" I replied, my voice louder than it probably should've been.

"Hey, how's it going?" she asked, her eyes narrowing and moving shiftily from me to Peter and back.

"It's going good. Even better. Is it? Yeah, I guess. Good. Really good. Totally better," I babbled, while Peter could only manage a raised hand in greeting and a weird phrase like, "Down the basement."

Liz rolled her eyes and trudged off, calling back as she vanished from view, "I want the results of pregnancy tests from both of you by the time I get out of the shower!"

That day, though, a pretty nasty surprise awaited me when he drove me home after pizza. I'd been praying like hell that no one would be home because I seriously needed to be physical with my boyfriend. That was what happened whenever said boyfriend teased me with a hand rubbing the inside of my thigh while gobbling down gigantic slices of mushroom pizza. Seriously, how much more Freudian could he get? So when we drove up to the sidewalk directly in front of my home, I nearly screamed inside the car.

"Oh, you've *got* to be kidding," I said, my jaw dropping, as I stared at a scuzzy-looking station wagon parked in front of us. It looked like a damn hearse, which was perfect for the guy who owned it. I wouldn't have been surprised if it used to be a hearse that was converted to make it look harmless and suburban in that Stepford Wives kind of way.

Peter stared at me, shocked. "What?"

"It's him. He's here."

He looked back at the car. "It's an old station wagon that looks kinda like a hearse in disguise. What's the big deal?"

I turned to him. "Can I move in with you for a while? Like, till after Liz breaks up with Scanlon...or maybe marries him and moves out?"

"Who's Scanlon?" Peter's gaze dropped to my hands, which had somehow developed a mind of their own and had attached themselves to his right arm. My fingers curled into his jacket sleeve, looking like pale, bony claws. I didn't even realize that I'd grabbed him.

"My sister's boyfriend. Sort of. He wants to be with her, anyway, and he's trying really hard, but he's, like, something from a midnight carnival, and he won't go away, no matter how much garlic I hang around the door." I stole an anxious glance at the front door. "Please? Can I hang out with you for a little while longer? Until he goes away?"

Peter looked lost as he continued to grip the wheel with both hands. I had a feeling that I'd planted seeds of panic in him. "Eric, you know I can't do that. The heroes have a powwow coming up, and I can't be late. Maybe you should enter the house from the back. How about the fire escape?"

Beads of sweat actually broke out on my forehead.

"I can't. The back door has its own lock, and I only have the key to the front door. The fire escape only goes so far down, and I can't jump it without making enough noise to catch Liz's attention. Besides, my bathroom window's shut and locked from the inside." Note to self: never, *ever* do that again.

"Eric, calm down. Eric?" Peter pulled my hands away and took my face in both of his, forcing me to stare at him. "You'll survive. Just go through that door, say hello, and run like hell up the stairs. Or pretend like you're sick and make all kinds of gross puking sounds."

"I'm going to die, Peter," I said, my voice finally cracking. "I'll never make it to the stairs. Scanlon's vibes are like a vacuum from hell. He took me out for ice cream one time—ice cream, fer chrissakes! He thinks I'm ten years old!"

Peter blinked and then frowned. "We take each other out to ice cream all the time."

"Not at the Krazy Klown's Kreamy Karnival, we don't. Have you ever had ice cream with a complimentary clown's nose devaluing your manhood, Peter? Or that red curly wig that they give out to customers on Fridays?" I shook my head, shuddering from the memories. "God, I swear, I'm going to throw myself under the nearest bus if Mr. Stepford Cthulhu subjects me to more humiliation like that."

"Then suggest someplace that's more grown-up."

I couldn't believe what I was hearing. "Peter, you obviously don't get it."

No amount of begging, bribing, or self-whoring

would sway him, though. I guess I'd have to take the issue up with Magnifiman and voice my grievance over Peter's indoctrination into virtuous living. I mean, seriously, folks...what the hell?

So before I knew it, I found myself alone, abandoned, and staring helplessly at the front door, my house key in hand. I told myself to do exactly what Peter suggested, so while turning the key, I mentally calculated how many seconds it would take for me to cover the length of the hallway from the front door to the bottom step of the stairs if I were to break out into a run at full cheetah speed. I guessed somewhere in the five-second range. Two, if I were to not just run, but leap like a freaked-out gazelle on steroids.

The front door didn't open properly. It *still* doesn't. It used to, but the top hinge somehow got messed up from moisture or rust or whatever, and the door itself tilted in its frame, so that pushing it open always required a little bit of brute strength. It also goes without saying that it didn't open quietly. In situations like this, that would be something close to a tragedy.

I opened the door and held my breath, wincing when it moved with that familiar "eerk!" sound. There was no sign of life anywhere up and down the hallway, but I could hear voices in the living room. Crap. I opened the door some more but took care to keep the gap at a minimum—just enough for me to squeeze myself through. I slipped inside and closed the door, pressing myself against it as I braced myself. I thought of using the door like some kind of trampoline by pushing against it and then set a high enough speed for my desperate run.

"Okay, ready, set...go!"

I pushed and threw myself forward, only to be yanked back with a cry because the crooked door had caught the end of my jacket when I shut it. I fell back against the door then landed on my ass with a loud *Whump!* Bright stars exploded behind my eyelids.

"Eric? Is that you?" Liz called out from the living room. "Hey, come on in! We've got a visitor! Guess who?"

Dracula, that was who. The undead. The damned.

I sat on the floor, my jacket anchored to the door, while I reached above me and fumbled for the doorknob in a panic, the stars slowly fading before me. I stared at the living room door, praying that no one would emerge. Unfortunately, when it rains, it fucking pours.

Scanlon appeared, greasy head poking out of the door. He saw me and smiled, his white picket fence, freckled face glowing, his perfect teeth sparkling as brightly as his Richie Cunningham-styled hair—or, rather, helmet. "Oh, there you are, you little scamp," he said, stepping into the hallway. "Need help?"

Ohmigawd, yeah, I did! Where was Van Helsing when I needed him? I shrank against the door as he neared, the sight of his too-familiar outfit—crisply-ironed, short-sleeved oxford shirt tucked into crisply-ironed slacks with pleats down the front that were so defined, they could slice your legs into ribbons if you weren't careful—filling my immediate world. I felt faint. When he stopped in front of me and started fiddling with the door while cheerfully engaging me in conversation, my vision began to fade.

"You silly little goose," he said, laughing, when I was finally free. "You should be more careful when you close the door behind you." He stopped laughing to inhale sharply between his teeth, as though he were trying to suck up all the excess drool that had collected there. He always did that. It was, like, "Ha-ha-ha-ha! Slurp!" Really gross.

And...silly little goose. Who called anyone "silly little goose" in this day and age? I mumbled my thanks as I crawled away, trying to place some floor between him and me before I spontaneously combusted. My vision slowly restored itself. Then I felt a hand take hold of one of my arms. "Here. Let me help you up."

He gave me a sharp tug, and I stumbled to my feet.

"You okay, champ?"

Champ. Who called anyone "champ" in this day and age?

"Yeah, thanks."

"Be careful when you close the door next time, okay?" he said, laughing. He even mussed up my hair. "You funny bunny."

OMFG. I just flailed and went, "Gak!" then staggered away, my senses completely overcome by the too-strong essence of 1950s wholesomeness that always oozed out of him. I think he said something else, but I was too disoriented to pick up on what it was. I just headed first to the kitchen to get something to drink, restore my strength, and then scrounge around for garlic bulbs that I could string together. Mom always bought those things in bulk, anyway, so using about a hundred of them at a time wouldn't be a problem. I poured myself some apple juice, gathered several bulbs, and, using my shirt to haul my treasure up to my room, I hurried upstairs. Behind me, in the living room, Scanlon said something, and Liz burst out laughing. Maybe they were talking about the silly little goose who just had his jacket caught in the door, the little scamp. Whatever. I had a house to protect, a soul to save (mine!), and a collection of garlic to string together. Maybe, on a Saturday, I should swing by our parish church between masses and see if I could steal some holy water from the fount. I owned a pretty good collection of old-fashioned bottles with cork stoppers, and I could use one of them for my purpose.

I stayed in my room for the rest of the afternoon and spent pretty much all that time surfing and playing retro games. I'm totally addicted to Asteroids, and I asked Dad once if he used to play the game, when Atari came out with it centuries ago.

He lowered the newspaper and peered out at me. "Son, I was too busy surviving on ramen noodles, a part-time minimum-wage job, and suffering through college for a degree that turned out to be a useless waste of time and money. Besides, your mother and I were dating. Even after we got married, we had to wait a while before starting a family. Living off ramen noodles didn't exactly end after college, you know. If anything, my daily nutrition expanded itself to ramen noodles and peanut butter and jelly sandwiches."

'Nuff said, Dad.

Remind me to skip over the 50s decade when I get older. I think people get all bitter in their 50s and then kick back and turn cool again in their 60s. I guess, after living on this crummy earth for forty years, they really can't help but look back at their lives and wonder what the hell went wrong, just as they get closer to retirement age.

After playing, I opened my inbox to find this message from Althea: *Hey, Eric. What do you think of bingo?* I sighed and sent my response: *I don't. Life's better that way. Aren't you supposed to be saving humanity from the scum of the earth right now? Quit messing around and do your job.*

Scanlon stayed for dinner, by the way. I guess spending all that time on the computer, lost in complete denial of his existence, didn't alter the course of reality. When Mom called for me to help out in the kitchen, I went all obedient son on her and hurried downstairs, only to be told that we had a guest for dinner, and that I was needed to make sure that we had enough food to serve.

In brief...

"Here you are," Mom said, marching over to the table, where her purse and a writing tablet sat. She read what was on the tablet and then scribbled something on it before tearing off the top sheet. She handed it to me and then rummaged through her purse for her wallet. "Make sure to tell Mrs. Zhang that Scanlon can't take very spicy food. Remember the time we served him Kung Pao chicken? The poor dear came down with the worst diarrhea, I heard. Just...nasty."

"Mom, I might have to call child protection services or something if you continue with that story," I spluttered, totally grossed out. Who in the world would want to subject young, impressionable minds to Scanlon's toilet experiences?

"Anything on that list that's spicy, make sure that she cooks a special batch for us without the red peppers and whatever else they use to, you know..."

"Cause people to blow fire out of both ends," I said glumly, staring at the list.

"That would be a less subtle way of putting things, but yes. Here's the money. And don't dawdle like you usually do." She narrowed her eyes at me as I pocketed the cash. "I know you tend to get pretty chatty with Mrs. Zhang, Eric, and while that's fine when we don't have guests over, it's completely unacceptable tonight. Okay?"

"Yeah, okay." I sighed as I shuffled out of the kitchen.

Unfortunately, on my way out, I had to pass by the living room, where Scanlon, Liz, and Dad hung around, watching TV.

"Hey, Tiger! Where you goin'?" Scanlon called out.

"To hell and back, judging from tonight's

schedule," I muttered, but I pretended like I didn't hear him. It helped that I was nearly running for the door that time, so I had an excuse for snubbing Mr. Happy Days.

As much as I'd have preferred to chill with Mrs. Zhang, I didn't really have any other choice but to follow Mom's orders, so I gave her the list and told her Mom's instructions for spicy stuff.

"What, your guest too wussy for my spices?" she snorted. I shrugged and looked sheepish. "Humph. You Westerners. Don't know *real* Chinese food if it bit you in your white asses." She marched off to the kitchen and barked out orders to her husband, who was also the chef.

The only comfort I had then was the little bowl of wonton soup she gave me, while I perched on one of the stools scattered inside her takeout place, waiting for my order to be cooked. She always gave me freebies like that when I had to wait for my order. She said those freebies were good for my weight problem. That is, they were supposed to add between twenty to fifty pounds after consumption.

Let me say that I was glad as hell that those hoped-for pounds never materialized after downing her soup.

Every so often people would come in, ogle her steam counter, and buy heaping containers of greasy but freshly cooked Chinese food. From where I sat, I also noted that pretty much everyone ordered the same stuff that my family tended to default to— beef with broccoli, chow mein, sweet and sour pork, and hot and sour soup. It was kind of a sad testament of how little we Westerners really knew or maybe wanted to know about Chinese cuisine. I made a mental note to write down a list of alternate dishes that Mrs. Zhang might want to serve. Or maybe "mistakenly" substitute for one of the more common and boring stuff. The upside would be a pleasant surprise for the customer, who might ask for more new things from her next time. Of course, the downside was the total mind-fuck factor, which would mean angry complaints and demands for refunds or a night-long odyssey in one's toilet.

When my order was finally put together, I marched outside and walked in the direction of police sirens. No surprise there, given the overall sleaze quotient of the general area. A break-in? Sure! A carjacking? Oh, yeah! A murder? Pfft—why not? Sometimes I wonder how the Disney studios would interpret my city and especially neighborhoods like these. I figured that they'd make my trip to and from Mrs. Zhang look like a really edgy Little Red Riding Hood. You know, with the studio artists all toked out or something.

I didn't have to walk too far. Beck Street, which was kind of known as a haven for the criminally whackjob-y types, was also a favorite police hangout. It was also a part of my route home, and I couldn't avoid it even if I wanted to. Two streets down from Mrs. Zhang's takeout joint, I trotted over to the corner and found myself huddling with a handful of homeless dudes. I thought they were just residents loitering in a street corner, but I was *so* wrong.

"What's going on?" I asked, pointedly ignoring

the strange looks my family's dinner was getting from my impromptu peeps. One started flapping a hand in front of his face, as though he were shooing off flies.

"Dunno," someone grunted, and I instantly smelled a really potent mix of alcohol, cigarettes, and rotting teeth that nearly knocked me out. The hunched lump standing beside me pointed a gnarled finger down Beck Street. Well, he looked like a lump because he was, you know, hunched, and he wore ten layers of filthy coats. "Looks like a mugging or somethin'. Probably a rob'ry. Or a thief."

I inched away from them when I realized that their attention had completely shifted from someone else's crime spree to one that was possibly theirs. Yeah, like another mugging. This time, with non-spicy Chinese food for their target. I tried to look calm and a little more grim because I figured that I'd give off pretty intimidating vibes that way.

By the way, I also suck as a judge of my own vibe-giving. Instead of changing their minds about me, they inched their way closer, their eyes—those that I could see in the semi-lit area—fixed on the bag I carried, so that we kind of looked like we were practicing some weird group dance move in the shadows of a side street.

"Yeah, cool. Better get back there, you guys, or you'll get in the way of the cops. Know what I mean?" I said, raising my voice a little in case that helped make me look tough.

"'Ey, kid," someone barked. I thought I saw a large hand appearing from the mass of dirty bodies that was slowly bearing down on me.

"Hey, watch out!" someone yelled.

They all threw themselves down on the ground in a chorus of half-drunken grunts, while I just turned tail and ran down the street, keeping Mrs. Zhang's food close to my body.

"I said, watch out!"

I threw a glance over my shoulder. A couple of shadowy figures were running up the street as well, just several feet behind me. They were also in the middle of the street the whole time, while I ran along the sidewalk. I suppose the icing on the cake was that they were shooting at something behind them— or, rather, something above and behind them.

"You're not getting us, freak!" one of them yelled. He shot a few more rounds into the night air. Then he snarled and threw his gun away. His partner kept shooting till he ran out of ammo as well.

I dove against the nearest wall and pressed myself there, holding my breath, as the two men picked up the pace and barreled down the street. Anyone who happened to be outside did the same thing I did, and Beck Street was lined with confused and frightened people pressing themselves against grimy walls of rundown tenement buildings.

"Yeah, yeah, whatever," Spirit Wire called out from somewhere. "Sticks and stones, dorkwads."

I glanced up and found her hovering about two stories up, her steampunk-ish costume faintly gleaming in the night lights. I couldn't see her face clearly, but her goggles seemed to glow. She paused for a moment and then went still, like she was concentrating really hard. The two thugs continued to run, and I thought that Spirit Wire was letting them go.

Then I heard a sudden explosion of glass. A window on the second story of a grungy apartment building across the street had shattered, and shards of glass flew everywhere. From inside the room, a bunch of long cables shot out, tentacle-like, waving and looking like bizarre slithering snakes as they flew right at the two thugs. I imagined that they were all normal cables with limited length, but from what I saw, Spirit Wire's powers stretched them out to whatever length she needed. It was seriously like watching a cartoon, with everything taking on elastic qualities. It was so weird—but cool as hell.

I watched the cables loop themselves around the guys' waists, tighten, and then yank them back hard, like bungee cords. The two screamed as they catapulted the other way, flying low, as the cables whip-lashed back the other direction, carrying them in the waiting arms of the cops. Other people in the street with me also cried out in surprise or shock. The two were unceremoniously dumped on the ground, where they were immediately surrounded by men with drawn guns.

"Over here!" Spirit Wire called out, waving at the police. Then she pointed at the window where the cables had snapped back inside. "There's a room of stolen computers in there!"

I blinked. Wow, she was good. How did she know that? Superhero sense? Half of the cops followed her as she flew straight inside the broken window. The police had to use the front door, but I figured that they'd get there eventually. In the meantime, the two muggers were hauled off into waiting squad cars. Yeah, all in a day's work for a superhero.

I stumbled to my feet, still clinging to Mrs. Zhang's takeout stuff, feeling unashamedly proud of the fact that the superheroes once kicked my butt. When I got home, I helped Mom get everything laid out on the table while prattling on and on about what had just happened. She was also predictably freaked out.

"Are you okay? No, really. Are you...*okay?* Eric? Look at me. Let me check you. No, stand still, mister, or you're going to *get* it. Do you hear me? Oh, God, what's this mark? What about this? Where did you get this? Wh—is this a *hickey?* Eric!"

I didn't have the heart to tell her this, but if Hollywood were to do a remake of *The Exorcist,* I'd give them Mom's work number if they were looking for a more mature Linda Blair for the pea soup role. As it happened, I was too tired to argue, so I just let her go nutty on me while I stood there, glassy-eyed, ignoring her screeches and letting myself be subjected to her paranoid inspection. Exposing myself to physical harm as the Trill's sidekick once upon a time? Obviously, I could never live that one down. She wouldn't let me, anyway.

To add insult to injury, I was also given the thankless job of calling Scanlon to the dining room.

"Do I have to?" I asked. "I mean, I'm sure they can smell Mrs. Zhang's food from the living room. Can't they just follow their noses or something?"

Mom just placed her hands on her hips and leveled

me with that you-are-SO-going-to-get-it-young-man look. I sighed and walked out, taking care not to cross the threshold when I reached the living room door. I just peeked in and called out.

"Yo! Dinner time!"

"Hey, is that what's hot in urban speak, Tiger?"

I narrowed my eyes at him. "Yeah. It's, like, way up there with 'Brainsuck.'"

"Oh! Ha-ha-ha-ha-ha-ha-*slurp!*"

They made Scanlon sit beside me at the table, by the way. I spent my dinner getting my hair mussed up every ten minutes or so. At first I thought it was because Scanlon was just being, you know, Scanlon, but after a while, I began to suspect that he'd used up his napkin and needed a substitute for cleaning his hand and just didn't feel like asking Mom if we had any extras. If I could detach my nose from my face, hold it up next to my hair, and take a whiff, I wouldn't be surprised if my shampoo would come off smelling like soy sauce, garlic, and pepper.

I honestly can't remember how I managed to survive dinner. All I can say is that I did, and for that I was grateful to all universal forces that sought to protect me with soothing auras or clouds of purple calm or a generous dose of cosmic Valium.

After dinner, I went back online and destroyed Asteroids like whoa. I even beat my own record. I guess, in that sense, Scanlon really did play an important role in my life. Before I shut the computer down, I got another email from Althea: *Dude, you can win mucho bucks just for sitting on your ass, waiting for the bingo announcer guy to call out the right numbers and letters.* I cringed. What the hell was she going on about? So I typed back: *I can also earn mucho bucks by being a hustler, and I don't have to put up with some boring dude with a microphone. What's your point?*

Oh, yeah—I also washed my hair before I went to bed. Just in case, you know.

Chapter 3

Boredom: that excruciating limbo that fills up a boy's time in between school, his boyfriend, and whacking off. I wanted to set up a blog, but it wasn't going to happen, obviously, since the only things I could have talked about were classified stuff.

I mean, think about it. With a blog with all kinds of juicy things about superheroes, I'd have been getting tons of hits. I could have had those ad things on my sidebars, where people could click through, and I'd heard that I could make money off them. I didn't even have to go out there and find a real job, see? I'd be kicking back, tossing down some M&Ms while making mucho bucks off people's gullibility. I just wondered if I needed a special permit for the state because of those underage job law things and all that crap.

Of course, if one of my blog readers happened to be David "Gorilla Grip" Cohen from sixth grade, the gloves would've been off. Wouldn't it be cool if I'd posted something like this:

"Hey, Dave! I'm going steady with the hottest superhero out there! I'll bet you didn't think I'd have it in me, did you? Oh, by the way, I charge a reading fee if you want to check out the rest of my blog and how life is, practically engaged to be married to Calais, who'll kick your furry, weenie ass if you tried to beat the crap out of me the way you did after homeroom. By the way, how's life in Loserville?"

Too bad I couldn't have one. It would've been fantastic, imagining Douchebag Cohen scratching his head and dragging his knuckles across the ground, trying to figure out how an awesome superhero like Calais could possibly be a card-carrying faggot.

So I decided to just get a physical journal to write in. Better than nothing, really.

I took advantage of the time before the early morning scramble to pounce on Mom with my dreams. I got up before everyone else, which always takes her by surprise. When she was knocked off her center, I hit her with my request.

"Mom, can I have money for a journal?" I asked, trotting over to the stove where she stood, frozen, a spatula in one hand and the griddle pan held in another. She was staring at me, shocked, the whole time.

"Huh? Money? Journal?"

"Yeah," I replied, all casual and suave as I peeked

at the pancakes that were well on their way to getting burned, no thanks to my very timely distraction. "Look out. Breakfast is in danger." I gave her sleeve a quick tug.

"Oh. Uh—you're up early, honey," she stammered, turning back to her cooking and promptly turning the pancakes over. They were pretty cooked on one side, for sure.

"Yeah, sure. I guess it just happened, you know? So can I have money for a journal?"

"You've never kept a journal before. What's up?"

Adults are so cynical. And suspicious. One state of mind I don't look forward to when I come of age. I just shrugged and waltzed over to the refrigerator and claimed Mrs. Horace's jam and then dug around the pantry for bread. "I'm just, you know, being thoughtful. I figured that I'd be better off expressing myself in a private journal and not spending so much time online."

"What happened to your poetry?"

"Oh. Haiku? That's *so* last year, Mom. I'm on to bigger and better things."

"Uh-huh..."

I hauled my breakfast over to the toaster, taking care not to look inside the slots and be reminded of how disgusting the racks and heating elements looked. One would think that someone in the household would notice and actually try to convince Mom to cough up money for a new toaster, but no. All I could do was pray that nothing indestructible, blackened, spiny, and mutating would attach itself to my bread in the toasting process.

"Besides," I added, "it would make for great writing practice, wouldn't it? And Dr. Dibbs did say that while I've always been good in written communication, I still need to apply myself some more? Remember your last kinda-sorta PTA meeting with him?"

Mom watched me as she held a platter of steaming pancakes. Then she shook her head. "You're good, kid. I'll give you that."

"So, is that a yes?" I prodded as she walked over to the table to set the platter down. When she threw me another incredulous look and then nodded, I grinned, thanked her, and gave her a quick kiss. Nothing says love like your own mother telling you how good a hustler you are.

On my way to my tutorials—or, rather, "school"—I kind of took my time by detouring down one road that had a couple of pretty cool stationery shops. One of them was all about handmade stuff, which I wanted desperately, but I couldn't afford. Besides, a lot of their merchandise was all froufrou stuff. The other shop specialized in some pretty cool unique designs from all over the world. Also handmade, and I guess just as expensive as the other shop, but I really liked how they were more international.

I stood by the wall where they had blank journals displayed, my eyes being bigger than my wallet... or, actually, Mom's wallet. I think I inspected and fondled every single blank journal there was, and before long, I started getting the feeling that the salesgirl was getting weird vibes from me.

"May I help you find something?" she asked as she

walked up to me. She was a pretty tall lady, about my height. That said, she was also pretty intimidating even though she wore the tie-dyed baggy stuff that neo-hippies wore around Vintage. I mean, she even wore her hair loose and long and shaggy, with a little crown of flowers perched on her head. The only thing she needed to do was walk around barefoot, but this was Vintage City, after all. The stuff that people could bring with them from outside defied description. Still does, really.

"Um—yeah. I'm looking for a blank journal that's really cool, with a little window-thingie in the cover, where I can write stuff," I said, holding up a journal that, according to its label, was handmade in Chile.

"Oh," she said, suddenly perking up. "In that case, you might find something you want in this section, where—"

She stopped short when we heard a weird noise that sounded like something metallic and small skittering across the ceiling. I automatically thought of rats and shuddered. We both looked up, but the ceiling looked pristine and freshly painted. The only sound that could be heard at that moment was the air conditioner's quiet hum. She frowned and shook her head.

"Sorry about that. I think the vents are getting too old or something. Anyway, let me show you these journals." She smiled and walked to a table, where I followed her.

I thought I heard another sound, and I wasn't sure, but it seemed like a series of little scrapes against the ceiling. Like something dragging itself along, using claws or something instead of feet. I shuddered, but when the sounds didn't repeat themselves, I decided that they were nothing more than my imagination getting fired up over the previous sounds.

Within minutes I was loaded with new, shiny things and was running through traffic because I was late for "school." Pfft. I didn't care. I'd gotten myself a cool journal, and I couldn't wait to destroy it with my musings and crap.

When Mom arrived home from work later that day, I happily paraded my stash in front of her. Well, I guess I didn't really have much choice, when Mom demanded to see where her hard-earned money went.

Sitting at the dining table, I spread out my treasure and gave her the lowdown on each, while Mom settled herself down with her usual mug of coffee. She couldn't rid herself of the habit of drinking late-afternoon coffee despite our urgings. "See, this journal's from India—"

"India? Whatever happened to locally-made journals? Why do you need to go international and pay an arm and a leg for something that would've been cheaper domestically?"

See what happens when she drinks late-afternoon coffee?

"I didn't see any that looked nice. Anyway, this is, like, one-of-a-kind, Mom, and see the pages? They're all hand-made. The edges aren't even, and you can even see different kinds of weird fiber thingies embedded in the paper. Isn't that cool?"

"Uh, yeah. What's this?" Mom pointed at the wooden box with the Victorian-type logo on the lid.

"My pens!" I lifted the lid and pushed the box toward her, grinning proudly. Inside the box, a set of two pens with separate nibs lay cradled, along with two small bottles of ink. I had a tough time finding that pen set, by the way, which was why I considered them to be my crowning achievement in froufrou shopping.

Mom stared at the pen set. "Eric...these aren't ballpoint pens."

"No. Of course not! Why would I get myself some cheap, crappy ballpoint pens for this kind of journal? Check this out, Mom. They even have different sized nibs for writing. I can practice calligraphy if I wanted to, I think. Maybe even drawing if I really applied myself."

She continued to stare at the pen set. "Eric Steven Plath, how much was this pen set?"

"Oh." I paused and felt around my pockets for the receipts, which I fished out in a crumpled pile. I handed them over, while yakking away about my shopping adventures that day, as well as a regular update on my progress in "school."

"Dr. Dibbs said that I'm doing pretty good, but that maybe I'm just plain hopeless when it comes to Chemistry and Geometry, so not much loss there, I say. I mean, I'm passing, but not with As or Bs, which is better than plain failing. I guess it's best to just focus on what I'm good in and help me 'bloom' that way, right? I'll be back at Renaissance High after the summer, he also told me, which doesn't really sound very appealing right now, so I was wondering if I could talk to you and Dad about being home-schooled for the rest of my high school life." Mom looked like she'd just gotten zombified as she continued to stare at my pen set with her jaw hanging a little slack, so I decided to lay off for now. "Well, maybe another day, we can talk about it. But, seriously, Mom, it's something to think about."

"Eric..."

"Yeah?" I took back the pen set and put the lid back on, lovingly setting it down next to my brand spankin' new journal from India.

"Why do you have an oil lamp?"

"Oh, this?" I pointed at my third acquisition, which sat in all its gothic, atmospheric glory nearby. "Yeah, I figured that if I wrote long, private, and emo-type entries in my journal, I'd be best served using an oil lamp instead of boring electric lights. Remember all those horror films we used to watch when I was a kid? The ones with Christopher Lee as Dracula back in, like, ancient times?"

"Those ancient times were the 1960s, Eric," Mom said.

I shrugged. "Forty years ago? That's almost like a century, Mom. Anyway, I thought that—"

"I think that you need to take your stuff upstairs, mister, and get ready for dinner before I make you take these all back and get refunds for every one of them," Mom cut in, her eyes narrowing at me. She glanced at the receipts. "I'm not kidding."

"But what do you think of my lamp?"

"In addition to the fact that you squandered my money on something pointless? Using that lamp instead of electric light is bad for your eyesight."

I rolled my eyes. "Mom, it's not like my eyesight's peachy-keen. I mean, when was the last time I had 20/20 vision, anyway? Not counting my stint with the Trill, of course. Why even bother protecting what's already hopeless?"

Mom just gave me that look. I really can't describe it. It was like that look you got from Neanderthals like Douchebag Cohen right before they gave you the kind of melvin that'd set your puberty back by half a dozen years. And I knew that my mom was more than capable of doing that, too. I mean, she changed my diapers. It goes without saying that she could do an über-melvin if she was pushed into it.

It was awesome that Mom let me go squander some of her money on a really cool blank journal from India with a special decorative window on the front cover, a pen set, and a real, honest-to-goodness oil lamp that I found on sale at a lamp store that I checked out on my way home from my tutorials. It was seriously bitching, but what kerosene oil lamp isn't? I got myself a brass mug lamp, so I could carry it by its handle anywhere I went.

I wanted to test it out, too, in the dead of night, when everyone was in bed and the lights were all out. I'd wander from room to room with my lamp and make like some kind of gothic hero out on an adventure of some kind. Maybe even stand in a dark, dark corner really quietly and then scare the crap out of Liz when she stepped out of her room for her midnight snack. Hopefully it'd be raining hard, too.

Weird, what owning an oil lamp could do to one's brain. Later that evening, when I wrote my first entry, I realized that I wasn't writing in haiku. I thought that writing haiku was a study in discipline or something like that. Now that I stopped doing it, it was as though I were on a writing rampage. If anyone were to look at my first entry, which I'd never allow to happen, they'd see just how far I'd come in my artistry.

I don't know what Liz sees in Scanlon Dorsey, but she really should take him out more often before he opens a rift in time, sucks all of Vintage City into another century, and traps everyone there, just by showing up at our doorstep. I don't want to wake up one day and find myself looking like Frankie Avalon, half-naked and cavorting up and down a beach with squeaky-clean surfers around me. Okay, so I don't mind the half-naked bit, but I'd rather be cavorting up and down an empty beach with a totally naked Peter. Yeah, those were my opening lines. How many words did I write without stopping to rest my wrist? Did that mean that I was progressing in my artistry?

Incidentally, I found another Althea message in my inbox. I felt my universe get sucked into a black hole when I clicked on it: *You don't get served hot dogs when you hustle.* I snorted, shaking my head. Okay, this was too easy: *Oh, yes, you do—kosher and otherwise.* I sniggered the whole time, and clicking "send" felt like I was tap dancing on Althea's grave. Still had no idea where this whole bingo obsession came from, though, but that was Althea for you.

I really missed Peter's visits. I wished Mom hadn't had to make that "you can't be seen together when he's in superhero mode" rule because it stank. Stank! Now we had to see each other like normal people did, going out on dates and stuff, not sneaking around with him creeping into my room, all mysterious-like, or with me climbing up to the roof to steal some super-schmoopy moments with him during his ten-minute break from crime-fighting. Though I must say that I preferred him stealing into my room—very kinky. Dracula also came to mind, and I didn't mean of the Scanlon Dorsey kind. But Peter was a gazillion times sexier than an undead bloodsucker.

I wished my pens came with a quill on the side, actually, to go with the ink bottle, but that would have meant killing turkeys or ostriches or whatever big-ass birds they needed to get the right size feather for a real quill pen, wouldn't it? If that were the case, I'd rather not have had the blood of innocent big birds on my hands whenever I wrote in my journal, thank you very much.

I missed Peter. Good thing I'd just washed my collection of old towels.

I lay on my bed, sprawled, sweaty, and tired, staring at the ceiling and mentally watching that hot, hot, *hot* fantasy I'd just enjoyed involving Peter fade away. Once my brain cells got their crap together, I tried to think of what else I needed to do before going to bed. Nothing, apparently. I'd done my homework. Done my chores. Done the nightly boy-meets-towel thing. Oh, yeah. I could always write in my brand spankin' new...

Jeebus, my life was so *boring,* I could gnaw on my ankles. Why the hell did I buy a journal? At least one that didn't talk back to me? Writing longhand had already outgrown its charm. *Crap*. I even went so far as to wait for the off-chance that Althea might have some time to possess my computer and get all angry-straight-girl-buddy on me after homework and crime-fighting. Nope, nothing. Silence. Life could be *so* lame.

Man, I hated my journal.

Chapter 4

L ife in Vintage City couldn't be without one or two references to the Bad Guy du Jour. Or Bad Guy du Jour-Jour-esque. Seriously, supervillains lasted for more than a day, so how would one call the Bad Guy of the X Number of Moments in French?

Via online free translation site: Bad Guy de Beaucoup de Jours. Did I get that right? It's supposed to mean Bad Guy of Many Days or something like that. Anyway...

Since the attack at the mall, Bad Guy de Beaucoup Many Moments-esque still hadn't resurfaced, and the silence had been kind of creepy. Like we were all waiting for the other shoe to drop, and he was drawing it out for as long as he could. We hadn't gotten a manifesto from him yet. Trust me on this because Dad was totally on top of things when it came to supervillains and whatever narcissistic maneuvers they used to look like they were way bigger than they really were. I think he subscribed to around fifty different newspapers or something, from morning to afternoon to evening editions, and—get this—he even brought home the free indie ones. I liked checking those out because they got all the hot gay ads in the classified section. I was always tempted to cut out the really hunky guys and had been thinking of learning scrapbook-making, so I could have a really *smoking* gay scrapbook going.

I wouldn't add Peter's pictures to it, though. That would only tarnish his image. Yeah, even when he was in blood flow-constricting spandex. Besides, why ogle his picture when I could always have him there, in person, with me, and equally horny? Sucked that superhero work had to come first, though, but beggars couldn't be choosers, I guess.

We'd collected so many newspapers that it was hell taking out the garbage at the end of the day. It sucked that I was stuck with it because Liz said that she was saddled with that chore through her tweens and early to mid-teenage years, and as they say, crap travels downhill. I suppose the good thing was that the downward-traveling pile of poo got caught in rocks, roots, and other obstructions, seeing as how I'd be condemned to dumping garbage for a total of three years, unlike Liz, who'd been sentenced to five. No wonder she always bullied me around. I had a couple more years of this before I'd get to enjoy some real democracy in this household, and we'd all take turns dumping garbage after dinner. That would be adulthood in a nutshell, I guess.

Anyway, with Dad taking in every newspaper that

could be had, I now had to dump the garbage *and* haul out his recycling pile. Wouldn't this be a blatant violation of child labor laws?

Dad tried hard to keep up with supervillain shenanigans, and so far, with pile after pile of well-read and discarded papers to his name, he still didn't have a clue as to the new Bad Guy's identity.

"Well, he's definitely better than the Trill in messing around with people's minds," Liz said at tonight's dinner. "Then again, that's how it is with these supervillains. They get more and more sophisticated in their methods."

"Unless you're talking about the Deathtrap Debutantes," I said, and we both rolled our eyes and giggled. Yeah, that was one of those rare bonding moments I got to enjoy with my sister. Be totally catty and abusive toward other girls. I think there's something in estrogen that makes women behave like that toward other women, and we gay guys get to enjoy the snarky ride all the way.

"Yeah, no kidding. Dangle some bling from the darkest corner of the sewers, and they'll be there, clawing away at sludge to get to the so-called treasure."

Mom didn't want to hear about the gritty stuff tonight. She made a face and said, "Okay, that's enough of that. We're eating." She also didn't spare her maternal energy. "Eric, I know what you're doing with your meatloaf. Stop that, or so help me, I'll make you *cook* the stuff next time."

"I wish we had a dog," I grumbled. I was trying to spirit away chunks of my food when Mom wasn't looking, using my napkin to collect them in a greasy, soggy pile for disposal later. Apparently she *was* looking, because mothers are born with eyes in the back of their heads. Yeah, a dog would've helped me a lot.

I *hated* meatloaf. It was like something that Satan pooped out after an eternity of constipation. So I told Mom because I was honest that way. I sat back, squared my shoulders, and met her eyes, all confident-like.

"Mom, meatloaf's like something that Satan pooped out after an eternity of constipation. It should be outlawed, frankly, and serving it for dinner is like child abuse and should carry with it some pretty stiff penalties."

Liz stared at me. She even raised her glass in a toast. "That's a good one. I'm impressed."

Apparently honesty was a virtue that wasn't really valued highly in the Plath household because Mom made me eat the rest of the stuff right out of the loaf pan as punishment. Thank heaven Dad pretty much scarfed the whole thing down, and I was left with maybe three slices of Satan's poo. No, it didn't make the ordeal any better, but at least it was shorter.

"Any news on the Puppet or the Debutantes, Dad?" Liz asked.

"Nothing on the Puppet so far. I have a feeling that he's lying low after getting all his killer dolls blown to bits by the Trill." Dad sounded so official whenever he updated us on the goings on of Vintage City's more famous residents. I always wondered if he fancied himself a newsman or reporter of some kind, which would really work with my associating Dad with Les Nessman, given his appearance and slightly nervous energy.

"I wonder where he gets the money for all those things," I said, after washing down the nastiness of meatloaf with five glasses of water. Mom didn't even bat an eyelash when I looked at her and sulked. "I'm going to run away and *then* you'll be sorry."

"Don't be a drama queen, Eric," she said, blowing at the steam wafting from her coffee mug. Well, it was worth a shot.

"God knows, son. And as for the Debutantes, I hear that they're still out of commission."

Liz smirked. Oh, yeah, she loved that bit of news. "They seriously got their butts kicked by the Trill, didn't they? Man, I wish I saw the whole thing. It must've been *fantastic*."

Ah, women.

It was Liz's turn to wash the dishes tonight. I took out the garbage (No! Really?), and in the moonlight next to the recycling tub, I sifted through the indie papers and pulled out the classified sections, rolling them up and stuffing them under my shirt. Who cared if I looked like I'd gotten impregnated by a robot? Without Peter to cuddle and do all kinds of teenage skanky things with, my only backup was to ogle hot gay men in black-and-white print.

As a measure of my hormonal ingenuity, I'd also stocked up on old towels that I now made use of more regularly in order to spare my bed sheets. No one at home knew about my secret stash...for now, anyway, and as long as I got to wash out my own gene pool, I wouldn't have to worry about the usual tired complaints about teenage male libido and stuff.

As I still hadn't gotten around to replacing my old, dead bike, I walked to and from "school" everyday. The good thing about that was the fact that if I gave myself enough time to mess around, I could easily get quite a bit of window-shopping under my belt. By the time I got home after my tutorials, I'd have catalogued all kinds of stuff in my brain for future extravagant spending. It also meant that I really needed to go out there and find a job because talking to Mom and Dad about my needs—I desperately had to have four pairs of sneakers: two high tops, two low—was beginning to feel like talking to a couple of marble statues without arms and maybe heads. Actually, more often than not, they'd been more like a couple of marble statues with their ears gone missing because they never listened to a word I'd tell them.

So, yeah. I needed a job. I'd no idea how that worked, seeing as how I wasn't in *school*-school, and I understood that the state required permission from Renaissance High and my parents and other heads of state just so I could be allowed to slave away in minimum-wage hell. That was how Liz described her first job, anyway.

I tried to check out possible leads whenever I could. One of them was this gay and lesbian bookstore that was crammed into this tiny little shop space about five blocks from where my tutorials were held. It was Liz who gave me the heads up on it.

"If you're job-hunting, try them out," she suggested, right before she kicked me out of her truck once we reached Brenda's antique shop. "Mom and Dad already know you want to be productive, so why not start with your homies, know what I'm saying?"

She actually made sense for once. I mulled things over. "Okay, I'll do it. How'd you know about them, anyway? I mean, I'm gay, and I didn't know that my homies had a store of their own."

"It's called being good buddies with the Thursday morning Jumping Bean barista, dude, who's hot as hell and gay. Now scram. I'm late for work."

Yeah, it would be a good place to start, seeing as how I'd be working with my peeps. They could take me under their wing and get me all educated on issues and stuff. Then I'd turn into a vigilant, hardcore pro-gay rights activist when I got older and more cynical. Maybe my relationship with the bigger gay community would lead to the first steps toward a pride parade or something. We didn't have a pride thing every year, by the way. Vintage City wasn't called Vintage City for nothing.

Unfortunately I think the store was owned and managed by one person, and whenever I happened to swing by, he or she would always be out. "Be back in ten minutes" was the sign that I kept seeing taped against the glass door from inside.

I tried to wait a couple of times, standing outside

and peering through the shop window, but the interior was so packed with stuff and so gloomy that I couldn't really get a good idea of how well business was going. Even after ten minutes were up, the store manager or whatever was still missing, so I just had to leave before Dr. Dibbs punished me with more Geometry exercises for being late.

Anyway, on one of those days, I decided to walk by and see if anyone was there. I was shocked to find the door open and the "be back soon" sign not there, so I eagerly stepped inside and looked around.

"Wow," I said, sweeping my gaze across the area. The store was definitely tiny, with all shelves packed with books, and the center space also taken up by big tables piled with discount books and calendars. I didn't even know where to begin with my search for gay titles. I also figured that toward the back part of the shop was the adult section, with the screen and the somewhat obvious sign that said "adult section" hanging on it.

The lighting wasn't very good, either, and neither was the ventilation. The fluorescent bulbs kept flickering, and the vents above kept rattling, occasionally filling the quiet area with weird metallic scratching sounds.

"Hi," I said, walking up to the skinny, balding guy behind the counter. He glanced up from a ledger he was poring over and stared at me, surprised. "Um— nice shop." Cue big, brilliant, engaging smile.

"Hi. Thanks."

"I, uh, was wondering, are you hiring right now?"

Tall, skinny, balding guy waved a hand in the

direction of the main shop area. "If you know how I could sell all these books and magazines by the end of this month, I'll hire you."

I grimaced. "Really?" I glanced over my shoulder. "Why won't anyone buy these? It's not like Vintage City's gay and lesbian free."

"The recession's been biting us in the ass, and there's no support inside the community or outside. Not enough, anyway. Look around you, sweetheart. This store's been around for thirty years, and it's on its way to closing if things don't change." He paused and looked up at the ceiling, frowning deeply. "Goddamn it, what the hell's wrong with the vents this time?"

"Yeah, it's kind of irritating, but you know, this isn't the first place to have that problem," I replied.

"Well, I can't afford to have anything fixed up." He looked back at me, his annoyance melting away in an expression of defeat. "I'm really sorry, but you'll have to look for a job somewhere else. This store's closing at the end of the month."

I left the shop feeling all bummed out. If I had any money on me, I'd have bought one book to make him feel better, but I kind of needed to work first before I could do that. The walk to Brenda's antique shop was spent pretty much lost in sad gay thoughts.

"Hey, hon," Brenda called out when I stepped inside her shop. Despite the fact that there was a ton of creepy old stuff that littered the place and filled up the space between the counter where she stood and the front door, I was always amazed at how she knew that it was me stepping across the threshold.

"How's it going?"

"Fine," I said, my voice weak as I wove my way through her gloomy shop. "I'm feeling a little depressed."

"Ah," she replied as I drew near. "Dr. Dibbs isn't here yet, so you've got time to hang out with me. Tea and cookies, coming up!"

Without waiting for me to say anything more, Brenda turned around and marched toward the back, while I dumped my bag on the floor and perched myself on the bar stool in front of the counter. I'd long claimed that stool for my own, by the way. Brenda didn't have any use for it, frankly, but since we'd gotten to know each other better, she hauled that old thing out and set it where it now stood, so I could sit and chill with her while waiting for the time. She even stuck a piece of masking tape under the seat with "Eric" scrawled on it in thick, black permanent ink.

"So, what's up?" she asked, once the snacks were set on the counter, and I was busy chowing down.

I told her about the bookstore, and she just listened closely, leaning on her elbows and staring long and hard at me the whole time. I really liked talking to Brenda. She was sort of my private therapist without the sky-high fees, and besides, we had the same experience of being manipulated by whackjobs, so that was our real bond.

"Oh, sweetie, I'm so sorry," she said once I'd done. She watched me refill my cup with hot water. "Times are tough, and some businesses just can't cut it."

"Yeah, but where do kids like me go for stuff to read? I mean—there's the big bookstore downtown, but did you see their gay and lesbian section? It's so lame! I bought only one thing from them since I came out to my family, and I couldn't see anything else there except blue collar porn, and Mom won't let me get a copy." I shrugged weakly. "So far, I've been gambling on Olivier's to see if they've got anything new in their used book collection."

Brenda smiled and gave my chin a gentle nudge with her fist. "Then tell your friends about the store you went to. Get them involved, and see if they can get other kids in Renaissance High involved, too. I'm sure you and Peter aren't the only gay kids there."

I nodded, feeling a little better. I guessed she was right, but I didn't know how late any rescue efforts might be for that shop. Then again, I really shouldn't have let that doubt stop me. Any little bit helped, and if the shop closed at the end of the month, at least we could comfort ourselves with the fact that we tried.

"You know, I'm glad your store isn't falling apart the way other stores are," I noted after a moment of silence.

"Hmm?"

I pointed at the ceiling. "The vents."

"What about the vents?" Brenda asked as she blew at her cup.

"They're not making weird noises...like things crawling all over up there. That gay bookstore? I heard those sounds, and it was the same for that one store with all the handmade stuff from different countries. I figured that the buildings were just too old, and the ventilation systems were falling apart."

Brenda's gaze remained fixed on me as she sipped her tea. "This building's one of the oldest in Vintage City," she observed. "I've never had any problems with it. The vents work perfectly, and I haven't noticed anything weird about them."

I shrugged and snatched a lemon cookie. "It makes me think of cheesy monster movies, like, little flesh-eating critters invading ventilation systems and attacking people when the right time comes or something." I chuckled. Brenda just listened, sipping her tea and staring long and hard at me.

Chapter 5

A couple of days later, I finally got to play an online game with Althea. Blame it on my propensity toward the macabre, but I challenged her to a game of online Hangman. What I didn't realize then was that, since she *was* the computer, she also had the ability to manipulate the results.

Wrong! You're getting strung up, dude! Sure enough, I only had one limb to go.

I stared at the monitor, frowning. "What the hell is this crap?" I cried. "What's MU_B O_ _ _ Q U_U_ _ X_II_A_ _ _?"

It's a sentence, dill weed. Come on, choose another letter.

"I've chosen every single letter in the freakin' alphabet, you cheating pile of computer chips! I'm not playing anymore! This sucks!"

Man, talk about a sore loser.

I narrowed my eyes at her. It. Her. Whatthehellever. "Sore loser, my ass. Anyone with half a brain cell could see that you're messing up my chances of winning anything."

Beep. Sorry! Hangman!

Have I ever mentioned how much I sometimes hated the way Althea's powers evolved? Sure, they were pretty cool where thugs and crime fighting were concerned, but in this situation? Major, major suckage.

The limb on my "body" appeared, and the screen flashed in a burst of multicolored light. It was sort of like one of those TV game shows, where the winners were treated to an explosion of colorful confetti, while stupid, cheesy music was played. Then cables shot out of the monitor—and I'm talking cables that weren't real cables, but the kinds that were made of a collection of wild, pulsing, crackling light and electricity. So they shot out of the monitor, sending me jumping out of my chair and crying out in surprise. Before I knew what was happening, they looped around my arms and upper body and pulled me off the floor till I was dangling. Yeah, like Hangman, but not strung up by the neck.

"Ohmigawd, whatthehellareyoudoingyoucrazy b—" I shrieked, kicking. It was kind of sad, really, since moving my legs was the only thing I could realistically do, being wrapped up in pulsing light cable thingies. "LetmegoorI'llfuckingkickyourelectr onicass! Daaaaadddd!" Another "cable" flew out of the screen and wrapped around my head and over my mouth, muffling me.

I need your attention, Eric. I really need a favor. I mean, seriously. I'm totally desperate.

Everything that followed was a blur. I might have passed out, even, but maybe not. All I can say right now is that Althea was *so* on my crap list after our "talk" and "negotiations." I had to be un-muffled first, but it didn't make things any better from my end. She eventually released me and even gave me a consolatory pat on the head with one of the bizarre cables before withdrawing them. I couldn't even stand when she finally set me back down on the floor. I think I teetered a little before my legs gave out from under me, and I landed on my ass with a pretty embarrassing plop. I couldn't even feel the pain from the contact. I was too messed up to feel anything.

Thanks, Eric. You're a doll. I'll call you when Grandma tells me when the next Bingo Social will be at the senior center. <333

I couldn't remember how long it took for me to recover from the shock of being harassed into agreeing to accompany Althea to her grandmother's bingo night, but I recovered eventually. I had to stagger off to my bathroom, where I peed because I nearly literally wet my pants from my ordeal. After cleaning myself up, I staggered back to my room and sat down on my bed, all brain functions frozen.

It wasn't until after dinner, when I had sufficiently recovered, that I got back on my computer and fired off a pretty pissed-off email: *Coercion doesn't count. Go to bingo night on your own, girlie. And if you attack me that way again, I'm filing a restraining order against you. You suck so much ass.* I expected her to possess my computer again and slap me ten different ways for going back on my promise, but

I figured that Althea'd had a change of heart in the end. After all, what was the use of bullying a friend into making a stupid promise?

That was so uncool, and I was sure that she realized it.

Whenever I talked to Peter on my private phone, I always lay on my stomach. I don't think it's necessary to explain why.

"So how're things in good ol' Renaissance High?" I asked, smiling. I couldn't help it. I'm disgustingly schmoopy that way.

"Same old, but you're not there to harass anymore," he replied. "Althea's gone so far as to stick flowers in your old locker as a memorial. She's been talking about tacking on an old photo of yours and somehow figuring out a way to set up a votive candle somewhere, but I had to smack her upside the head and get her back on track."

"You didn't!"

He laughed. He was hot when he laughed over the phone. Reason number one as to why I had to lie on my stomach when we talked via landline. "No, of course, I didn't! You dill weed. I did drag her away using her shirt collar, though. I think that woke her up."

"Are people talking about me?"

"Meh. Not really. A few tongues wagged when the Trill was around, but not anymore. I think there's some kind of rumor going around about you needing special tutorial help or something because you've got a learning disability, which was why you got pulled out of school."

I made a face. "Well, considering how much I suck at Geometry and Chemistry, I wouldn't be surprised if that kind of rumor's making its rounds. Don't bother stopping it or correcting anyone."

"I almost did a couple of times, actually."

I sighed against my pillow. "Better to be thought of as a real dumb ass than a freak."

"Eric, you're neither. Okay? Stop it. I'm not going to hear any more crap talk like that about yourself. Come on..."

My jeans felt a little too tight. "Speaking of coming, are you free anytime soon?"

"I've got work tonight on top of homework. How about tomorrow? It's Saturday, and Mom and Dad will be at a friend's wedding or something."

Sweet. It had been an eternity since we last went out on a real, ordinary date. Like, about a week ago, and it had been a really short one—a whopping two freakin' hours—since it was a school night, and while Peter had already gotten some homework done, he was still expected to turn into Calais and battle the forces of evil after dinner. Somehow he managed to convince Trent that he was going to clock in a little late that night.

A week ago? Mom shouldn't have kicked up a fuss about that. So we settled on the what, where, how, and how much before I reluctantly let him go. I waited a while, still lying on my stomach and enjoying the blissful pressure of a boner against my mattress, and reflected on the conversation I'd just had with Peter. Thank God I'd taken care to lock my bedroom door. If Liz were to barge in to get me downstairs for dinner and then catch me dry-humping my bed...

I remember Wade, when she first introduced herself to me, saying, "I think Peter's a really lucky guy." She wasn't pulling my leg; Wade's just not capable of being a real jerk like that. She actually sounded slightly jealous, not in the sense that she had a crush on me or something, but that she seemed jealous that Peter and I were together. Of course, I also wondered what Peter had told her about me, and no matter how much I'd been prodding him, he kept that a big secret. It'd been pretty easy to throw me off the scent, anyway. All it took was a kiss and a hand down my jeans. Peter had persuasion down to an art form.

It was that one thought that sprang to mind whenever I reflected on any conversation I had with him. To wit, how lucky we'd been.

Now if I could only play matchmaker for both Wade and Althea without them killing me...

I was so brilliant, I could marry myself and spawn forever. I took a shower after Peter's call and then did the laundry. Only mine, though. Jeebus, I got enough problems, and handling my family's dirty underwear would be the proverbial straw on the proverbial camel's proverbial back. While waiting for things to dry, I went to the kitchen and prepared a part of tonight's dinner. That is, I snagged the bag of salad from the vegetable crisper and dumped the stuff in a big bowl.

I set it down on the table with the bottles of dressing neatly lined up next to it, and the icing on the cake was my livening up the table *with napkins*. Yeah, those napkins that we only saw during holidays. I was seriously good.

When everyone got back home, I was fresh and tidy, my laundry was neatly folded and put away, and I greeted everyone with an offer of ice, cold water to soothe frayed nerves after a hard day in the office.

"I've got a feeling that you're about to be hauled off to jail, and this is your way of saying goodbye," Liz said when I gave her a glass of water with a slice of lemon tossed in. She just stared at it. Then she stared at me. I mean, what the hell? That was gratitude for you.

"Oh, God, don't tell me you failed your Chemistry quiz," Dad croaked as he stood just inside the foyer. I didn't even bother to wait for him to settle down. He still had his hat and coat on, his briefcase still dangling from his limp hand, and I could still smell the familiar scents of old leather car seats and carbon monoxide on him.

"Honey, I'm not bailing you out of jail if that's what you're wondering," Mom sighed as she shuffled past me in the direction of the stairs. At least she took the glass of water with the lemon slice and nursed it on her way to her bedroom. "I didn't raise my children to be juvenile delinquents. And the answer's no."

Man. I lived with a tough crowd.

So I upped the ante and made dinner. Like frozen pizza that had been sitting in the freezer for a couple of weeks now because apparently Mom forgot about it, and I figured it was high time to put some factory-made goodness out of its misery.

Good thing it normally took everyone at least half an hour to wind down before shuffling off to the dining room. By the time they got there, everything was set: plates, silverware, *napkins,* glasses, salad, salad dressing, and pizza. I even cut the damn thing into nearly equal portions, fer chrissakes.

"Oh, God," Mom gasped as she froze at the dining room door. "Oh, Eric, please tell me you're okay. I don't think we can afford therapy right now."

I narrowed my eyes at her. "I'm fine, Mom."

"What do you need? Just tell me now."

"Can I go out with Peter tomorrow for a nighttime date?" Flash perky, dimpled grin. Exude squeaky-clean teenage innocence (whatever *that* means). Widen eyes very slightly to complete squeaky-clean teenage innocence look. Hope like hell that everything was working its magic. Remind self to vomit before eating.

"Mom, say yes and be done with it," Liz said as she cautiously sat down at her usual place. She never took her eyes off me, either, and she didn't blink. Maybe she didn't *dare* blink. "I don't think I can survive another creepy Eric moment like this again, and that's saying something."

From where I stood near the stove, I could feel the maternal energies vibrating in Mom. I could easily sense the yes-no battle going on in her head. Another five minutes of that, and her skull would've popped like a zit.

"But you just went out, what, a few days ago," she said. I figured as much.

"It was a week ago, actually. And we were together for only two hours, in a family-friendly burger joint, with creepy children running all over the place."

"Wow, that must've been a real threat to your manhood," Liz said, still looking uneasy as she scowled at me.

"Come on, Mom, it's not like we go against your curfew. We don't go to the same school anymore, either. By the way, would you like some red wine with your pizza? Hard day at work, you know..."

"Mom!" Liz cried, panicking. "Do it!"

"Okay, okay, yes, you can go out with him!" Mom actually pinched her eyes shut and flapped her hands in front of her as if she were warding off a swarm of flies.

Broaden perky, dimpled grin at confused mother. "Thanks, Mom. You're the best. One glass of red wine, coming up."

"Forget the wine," she growled, rubbing her temples as she sat down. "Do we have whiskey anywhere?"

I rocked.

So I celebrated my victory by staying up late after doing my homework, sorting through my growing pile of hot gay ads, ogling the models, and letting my imagination do the rest. Then I cleaned up and sat down to write in my journal. The night was a little on the cool side, with the usual acidic fog forming up and down Vintage, so it was perfect for setting the mood. My lights had all been turned off, and I sat by my window, looking out and finding inspiration in darkness and urban grime. Once in a while, I'd hear police sirens wailing. I figured that my superhero buddies were all out there, up to their ears with cleanup work.

I also wondered what the Sentries were doing, besides setting up the usual training grounds for the heroes. I knew better than to ask Dr. Dibbs for specifics, and Brenda sure wasn't going to let me in on anything, even though she was like my other sister. During moments like these, I couldn't help but think back on my adventures when the Trill was still alive, and I wondered how things would've turned out had I not let myself get suckered by my own demons. On the one hand, I'd have spared my family all that pain and grief. On the other hand, I wouldn't have learned anything about myself, even if those lessons came at a pretty high price—though I wouldn't call private tutorials a high price; I kind of liked being given undivided attention when it came to my education, and I didn't have to put up with high school drama and status quo crap.

I did miss hanging out with my friends, though, but since these tutorials were only to see me through the rest of the year, I was still set to return to the old high school environment afterward.

When I got tired of writing, I fired up my computer and checked out the local news. "International Crime Ring the Masterminds Behind Stolen Computers!" I grinned. Way to go, Althea! One of the things that I started doing was checking online news for tidbits on what my friends were doing. It didn't matter how small it was: mugging, carjacking, whatever. I guess I was really going through some kind of maturing, enjoying those stories and taking pride in what they did, rather than sulking over what would've been, had I been born with superpowers like them. I still had to remind myself of what Peter told me: "You ground me, Eric. At the end of a crazy day, when the world seems to have gone to hell, I turn to you for a reality check."

That had to be the best thing he'd ever said to me. Okay, it was actually second to "Your jeans are in the way."

"I know these guys!" would always be at the tip of my tongue while reading or watching the news, but of course, I couldn't say that to just *anyone*. Mom knew about Peter as Calais, but neither Dad nor Liz did. Beyond Peter, my family didn't know anything about Althea and the others beside the fact that Trent was Peter's older brother, Wade was Peter's good friend from another school, and Freddie was some kid I met while under the Trill's influence. They knew about Brenda, Dr. Dibbs, and only a few hazy facts about their role in saving me, but they were still ignorant about the Sentries, and I didn't want them to know any more than that.

So, no, even to my family, I couldn't admit to knowing the heroes. "I'm going steady with one of them!" always came a close second, but that was even more of a no-no.

Maybe someday, I'd be able to brag like that. For now, I found myself deep inside a different closet, and it was kind of hard, not being able to come out.

Chapter 6

One of those cosmic laws defining my existence involved paper-thin slices of red onion finding their way into my burger, even though I specifically asked for none. I really shouldn't have thought badly of fellow human beings, especially if they worked at some crummy, dead-end job in a fast-food joint. I ignored the possibility that they either forgot my request or decided that something in the way I looked said that I deserved to spend my entire date night blowing sewer breath down my boyfriend's throat.

Nope. I wasn't going to go there. Because I figured that I screwed up so much as the Trill's Worst-Sidekick-Ever and needed to balance my cosmic IOU with good deeds, I decided to believe that paper-thin slices of red onion slithered like gross, stinky, slithering things into my sandwich when the burger-making dude wasn't looking because red onions just sucked that way.

Now would that make an awesome horror movie or what?

The long and short of it was that I asked for no red onions on my turkey burger and got them, anyway. I spent the first five minutes of my date with Peter carefully taking my sandwich apart and lifting out drooping slices of those gross, stinky, slithering things with a plastic spork. Peter had to spend the first five minutes of his date with me watching the window beside our table, blinking and frowning. He tried a few times to take a bite out of his burger, but the distraction that came from the window pretty much kept him from progressing in his meal. In the end, he just set his sandwich down, sat on his hands, and looked all confused.

I also knew exactly what was outside the window, but I totally ignored it and pretended that nothing was out there. "How's your cheeseburger?" I asked without looking at the window.

I'd already gotten all the stupid onions out and raked them as far, far away from my sandwich as I possibly could. Much good that did. I took a bite of my turkey burger and had to ignore the residual onion taste in the lettuce.

"Um...can't say for sure."

"Try mayonnaise instead of catsup with your fries. Europeans do that all the time, and it's not as gross as it sounds."

He wasn't listening and just answered me with a series of "Err..." or "Uh...Eric?" When I continued to chatter away and pretend like everything was all normal, he cut in, "There's a very pissed-off girl giving you a pretty nasty look just outside the window."

I shrugged. "I don't know any pissed-off girl except for my sister, but she was born pissed off."

Peter frowned at me now. I could see realization dawning. "What did you do, Eric?"

"Nothing. Go on and eat. Your fries will get all soggy and stuff, and you know how cold French fries tend to taste." I stuck my tongue out and made a face.

I could also feel Althea's death glare. I didn't need to look at her to know how she stood outside, pinning me with her eyes and brain waves. I *did* mess around with the mental image of her being pressed so tight against the window so that she looked like one of those stupid Garfield plush car window hangings, arms and legs splayed out against the glass, eyes bulging out of their sockets, pupils small and frozen in that crazy-ass stare. I made a mental note to mention that to her once she'd calmed down—and then run like hell.

Anyway, even with the thick, industrial-strength glass that the little burger joint used for its windows, she was pissed enough to send all those "I'm gonna whoop your skinny ass till your sphincter fuses shut, gay boy!" heat waves through the window and right at me. Seriously, if I'd needed to get a tan, and trust me, my family would've killed to see that, all I would've had to do was sit there, naked, and get blasted by Althea's Death Glare Waves. Maybe rotating a quarter of a turn every five seconds or something.

I guess Peter tried to ignore her and even made another valiant attempt at taking a bite of his burger. No could do. He set his food down again and sat back. "Eric, I can't. She's really creeping me out."

"I can have her arrested for disturbing the peace," I offered, but he wouldn't have any of it. Sometimes Peter was a little too rational for his own good. Unless he was horny. Or pissed at me.

One of the employees appeared off to our side, wet towel in one hand and a growing stack of grimy plastic trays in another. As she walked past our booth, she stopped and gaped at the window, tickling my nostrils with that familiar scent of Eau de Grease that was the curse of fast food workers all over the globe. I wondered how many super-scented fabric softeners she went through to exorcise her uniform of its grill demons.

"Excuse me," she said. "I think you forgot your friend. She looks a little, um, upset. I mean—I'd be, too, if my buddies dumped me and had, like, burgers and stuff on their own."

I waved a hand and fished out a couple of French fries, dipping them in the blob of mayonnaise that I squirted onto my plate. "No worries. She's always upset. She was born on the rag, you know." Liz would have to forgive me for applying my favorite description of her to my best girl buddy.

"Really?"

Peter cut in before I could even manage a squeak. "Ignore him," he said, jerking his head in my direction. "He was born with an alien twin whose suckers were glued to his skull."

"You suck, Peter."

"No, your alien twin did. I should weigh your brain while you're asleep and see how much was vacuumed out of you before your mom gave birth."

Okay, we were *so* going to break up after this.

The fast-food girl, whose name was Sasha, according to her tag, shook her head and slowly crept away. Peter sighed and leaned forward, eyes flashing. Have I ever mentioned how hot he looked when he glared at me? Have I? Okay, my boyfriend was *hot*. Especially when I pissed him off, which was pretty often. "You have ten seconds to tell me what's going on," he said.

"It's stupid," I retorted. "I don't want to talk about it."

"Why not?"

"Because I don't want to. And it's stupid. Did I just hear an echo?"

"Your best friend's out there, staring at you, screwing up our date, and freaking out the staff. Tell me."

"No."

"I brought a clean towel."

I smirked while gnawing away like an anemic cow that just stuffed its face with a bucket of plump, juicy, organic grass. "Big deal. You bring clean towels all the time."

Peter didn't miss a beat. He didn't even blink, the shameless bastard. "It's a *beach* towel."

"She's making me go with her to her grandmother's bingo night, and I told her no after I said yes! There! Happy? And that towel had better be shredded by the time we're done this evening!" I paused and then backpedaled. "Condoms? Did you say that you brought condoms, too?"

"You wish," he said. "Sorry, no condoms. I believe in waiting for the right moment because I'm old-fashioned that way." Yeah, *right*. He slid down his seat and stumbled to his feet. "And I'm hauling Althea's pissy ass in here because I'm starving, and I can't stand another second of being put off my dinner because of some stupid promise about bingo night."

I sat there, watching Peter saunter off. "You tricked me again? I *hate* it when you play dirty!" I snarled, but by the time the words came, he'd already stepped outside.

I suppose the only comfort I had then was his mention of a beach towel. Not a bath towel, mind you, but a *beach* towel. You know, like Aladdin's flying carpet. Okay, so it wasn't exactly as awesome as airborne Arabian rugs, but my point is that beach towels, by their very nature, promise any horny sixteen-year-old the moon and the stars and an infinity of amazing cosmic supernovas between him and his boyfriend. I turned the idea over and over in my mind, barely noticing the two figures shambling past the doors and making their way to our booth.

"Watch out," Althea's voice cut through my thoughts. "I know that look. Eric's up to something again."

"Whatever it is you're planning, forget it," Peter said as he slid back on his seat, Althea taking her place beside him.

"If you check under the table," she said, "I'm sure you'll find that it's got something to do with you."

I coughed, nearly blowing soda through my nose. "Shut up, Horace."

"Nice to see you, too, Mister Senator." Althea glanced at Peter. "He's starting out pretty young, you know, breaking promises left and right."

I rolled my eyes. "If I promised you something, Althea, it's because I was coerced. Yeah, you heard me. Coerced. So I'm taking my promise back."

"I didn't coerce you!"

"Uh, should I remind you about the—" Here I raised both hands and made the quotation marks sign with my fingers. "—accidentally-moving cables that got me in my own bedroom and held me up like a human burrito for a gazillion seconds till I had to scream 'I promise I'll go with you'? Seriously, all this time I was under the impression that Peter's the dirtiest player on the planet. He's got nothing to you and your criminal mind." I turned to Peter. "Did she tell you what happened? How she cheated me in a game of Hangman and then made my computer puke out cyber cables or something that attacked me? You know, I've heard about tentacle sex online, and what Althea pulled with her crazy cyber cables came pretty close to that."

Peter shook his head slowly. He looked like he wanted to go home and pretend that this evening never happened.

"Well, it happened exactly the way I described it. She cheated, and then she turned cyber terrorist. Before I knew it, I was wrapped up in her creepy tentacle cable thingies, pissing myself, while she made me promise to go to bingo night. It was total abuse of power! I should file a complaint with the city!"

"Okay, my bad." Althea sighed. "I shouldn't have held you up that way. I'll truss you up like a Thanksgiving turkey next time."

"There! I was terrorized into a promise! And she's *still* terrorizing me! Case closed! Now can we have our date night back? Our dinner's already ruined, time's ticking away, and we haven't even had sex yet," I said, throwing my hands up.

It was Peter's turn to choke on his soda.

"You're definitely not going to get any tonight, Plath," Althea said, reaching for a couple of now-soggy-and-semi-cold French fries. "Look what you just did."

"And whose fault was that?" I retorted.

Althea sighed. She actually looked beaten and tired. "Okay, okay, I'm sorry I forced you into promising to come with me to Grandma's bingo night. But you gotta understand, Eric, if you make me go alone, I'll totally go nuts. You know how much of a brain suck bingo night is for anyone under forty. And I don't want to go postal and mow down a bunch of seniors in the church's community hall." She leaned over the table and gave me that deer-in-the-headlights look. "I swear I'm gonna lose it if you don't come with me."

I scowled at her. "You lost it a long time ago, girlfriend. Try again."

"Please? Pleasepleasepleaseplease? I promise I'll

treat you to ginormous pizza slices for a month. Please?"

"Talk to the hand." I actually raised a hand when I said that. I surprised myself with these slips into corniness sometimes.

"Will good karma be motivation enough? Think about it. In your next life, you'll be married to the hottest, sweetest, richest gay man around—"

I sniffed. "I could come back as sewer sludge in my next life."

"Well, that's only because you're not helping a good friend out."

"Ha. Try again." I pointed at my watch. "You've got three seconds to make me change my mind. Tick, tock, tick, tock...oops. That's four."

Althea glanced at hers and turned to Peter, who was still coughing. "I gotta go and pick up some stuff from the grocery store for Mom. Peter, talk to him, okay? Please? I already told you the details."

"Most likely blown out of proportion," I cut in, biting into my turkey burger. "Time's up, girlie. Buh-bye."

"If worse comes to worst, threaten celibacy for the rest of your teenage years." She turned to glare at me. This time around, I was ready for the heat waves and made like I was fanning myself with my napkin while looking bored. "That oughta learn him."

I rolled my eyes again. "Whatever, dude. Now scram. We have a date to finish."

Althea slid off the seat, fixed her shirt and jacket, slung her messenger bag across her torso, and said, "I won't be using cyber cables next time, Plath."

"Your powers should be revoked—or something. Terrorist."

I watched her march off in a huff, while Peter heaved a sigh of, what, relief? Exhaustion? I figured it was the latter because he raked his fingers through his hair and gnawed on his lower lip till it swelled up, making my jeans tighten. Again. Then he slumped in his seat and leveled me with that extremely-patient-but-gently-disapproving-boyfriend sort of look.

"Eric..."

"Oh, come on, Peter," I sighed, rubbing the back of my neck. "I really hate bingo night. I've already been to one of those with my dad, and they seriously *suck*. And I'm not lying when I say that Althea bullied me into saying yes."

"Yeah, I know she bullied you. That's really the only way to get you to listen. She knows you too well. Anyway, it's only once, you know, and it's her grandmother's special monthly thing."

"That sounds menstrual."

Peter raised a brow. "Are you forcing me to make you celibate for the rest of your teenage years?"

I considered it while taking another bite of my turkey burger. "Can we have wild monkey sex on your beach towel first and then discuss that afterward?"

"No."

I set my food down and leaned forward, holding Peter's gaze because I was desperate. "Have you ever been to one of those movable potties in public parks? Do you know that they're actually, like, rifts in space that take you directly to Satan's lair? They're seriously inter-dimensional portals...well, the toilet seats and whatever's boiling under them, are. Bingo night's the less disgusting version of those. I'm not kidding, Peter. It's like purgatory on earth. And they serve rubbery hot dogs."

"I like rubbery hot dogs."

I sighed, feeling the hot, sweat-slicked hold of promised not-quite-full-on-sex—i.e., we'd never gone all the way yet—slipping away. I could never win in stupid moral arguments like this. It was so unfair.

"Peter, I don't want to go!"

"You'd do it for your grandmother."

I figured as much.

"Look, Althea screwed you over. I know that. But what about Grandma Horace? Remember all those little treats she used to make you when you and Althea were in grade school? And don't forget Mrs. Horace and her special jam..."

I threw my hands up. "Okay, okay, fine! Fine! I'll go! God!"

Peter broke into a broad, sparkly grin. "Atta boy. I knew you'd come around. Don't do it for Althea. Do it for her grandmother. Just think of it that way, all right?" He reached across the table and took my hand in his, giving it a tight squeeze.

I sulked. "I'll have to sneak in some Jack Daniels or something. You know, I've got a feeling that you're really a closet Catholic, the way you work that guilt trip on me all the time."

Peter merely laughed, gave my hand one more squeeze, and then prattled on about...well, whatever.

His mood had improved, he seemed proud of me, and he dove into his now cold burger and fries with an appetite that would make Mom adopt him on the spot.

By the way, we didn't shred the beach towel later that evening, but it sure was soaked. The location was perfect, too, with us tangling at our favorite little beach hideaway in full view of a clear night sky and a crescent moon.

For all that, though, we still returned home virgins. Yay, restraint. Backward slash, end sarcasm. Someday, down the road, maybe I'd look back on this and laugh. How's that for optimism?

Chapter 7

In spite of my previous wibbling over my journal—how bored I was, and how it was pointless to own a stupid blank book with stupid pens and a stupid oil lamp—I gradually fell into a nice pattern of scribbling almost every night. It was kind of nice, really, being able to unload like that, now that I really didn't have my friends to chat up the way I'd used to. I was still mulling over the online blog thing, though. I mean, come on. Earning money from people clicking on links? It was a brilliant idea! Besides, being online was *the* way to meet new people, and maybe I could create a new network of friends via my blog. But I guessed, if I'd spent Mom's money on my stuff, I might as well put everything to good use.

The downside to all that private writing time was that my wrists grew sore after a particularly long and detailed journal entry, which was mostly about Scanlon Dorsey and how much garlic he'd cost my family so far. Yeah, I'd been keeping tabs. Mom had already begun noticing her dwindling garlic supply, but I wasn't about to talk. Well, not unless I got caught, anyway.

First test for wrist strength came when Mom and I went to Uncle Chung's for some Chinese food dinner. It was payday, so, yay for us. No frozen pizza.

"Good evening, Mrs. Plath!" Mrs. Zhang called out from behind her steam-filled counter. I wasn't sure if it was just me, but her little take-out place seemed to get foggier and foggier every time I went there. I could barely make out her silhouette as she waved a ladle above her head. "Haven't seen you in a while! I only see skinny boy here! What, no boyfriend with you tonight? You two not an item anymore or something? You real heartbreaker, huh? Tsk, tsk!"

"Good evening," Mom said as we stood before the food counter. "I've been busy with work, Mrs. Zhang. And, no, Eric's solo tonight. No boyfriend anywhere. It's a bit of a miracle, actually."

Yeah, thanks, Mom. I glowered at the steaming trays of greasy food before me. I guessed adults forgot how it was, being sixteen and in a first relationship. Sometimes I thought that they were jealous because when a person was young, everything was pretty intense. You couldn't say that about adult romance. Older people were more, like, sly and conniving even when they flirted with each other. Then they jumped into bed and then woke up in the morning to realize that, hey, they had a spouse and children back home! So whom were they really in love with?

Okay, so I'd just made all of that up. I was a little inspired because I was forced to watch some horrible, sappy-ass chick flick on TV while waiting for Mom to get ready for this trip to Uncle Chung's. Liz was watching, anyway, and I didn't have a choice. Then again, I supposed I'd rather suffer through some sappy chick flick than be dragged to the kiddie ice cream parlor by Scanlon Dorsey because he figured that spoiling me would earn him brownie points with Liz.

"Special for today—buy two potstickers, get one egg roll free!" Mrs. Zhang said proudly, waving a hand before her face to dissipate the clouds that continued to roll between us. I still could barely see her in the fog. "Good treat for kid here. He needs bulk. If you let me keep him for a month, I'll make sure he eats everything I cook, and he goes home all fixed."

"I don't want to be fixed," I gasped. "Dude, are you kidding me? I'm not a stray animal!"

"Eric, Mrs. Zhang's not a dude." Mom leaned closer to Mrs. Zhang. "You're welcome to keep him for two months. Just make sure that he does his own laundry because, well, you know how teenage boys are."

Whatever, Mom.

Anyway, Mom finally got serious—though, frankly, I had a feeling that she'd been pretty serious about giving me up for two months—and ordered tonight's dinner. Before long we were walking back home, with Mom humming to herself while I struggled with the two plastic bags that Mrs. Zhang packed. My right wrist...holy cow, it felt like my whole hand was about to tear off its joint. I cursed under my breath the whole time, hoping pretty much that the next eventful moment that required a blow-by-blow entry in my journal wouldn't happen for at least another week.

Along the way, we nearly got run over by a stolen car. We heard the tires screeching behind us, and Mom and I automatically jumped away from the edge of the sidewalk. I almost fell into a pile of trash cans that were old and battered, and they looked like they hadn't been emptied in a month. Even in the early evening hours, the whole thing was just gross. I didn't need to see all that accumulated crap in detail. Besides, I wasn't sure if it was a trick of the dying light, but I could've sworn those garbage heaps actually *breathed*.

Mom grabbed hold of my left arm to steady me and to pull me closer to her while she froze, waiting for the car to fly by. It did, careening all over the place and nearly running over some drunk who was passed out and lying half on the sidewalk and half on the road.

"Stop right there!" someone shouted from somewhere above us.

A familiar shadowy figure flew down and landed several feet in front of the car, and it was like ballet. Magnifiman stood in classic superhero pose with legs apart and hands on hips, cape flapping jauntily behind him, which made me wonder if his superhero powers also came with his own breeze that made him look perfectly cinematic every time he struck a pose. The car didn't slow, and all we saw was it going straight for him and then getting swept up in one fluid motion. Magnifiman held it up above his head like it weighed nothing and flew off with it.

"Good evening, ma'am!" he called out.

"Good evening! Thank you!" Mom yelled back, waving. I just stared.

When the street was again safe, Mom and I moved forward. Her mood restored itself, and she was once again humming while I struggled with the two bags of Chinese food. I think we were about a block away from home when Mom suddenly stopped. I had to walk another ten feet forward before I realized that I'd just left her behind, and my wrists throbbed. Irritated, I stopped and turned.

"Mom? What's up?" I said.

Mom didn't answer right away. She just stood there, quiet, as if she were listening for something that only she could hear. She looked up, sweeping her gaze along the top of the grungy apartment building across the street from where we stood. I stared at it, frowning. I didn't see anything unusual there. It was typical lower-middle-class housing, with decaying bricks and some broken windows, the lights all yellow and murky. Nothing looked suspicious on rooftops anywhere, either.

"Mom!" I called. "Come on, these things are heavy! And I'm starving!"

She didn't seem to hear me still, but after several more seconds of standing, listening, and searching, she finally sighed and walked toward me.

"I'm sorry, honey," she replied, taking one of the bags from my hold and gently guiding me back home with a strangely firm hold around my free arm.

"What's wrong? Did you hear something?" I asked.

"Hmm? Oh, no. It was nothing. I thought I saw something move up there, but it was just my imagination." She ended that with a small laugh that sounded a little tight and forced, but I didn't push things. We just fell silent for the rest of the way, and once we crossed the threshold, I suddenly realized that I was panting and a little sweaty. That was because we'd practically run the rest of the way home, or at least Mom had made me pick up my pace for whatever reason. Like we were running away from something.

I was a little unnerved by that, but I said nothing to her when I followed her to the dining room and helped her set the table. I did try to watch her, though. Nothing appeared out of the ordinary other than the fact that her hands trembled a little, and she didn't bother to hide it.

After dinner, I called Peter and got his voice mail. No surprise there, but I did make sure to stay up kind of late to wait for his call back. It didn't come till about eleven, and he sounded dead tired.

"Hey," he said, yawning. "What's up?"

"I'll keep this short, I promise. Sounds like you had a pretty rough day out there."

He chuckled. "Comes with the territory."

"Okay, did Trent say anything about the neighborhood where he nabbed a carjacker? Mom and I were out, and we saw everything. But other than the carjacking thing, was there anything else he mentioned to you about the area?"

Peter was silent for a moment. "Uh, no, really. Why, did anything else happen?"

So I told him about Mom's odd behavior and the rush home, as though she were running away from a threat.

"I wonder if she saw something," I said. "She really looked like she was suspicious of something in the area, but when I tried to look around, I didn't see anything weird or out of place. Then again, it was getting dark, so the shadows didn't help. Mom still seemed freaked out when we were at home, but she wouldn't talk." I shivered. "Talking about it kind of makes my skin prickle. It was just creepy."

"Okay. I'll tell the others about what you said. That area's always been bad news, Eric. I wish you and your family would take the longer and safer route to Uncle Chung's."

I smiled. "I know. After tonight, though, I wouldn't be surprised if Mom forced me to take the bus just to get some takeout Chinese food from now on."

"Just be careful, okay?"

I promised. After saying goodbye, which always took us around five more minutes before actually hanging up the phone, I decided to get a little more involved in superhero work, even if only as a "casual observer" of the unusual. Maybe I could recruit Freddie, seeing as how his chameleon powers could work pretty darned well for my purpose.

Too bad I didn't exactly know the first thing about detective work, but, hey, I was open to on-the-job training. Or whatever.

Chapter 8

You know, there's a special place in hell for bullies of all stripes. I mean, Gorilla Grip Cohen has reserved seating waiting for him when the time comes, and I'm sure it'll be at Satan's right hand. Hopefully inside his Latrine of Fire. For other jerks, though...

I was on my way home from my tutorial with Dr. Dibbs, when I spotted a kid who looked about my age or slightly younger being taunted by a couple of older ones. He wasn't really responding to them, and I guess that was a good sign that he was smart enough not to lower himself to their level, but it still pissed me off. I mean, I'd been there before.

The kid was overweight. Not obese, but overweight enough to be picked on. He also had tons of freckles along with curly red hair, which made him an even bigger target for stupid jokes. He didn't look poor or anything. He was actually dressed up pretty nice, a backpack slung over his shoulder, but that didn't stop those morons. They looked like total punks who also might have been jocks at the same time. I mean, they were pretty built for their age, dressed in tattered jackets and denim. I wouldn't have been surprised if they'd carried those little switchblades in their pockets. Seriously, I couldn't get any better in describing a couple of clichés.

"Hey, have you seen pigs fly?" one of them asked as they trotted behind the kid, every once in a while reaching out to tug at his backpack or give him a "playful" shove.

"Nope, but maybe ol' Big Bird here might want to show us how it's done," his buddy replied. "Hey, Biggie, how about jumping off a roof and showing us how it's done, huh?"

They went on for a couple more moments, poking and laughing, calling the kid names, and I saw that among those who were walking around the general area, no one seemed to be aware of what was going on. Then again, maybe they'd grown pretty indifferent to other people's misery. We were at a small side street that didn't have a lot of pedestrians since rundown tenements surrounded us, not shops. I kind of figured that those idiots hung around the area and just decided to have fun at this poor guy's expense. Since I was at the cross-street, waiting for the light to change when they appeared, I decided to jump in.

"Hey! Leave him alone!" I called out.

"Huh? What? Leave who alone, faggot?" one of them yelled back, and his friend laughed, giving me the middle finger. "Oh, you mean Baby Huey over here?" He gave the kid another quick shove. The boy stumbled forward a couple of steps, but he just set his mouth in a grim line and adjusted his backpack. He didn't break his stride, otherwise. I felt really bad; I was sure he was used to crap like this.

"It's all fun and games," his friend added. "Speaking of fun and games, how about giving us some fun, huh? It's been a while since I got to blow off steam."

"Dude, seriously? That's lame," his buddy said. I thought that was lame, too, but funny as hell. I mean, who'd want to get it on with that loser? I wouldn't be surprised if his hands had already filed a restraining order against the rest of his body.

"Shut up. So how about it, huh, princess? You look a little anemic and skinny, but I'm sure you're used to kneeling down, and I'm not talking about praying, either." Neanderthal Number One walked up to me and draped an arm around my shoulder. He looked me up and down before pointing at my legs. "You think he's got some pretty strong knees?"

"You're an asshole," I said, surprised at how calm I sounded despite the fact that I was crapping myself.

Neanderthal One, who was as tall as me but way heavier, smacked me upside the head pretty hard. I yelped as I staggered forward, and he laughed, "What? What did you say? You want my asshole? You all hot for a poke, faggot?"

"Damn, dem queers are getting pretty brave, proposi—eeeyyyargh!"

I ducked with a little cry just as something whooshed down, plucked those two troglodytes off the street, and flew off with them. I glanced up to find them sailing away, each goon held in one of Magnifiman's meaty arms. I smirked as I watched them flail and scream.

"Serves you right, jackasses," I crowed, gingerly rubbing the back of my head. It throbbed from the major smacking I'd gotten. "Give 'em hell, Magnifiman!"

I sighed and brushed off my jacket as I stood back up, reminding myself to take some aspirin when I got home. Then I remembered the other kid and turned around. He was still standing there, watching the sky and looking pretty impressed. He was also very, very calm about the whole thing, which I thought was amazing.

"Hey, are you okay?" I asked, and then he turned to me with a frown. No, really. That's gratitude for you.

"I can take care of myself. I've got what it takes to beat those creeps," he huffed. Adjusting his backpack once more, he walked on while I cocked an eyebrow at him.

Wow, you're very welcome. It's no problem at all. My pleasure, really. I shook my head and muttered a few choice words about people who wouldn't know class if it bit them in the ass. I carried on, my mood a little sour, and things didn't get any better when I passed by a small electronics shop with a bunch of old, used computers sitting behind the display window.

Just as I walked by, the computer monitors flashed a bright white, startling me. I turned and saw the screens of about four monitors flickering before fading into black. Then white text marched across the screens, so it looked like I was seeing echoes of the same dumb message.

Remember bingo night! I'll call you when the time comes! <33333333

I rolled my eyes and walked on. Before rounding the final corner into my street, I passed a couple of shop owners who stood, smoking, on the sidewalk, looking pretty grumpy.

"I can't afford to have the ventilation fixed," one of them said. I recognized him. It was Mel Bryant, whom everyone in the neighborhood called "the gentle giant" because though he was this big, hulking guy who could intimidate anyone with just his presence, he was the nicest, most generous mechanic who'd always shared some down-home cooking with me when I was a little kid. He was Dad's mechanic, and I used to get treats from him while Dad and I waited for him to change the oil or something. From a poor, rural region, where blacks were still being treated like crap, he never talked about the bad stuff he put up with all his life.

The other guy was Francisco Hernandez, who owned the tiny grocery next to Mel's garage. He listened in silence, his hands in his filthy apron's pockets the whole time. "Yeah—I keep telling Mr. Rush that the building—our building—needs repairs. He doesn't listen. He even said that if the roof hasn't caved in, we shouldn't have anything to worry about."

Mr. Bryant shook his head as he threw his cigarette

on the pavement and squashed it with his foot. "Landlord, my ass. As long as he gets the money, he don't give no crap about vents making noise."

"I'll have to do the repairs, myself," Mr. Hernandez said, wiping his nose with his sleeve, and grimacing. "Once I find the time, I'll do it. Right now? No time."

"Hell, who does?"

I passed by and waved at them both. They stopped their conversation and greeted me, but I didn't bother engaging them, seeing as how they seemed a little upset over the shabby conditions they were forced to put up with, day in and day out.

Mom and Liz were set to watch *The Sixth Sense* that night. Talk about a miracle. Mom, who was always too freaked out to watch horror movies, agreed to watch *The Sixth Sense*. She even looked kind of smug when Liz announced it over dinner and invited me and Dad to watch with them.

"Really?" I said, blinking at Mom. She just grinned at me.

"Honey, what's there for me to worry about? I'm not going to be in a dark theatre, the lights will be on, and it's in the living room."

"Besides," Scanlon piped up (did I mention that he had dinner with us tonight?), "I'll be there to keep you ladies company."

Liz flashed him a tight-lipped smile, and Mom laughed. Across the way, Dad looked a little puzzled but kept quiet, while I narrowed my eyes at my food. I'd have given Scanlon another death glare, but since he sat beside me, it was a little hard trying to mask it without looking like I had some weird visual defect.

"So how about it, scamp? You up to some goose-pimply entertainment tonight? Ah-woooooo..." he said, the final bit being a cheesy moan that was supposed to make him sound like, you know, a ghost.

"I'm actually getting all goose-pimply right now, thanks," I said, instinctively stiffening when he reached in front of me to take the pepper shaker.

Man, Disney's Haunted Mansion had nothing on the Plath dining experience. I looked at Liz with my best why-can't-you-marry-him-now-and-convert-him-to-normalcy look. Unfortunately, she was too busy giggling at Scanlon's cleverness.

I sighed and lightly toyed around with my dinner for a bit. We were having tuna fish casserole, which never agreed with my stomach. I expected a miserable night on the toilet later. "Mom, can we have a dog?" I blurted out.

"So you can feed him your food while I'm not looking?" Mom replied, all smiles and sweet motherly vibes mowing me down.

I shrugged. "Well, yeah."

"Nice try, but sorry. I'm afraid you'll have to eat what's in front of you, honey."

"Oh, and it's your turn to wash the dishes, Eric," Liz said, and to add insult to injury, Scanlon turned to me.

"Hey, want some help with the dishes, sport? If the ladies don't mind waiting, I'd be more than happy to give you a hand. I mean, what are bosom buddies for, right? Birds of a feather, you know? All for one, and one for all, right?" He actually made some weird gesture with a hand, which I figured was his way of being ghetto. "Yo, dude! Aha-ha-ha-ha-*slurp!*"

"Ohmigawd, no. I'll survive. I've done this a gazillion times before. Jeebus."

He shrugged and then reached out to muss up my hair. For the third time in one night. "Okeedokee, artichokee. Just holler, though, if you need an extra hand."

I looked at Mom while gripping the edge of the table till my knuckles turned white. "Mom, make him stop," I hissed.

She only rolled her eyes, and Liz giggled even more. Dad looked like his head was about to pop. Too bad for me, I'd yet to master the fine art of masculine control the way Dad had it. He just soldiered on with his dinner, while I sulked and groused. Whenever Scanlon leaned close to mock-whisper in my ear, I'd growl at him like a rabid dog. Not that it mattered, anyway, since he was completely oblivious to my pain, all for my sister's sake.

In fact, now that I thought about it, I wouldn't have been surprised if Liz and Scanlon weren't really dating, and that Liz had hired him just to make life miserable for me till I turned eighteen or something. My sister wasn't above criminal maneuvers like that. I mean, we were cut from the same cloth, you know. I shouldn't have been surprised.

So I just suffered in silence till everyone was done,

and I literally shooed them out of the dining room, so I could have some quiet time to myself. Dishes and garbage-dumping—I was living out a feminist Cinderella story, with Prince Charming out there somewhere in the dreary badlands of Vintage City, all decked out in tight-tight-*tight* spandex that made me hard every time I thought about him.

I actually started zoning out a little while I was up to my elbows in soapy water. I didn't even catch myself till I thought I heard a voice singing behind me, and I snapped out of my trance only to realize that, good lord, it was *me*. Singing. Like Snow White or Cinderella while they did their chores around the house or cottage. That realization gave me my second creepy, spine-tingling moment of the evening.

"Ugh! Gross!" I spat, shuddering, before scrubbing more violently at the casserole dish. When I took out the garbage, I made sure to rescue the usual gay ads from the soft porn section (as I called it), which pretty much roused me from that momentary icky Disney moment. Or maybe I should say aroused me instead because, damn, those ads I found were total scorchers.

I passed the time in my room, reading for a bit after my usual gay ad gawking. I thought that being at my computer would be courting danger, with Althea dangerous and loose out there. In fact, not only did I unplug my computer, I also covered the thing with an old afghan that Mom made after she gave birth to me. It was made of cheap, scratchy acrylic yarn that had made me yowl and yank at her ears and boobs while breastfeeding when Mom wrapped me with it. At least that was what she told me. To what extent a computer-morphing superhero would feel the itchiness of cheap acrylic yarn against a computer, I sure couldn't tell, but I thought that it was just as good a protection against evil forces, the way strung-up garlic was a defender against vampires and Scanlon Dorsey. Then again, seeing as how Scanlon spent the evening with us and was even set to "chaperone" Mom and Liz through tonight's movie, there was something to be said about the real effectiveness of folk remedies, or whatever strung-up garlic was called by superstitious rural types back in the day.

I couldn't wait to hear Liz's report of tonight's horror extravaganza. I figured that she'd be in pain tomorrow, with bruises or whatnot where Mom grabbed hold of her because Mom just totally freaked out.

Incidentally, I also wondered what Magnifiman had done with those two jerks. Sensitivity training might be too little, too late. I hoped they'd come back as black mold in the next life.

Chapter 9

It was sort of like Minimum Day at my "special school" today because Dr. Dibbs said that he was needed for some undercover medical work, whatever that meant. My human chameleon buddy, Freddie, had to be recruited. So that left me with Brenda, who remained tight-lipped about what the Sentries had been up to lately, and who pretty much bribed me into shutting up by telling me that Dr. Dibbs didn't leave instructions for homework, which meant that I had the rest of the day to squander.

"You're not really that off the hook yet, kiddo," Brenda said as she pulled out a folder from under her counter. I felt the blood drain away from me.

"You're kidding!" I protested. "Why can't I have a day off, too?"

"Because you can't, and that's that." Brenda smiled sweetly. "You might not have any homework, but you do have some exercises to do. You can work in the shop area if you want a little atmosphere, but you're also welcome to use the back room if you prefer the privacy."

Being surrounded by old, old furniture and knickknacks whose owners were now most likely dead while working on school stuff proved to be a bigger draw, so I did my exercises perched on one of the high bar stools in front of the counter, while Brenda talked shop with customers. An elderly lady spotted me and asked if I were a foster kid in Brenda's care and why on earth wasn't I in school? I figured that if I looked slumped and pale and pathetic enough, she'd leave the shop convinced that I had TB or something.

I was out of Brenda's antique shop by 11:30-ish, and with the afternoon suddenly free, I didn't really feel like going home yet, so I did a little window-shopping in the downtown area, taking care to avoid the main square, which was always packed with the lunch crowd by that time.

Some of the coolest shops could be found on the smaller side streets. I guess being pushed aside by the bigger and swankier stores pretty much made them grow some mighty big balls and bask in their fringe status.

I decided to explore Sycamore Lane, which was this narrow little street a couple of blocks or so from the main square. A bunch of shops ran the length, but only about half of them were actually open for business. The rest were empty spaces, with the display windows getting all filthy and difficult to see through. The good thing was that none of them were boarded up like in the dingier alleys in the seedier parts of Vintage. The empty shops were just empty and dirty, with "for lease" signs tacked onto the display windows.

At the end of the street was an adult bookstore. I thought of walking in and pretending like I was twenty-one, but because the window was covered up, discreet-like, with pink paper, I had to steal a quick look through the front door. The tall, tattooed woman at the counter caught me staring, and judging from the way she looked at me, I figured she wouldn't be convinced that I was old enough. She even moved her arm to show off her "Devil's Angel" tattoo with the bloody knife filling up her entire upper arm.

Okay, okay, I got the hint.

There was also a New Age bead shop a few doors down, not to mention a leather store that also sold all kinds of bongs in different designs and shapes. There were a couple of edgy urban wear shops with eardrum-shattering music screaming through the doors.

The highlight, though, was the new retro arcade about three doors down from the bead shop. At that point I realized that I was getting pretty hungry, so I could only manage a quick jealous look through the window while making a mental note to tell my friends about it the next time I saw any of them. It would be great for the whole gang to go there and spend a couple of hours chilling and wasting money on awesome games like Pac-Man or Tron or whatever. Of course, I'd still have to go online, find free cyber versions of these games, and familiarize myself with them before tackling the real deal.

Except for Asteroids. I could whoop major ass with my eyes blindfolded with that game.

I decided to go to the lingerie store where Liz worked. It was the one that Althea tried to get me to work for a while ago. There I found her folding T-shirts and looking bored as hell.

"Hey, I'm hungry," I said, waltzing up to her. "No school today. Feed me."

She just scowled. "You're playing hooky. No deal."

"No, really. You can even call Brenda if you don't believe me. By the way, how're the bruises coming along?"

She sighed and held up her injured arm, her scowl deepening. "I don't know how long it'll take for them to go away, but it's been embarrassing as hell. People look at me funny, and I've had a couple of girls pull me aside and suggest that I report my abusive boyfriend to the police."

"Lesson learned, I guess. It's not worth literally risking life and limb over bonding moments with Mom."

Liz nodded, rolling her eyes. "I never thought that she'd have that kind of a grip. Man. The movie wasn't even a third done, and she'd already turned into a human barnacle. I had to threaten her with wasting a stick of butter just to pry her fingers off my arm. Seriously, if you want to see Mom back off, hold the household budget hostage. She'll listen."

"What, didn't Scanlon help?"

Liz shrugged. "His idea of helping was resting an arm around my shoulders and asking me if I was getting scared every, well, five minutes or so."

"He's a real Romeo, that Dorsey guy," I noted, which earned me a pretty lethal sort of look from my sister.

"Lay off him, Eric," she warned. "Or I'll tear your balls off with my teeth."

"Sweet. I like your subtlety." I looked around and took in all the froufrou underwear and casual clothes that packed the store. I never realized that so much lace and silk could exist within four walls. I was getting dizzy. "Take your lunch, dude. I'm hungry."

"Then go home and nuke something."

"No, it's time for your lunch, and I don't want any more microwaved crap filling my belly. Come on, Liz. Please? I promise I'll treat you when I get a job—well, when Mom and Dad let me, anyway."

She actually hesitated. I mean, figure *that* one out. There it was, a golden opportunity to slack off, and she wasn't taking it? What perks come with adulthood again?

At that moment, a group of four women in designer clothes swept inside the store, chatting and looking down their noses at everything around them. A cloud of horrible perfume, probably four different kinds, surrounded them like a poisonous bubble. Even though I didn't work retail, I knew right off the bat that these women spelled High Maintenance Trouble. I gave Liz's arm, the uninjured one, a sharp tug.

"Let's get out of here, quick!" I hissed, and we did. Liz gave one of her co-workers a quick word, ran to the back to clock out, and then made a beeline to the front door, dragging me behind her. Now *that's* the spirit.

We went to Dog-in-a-Bun, where I had a turkey dog. Pretty decent, certainly way better than those rubbery horrors that they served during bingo night. Which reminded me—those poor seniors who were subjected to those nasty things needed to pool their resources together and file a complaint or something. I mean, think about it. They were old and frail, and they still had to put up with crap food like that, as if that was society's thanks for all those years of their lives spent working hard and making this crummy world a better place for everyone else.

Back to lunch, during which something kind of weird happened...

The whole time I was with Liz, I didn't feel comfortable, and it had nothing to do with the fact that my sister sat across the table from me, and I had to see those bruises on her arm. In fact, even Liz seemed a little off-kilter. Sure, she was born that way, but at that moment, she seemed in a weirder mood than usual.

We hardly spoke the whole time. I think we spent most of Liz's lunch break gnawing, drinking, swallowing, and squirming in our chairs without really knowing why. Every once in a while we'd meet each other's eyes and then frown quizzically. There was something strange that kind of hung above us the whole time. Like electricity that crackled non-stop but that was also very quiet and subtle. It made itself felt but not enough to be jarring or to make us panic. It was like an anticipation or a lingering dread that we couldn't put our fingers on.

"What's wrong?" she asked after several minutes of this. I shook my head.

"I don't know. I just feel strange. Like something's about to happen, and I don't know what, when, or how. Know what I mean?"

She nodded. "I know. I feel the same. Let's finish lunch and get the hell out of here."

We did and hurried out, but nothing out of the ordinary happened. I thought about it more when I got home after dropping Liz off at the lingerie shop that it was that same feeling of waiting for the other shoe to drop. Only this time it was much stronger than before. Much, much stronger.

I got on the phone with Peter at the right time. I told him about today—the weird feeling that came over me and Liz, and he took me seriously, bless him. At first I wasn't sure if I could share it because I thought that he'd just laugh me off or tell me that I was just being paranoid or something, but he didn't.

"I learned early on to trust gut instinct," he said as I fidgeted with the phone cord, wrapping it around my fingers nervously. "Did it feel stronger when you were at different places or something?"

"No. It was pretty steady."

"Okay. I'll tell Trent and everyone else, and keep an eye out. It's been a while since the last attack, and nothing's come up yet. So far we've been busying ourselves with the usual stuff up and down Vintage."

"Did anything weird happen at that street I told you about? You know, with Mom freaking out over nothing?"

"Yeah, Freddie went undercover to scope out the area, and he found nothing strange, though he almost got picked up by some sleazy john."

"Huh?"

"Um...Freddie decided to blend in with the crowd, sort of, and transformed into a hooker." Peter coughed. I could actually hear his skin turn red over the phone. "I thought he was going to turn himself into a homeless guy, but I guess he was feeling a little, uh, adventurous that night."

"And you guys let him do that?"

"Hey, we didn't know what he was up to till he buzzed us after taking down this drunk and nearly breaking the guy's arm for groping him. Frankly, I think he kicks ass in his female masks, but that's just me. Ahem."

I needed some time for all of that stuff to sink in, so I urged Peter to continue while I rubbed my temple and grimaced. He said, "Wade volunteered to keep an eye on the place, too, and she came up with nothing." Peter fell silent for a moment. "It *is* kind of bizarre that you've been getting all kinds of bad vibes about different places. That says something, even though we haven't found anything yet."

I watched myself play around with the phone chord once the throbbing in my temple faded. "Well, I guess it's something like a building up of tension, you know? I talked about it with my family before, and since the last big attack at the mall, nothing's happened yet, but that's only because whoever was responsible is just waiting for the right time to make his next move."

"It's kind of overdue, isn't it?" Peter replied. Then he drew in a sharp breath. "God, I just gave myself goosebumps."

"I guess we just need to keep our eyes and ears open."

"Hmm. I thought that you guys had super sense or something like that. At least, I wondered about it when I watched Althea uncover those stolen computers in Beck Street."

"No, we don't have that. Like Spidey Sense or something? Nah. Althea just happened to hook herself up to the computers in that apartment because it was the closest source she found. She didn't realize they were stolen till the moment she took over them."

I remembered yesterday's incident with the redheaded kid and asked, "By the way, did Trent say anything about the two bullies he picked up?" I gave him a quick run-down on the incident in case Trent hadn't been able to update the other heroes on his part in keeping the city cleaned up. That had to be one of the funner aspects of being involved with a superhero. I got to be in on all the gossip and little behind-the-scenes things, which I thought was always cool.

Peter chuckled and said yeah, Trent had. As Magnifiman, he took those two punks to some youth club at the far end of the city and actually stayed around while they grudgingly signed up for a weekend of community service work. I'd absolutely no idea what that community service work was all about, but I couldn't help but laugh whenever I thought about Tweedledee and Tweedledum trying to do something productive for underprivileged kids. Or cleaning Vintage City's streets, literally. Maybe they'd be given latrine work or something like that— you know, cleaning out all the porta-potties up and down the city and public park. There you go.

It was once again time for—guess what! Superhero practice! This time, instead of the Trill's old subterranean hideout, we were in one of the old warehouses that the mayor had handed over to the superheroes. This one was an old warehouse that was about to be converted into lofts, except that the company had gone belly-up after a major scandal involving stolen money and other things that slimy, white-collar crooks usually did. So the place was abandoned to graffiti artists, time, stray animals, and the weather, till it was nothing more than a rotting shell of a partially finished luxury complex.

I've already mentioned that the place was a serious safety hazard, a situation that someone genetically-altered would've been able to put up with without a problem. Too bad for me, I wasn't genetically fixed up in any way, so should there have been a cave-in before the heroes found me, I'd be gone.

I pretty much voiced my concerns while Dr. Dibbs was showing me where to make myself comfortable. He chose one of the loft spaces for me to hide in, which didn't really sink in too well because it was cold, dark, and creepy.

I looked around me, swallowing, as he let me take in the surroundings. "Hey, listen," I said, "I'll stay here all nice and quiet, but can we skip the whole tying up bit? This place gives me the creeps, and if I'm tied down, I know I'll just have a major meltdown."

Dr. Dibbs cocked his head. "Interesting. I'd have thought that simply being in this place would cause a meltdown, but I suppose I was being much too harsh on you, Mr. Eric."

"Um, actually, if I could hang out at the Jumping Bean while everyone else practiced search-and-rescue here, that'd be way better." I flashed him a hopeful little smile. As they say, though, hope springs eternal. In my case, it was always out of reach because my Jumping Bean suggestion apparently didn't leave its mark in Dr. Dibbs; in other words, he completely ignored it.

"Young Mr. Peter has already argued pretty convincingly to keep you free on the condition that you stay put and not mess around with the day's agenda."

"If I promise to stay put, will you let me have a mocha or something?" I'm nothing if not insistent. That said, Dr. Dibbs was nothing if not selective in his hearing.

He merely adjusted my jacket (Peter's jacket, that is) and ordered me to put my hood up. I wore a hoodie under the jacket; it was *that* cold in there. Then he gave me this gigantic flashlight. "It's got brand new batteries, Mr. Eric," he said with a satisfied grin. He nudged his glasses up his nose. "It's a mighty powerful thing, that flashlight is, so you've got nothing to worry about should the lights outside go dim." With another quick inspection of the room, Dr. Dibbs left me alone.

I stared forlornly at the massive flashlight in my hand and guessed its length. Seriously, if I were to make a convincing enough picture of a boy who was trying to overcompensate for something, that would be the moment. I think the flashlight was around two feet long, with the main lamp thingie being five inches in diameter, give or take an inch. I pushed the button to turn it on and nearly dropped the whole thing, screaming and blinded.

Note to self: never turn on a ginormous flashlight while staring straight at the bulb. Jeebus.

I suppose there was some comfort there. I could be abandoned in that decrepit old warehouse and still be able to find my way out, thanks to this thing. Besides, the mere size of the flashlight was enough for me to marvel at its other use, which was that of a weapon in case I had to fight someone or something.

From an old speaker that had been set up in one corner of the room, Magnifiman's voice blared.

"Hello, innocent victim," he said, his voice slightly breaking up. I'd always thought that the speakers they used in that warehouse were a little too old for their purpose.

I held up a hand. Then I realized that he couldn't see me. "Hi, Magnifiman," I said, blushing, as I lowered my hand sheepishly. "I'm in position and ready."

"Good. The others are being briefed at the moment, and they'll begin today's practice in around five minutes. Stay put, and be patient. They'll come for you. Magnifiman out."

I was alone again. I looked around and saw nothing that I could sit on comfortably, which was a real bummer. I didn't know how long the others would take to find me, and I wanted to be as relaxed as I possibly could be under the circumstances.

No such luck. The room was completely empty. The only things that made the area slightly less psychologically traumatic were the gigantic cracks in the walls and floor. Then again, if mutant caterpillars suddenly crawled out of those cracks, the Psychological Trauma Meter would shoot right through the roof.

There were four large windows with no glass, so the wind blew in and chilled me. I pulled up my hood and walked over to one of the windows and gazed out, scanning Vintage City's grimy landscape. It was also overcast, so there really wasn't much light coming through, but I kind of liked the way the scene looked, all urban and filthy and rundown, with rain clouds hanging above. There was nothing but warehouses surrounding me because we were in the old industrial end of the city. From where I stood, I could see the rooftops of the shorter ones. I noted piles of rotting crates, boxes, and miscellaneous industrial materials scattered all over. There were also those giant industrial ventilation duct things that jutted out of the roofs like massive periscopes. Every once in a while a few black birds would flitter from one thing to another, which startled me at first into thinking that they were bizarre shadows.

From some distant part of the warehouse, I could hear tiny fake explosions and gunfire, so I figured that the heroes were already on the move. In the meantime, I could enjoy the view a little more.

I guess I zoned out after a couple of minutes of just staring out because I didn't realize that the shadow creeping across the rooftop of one of the other warehouses across the way was actually alive till I blinked, snapped out of my trance, and looked again.

"What the..."

Nope, it wasn't caused by a flock of black birds. I pinched my eyes shut and then looked one more time, leaning out as far as I could. Holy crap. I wasn't hallucinating. It was a giant spider, moving over boxes and crates and other junk. I couldn't guess what its size could be, but I was sure that there was something human-like about it. It moved so quickly and so easily that I could've sworn that it was actually gliding, not walking on all eight legs.

It paused once it reached the edge of the roof it was on. Then it raised itself on its four rear legs, the front four waving in the air. Was it smelling the air or something? I wasn't familiar with the way spiders worked, so I couldn't say for sure. Then it heaved its humungous body and leaped from that roof and landed on the next one.

The sudden downpour rattled me out of my shock. The rain came down hard and fast, a solid curtain of gray that forced me to stumble back into the room.

Once I managed to gather my wits, I quickly turned on my flashlight and hurried out the door, yelling for the others.

Chapter 10

I couldn't look at Peter as we sat in his car. We'd reached my house by then. The car idled, I was a little drenched, and it still poured outside. My clothes, including Peter's jacket, were a mess. There were scorched patches here and there. I could still smell burned fabric, and I could've sworn that some of the damaged parts still smoked.

"You okay?"

I nodded, sinking in my seat. "I am, yeah. Just embarrassed as hell. I'm really sorry I screwed up your training today."

"We've got plenty of other days to train. It's just...when you decide to run from your designated hideaway, don't get in the line of fire. We almost blew you away back there."

"I know, I know. I'm sorry. I just wanted to tell you—"

Peter sighed. "We all scoured the area, Eric, and we found no sign of a giant spider anywhere. It doesn't mean that it wasn't there, though."

I looked at him, finally. "You believe me, then?"

He chuckled. "Of course I do. We all do. But that was reckless, Eric. You could've been seriously hurt, probably even killed, by running straight for our practice zone. Remember, for the bigger warehouses, we use eighty percent of our powers. God, even Freddie as G. I. Joe was nearly on full blast."

What happened in the past hour would live on in infamy—in my immediate world, anyway. It was about to be counted on my growing list of What Not To Tell Your Parents. I could still see everything happen in slow motion. The exploding dummies and the noise of simulated gunfire suddenly crashing around me as I ran into the open area on the main floor of the warehouse, while I waved my arms and shouted at everyone about the giant spider I saw. Everything was a blaze of white and color, fire, speed, electronics, and in G. I. Joe's case, improvised weaponry (a hammer flew pretty damned close to my head) because Freddie was told not to use his grenade launchers for any kind of exercise. Then came the scattered cries of "Gah! What the hell is he doing here? Shouldn't he be kidnapped?" and then the too familiar sensation of getting swept up by Calais in hyper speed and taken to safety, while Magnifiman bellowed through the speakers: "I think not tying him down is a bad idea, Calais!" Then Dr. Dibbs and Brenda yelled at everyone to stop destroying things because the innocent kidnap victim somehow found a way to escape his captors, the crazy kid. When I said that it was embarrassing, I meant it.

"I promise I won't do it again." I mustered up enough courage to lean close for a kiss. One of the things that I'd yet to get used to was coping with extremely humiliating situations like what had just happened. I always defaulted to believing that Peter was mad at me, so trying to make the first reconciliatory move was always so hard.

He held my face and kissed me again, this time the usual full-on, wet, tongue-in-throat kind that made me melt. And get so goddamned horny. The fact that it was raining hard kind of added to the swoony, slutty moment. We ended up making out for a couple of minutes in the rain, breaking apart only because moving had grown extremely uncomfortable with a raging boner in a small car.

I pulled away and rested my forehead against his. We were both breathing heavily, and a quick glance down at his mouth nearly drove me into attacking him right then and there. A lot has been written about kiss-swollen lips, but I was there to attest to the truth in all the purple prose descriptions of what those looked like.

"I gotta go before I have an accident in my pants," I whispered. Peter didn't say anything, but he gave me one more deep kiss for the road.

I couldn't remember getting out of his car, but I wouldn't have been surprised if I just tumbled out and crawled blindly toward the front door of my house. I was just glad that Scanlon wasn't around to catch me all disoriented, half-burned, and totally hard.

The good thing about embarrassing stuff like that

was that the heroes were pretty cool about it. Well, after a few hours, anyway. Wade pinged me later that night for a nice chat, and it was like bonding with a really cool gal pal about silly stuff. She was sweet enough to tell me that what happened didn't screw anyone's practice time—merely rescheduled it.

"I'm monitoring the industrial area, Eric," she said. "That spider thing you saw could be using one of the warehouses for its hideout. Or it might not, if it's smart enough to learn from the Trill's mistakes."

"Hey, don't do it alone. It looked pretty formidable, and God knows how strong it is."

"No worries!" she said. "Magnifiman's on it, too. Then again, he's pretty much spread out over Vintage City, while everyone else has specific areas they're assigned to watch."

Yeah, that sounded pretty reasonable. I figured that Magnifiman wouldn't agree to being limited in his scope. He was such a Type A, and if he could, I was sure that he'd give himself another major city to guard over, in addition to this crummy dump.

"By the way, boyfriend, you should see my fire blades. They're the brand spankin' new addition to my arsenal. I can kick the Debutantes' dual butts now that my powers have expanded some more."

Girl fight! I couldn't wait!

I'd been thinking about that retro arcade. Okay, I'd been obsessing about it since I discovered the damn place. Whenever I could, I tried to go online and try my hand at some of these old games. I totally sucked at Frogger. How lame is that? I hadn't tried Super Mario yet, but Donkey Kong was next on my list, and I thought Pac-Man was like crack. I was also seriously whooping major ass with Asteroids.

I'd make sure to tell Peter about it the next time we went out on a date. He was geeky enough to want to take on a challenge from me before, and I'd kicked his hot ass more than once in online games. I guess it was a good sign that superpowers have limits.

I also hadn't forgotten about bingo night. How could I? I'd actually had a dream, fer chrissakes, that involved me stuck in a big hall, surrounded by zombified seniors, playing bingo. The guy calling out the letters and numbers was Jabba the Hut, and he had some strange half-naked undead woman, whose jaw seemed to have rotted away and fallen off, chained to his chair and wearing a tattered bikini. Then anyone who staggered to their feet and squawked, "Bingo!" without any body parts dropping off because of the sudden movement, would go up to Jabba and then get eaten up. I mean, really—crunch, crunch.

I just sat there, freaking out, surrounded by groaning reanimated corpses and completely frozen. I couldn't move a finger, let alone run. Body parts and rotting tissue were dropping around me. It was *gross*. I woke up just at the moment when I turned to the zombie sitting next to me to puke all over him. Or it. Whatever. At any rate, I decided to do something about my predicament.

Sometime after breakfast I went back to the kitchen and started rummaging through cupboards.

It was a Saturday, so Liz had to go to work, and Dad went golfing with his buddies. Mom and I hung around the house. Things were pretty quiet and dull, so I went on ahead with Operation Blow Bingo Night and started hunting around in the kitchen.

"Oh, my God!"

I whirled around, startled, a box of oatmeal and a bottle of expired aspirin in my hands. "Hi, Mom. Sorry, I was just looking around."

She stood at the kitchen doorway, jaw hanging, a hand pressed against her chest. It took her a moment to find her voice because I'd apparently shocked her speechless. She actually looked like she was about to faint. I asked her what was wrong while going back to my shelf-scanning-and-rummaging.

"Good grief, Eric, don't ever do that again!"

"What? Do what?"

"Frighten me like that!" Mom took a deep and loud breath before walking up to the sink and filling up a glass with tap water. She scowled at me as she downed it.

I looked around. "Like what?"

She waved a hand around the kitchen. "Like that! Opening every cupboard and drawer and leaving them open! I haven't gotten over the movie, you know!"

Oh, that. I forgot about the movie. I figured that she was still freaking out over the kitchen ghost and all the open cupboards and drawers in one of those scenes. Now if anyone wondered about where I got my tendencies toward drama queen-ness, you know the answer. I frowned at the two items I held and then showed them to her. "Mom, do you think that mixing oatmeal and expired aspirin will make me sick? I mean, like, incapacitated?"

"I don't think so," she replied as she went about, nervously shutting every open drawer and cupboard. "Why?"

"Do we have expired food that I can eat and get sick on?"

She stared at me. "Eric, what on earth are you trying to do?"

"I want to get sick." I had to stop myself before I blurted out "because I don't want to go to bingo night with Althea," knowing the kind of sermon that Mom would likely unleash on me if I did.

Apparently holding back proved to be a bad idea. Or at least being honest didn't pay off *again*. It never did, seriously, even with all those early childhood lectures about being a good boy all year long and getting massive karma points from Santa Claus come Christmas time.

"Okay, I'm going to count down from ten. When I get to one, you'd better have a clear, rational explanation that's good enough to qualify you to be the next Dalai Lama," Mom said, raising a hand and closing her eyes as she counted under her breath. "Ten...nine..."

"Just kidding! I was only messing with you, Mom. No need to count. Or send me to Tibet."

Mom opened her eyes and glowered at me. "If you see anything expired, Eric, throw it away. There's no need to be so sarcastic about our storage habits and saying things like you want to get sick." She went back to closing the cupboards before retrieving her mug and pouring herself some coffee.

Okay, things were getting more and more desperate from my end. I threw away the expired pills and thought about finding comfort in toast and Mrs. Horace's "Eric's Special Jam," but the fact that I was going to eat stuff that Mrs. Horace gave me cut me to the quick. POW! went my Catholic conscience because, apparently, you can take the boy out of the Catholic Church, but you can't take the Catholic Church out of the boy.

I hate my conscience. The Pope has a lot to answer for.

So I just stuffed my face with tortilla chips and racked my brain for more ways of getting out of bingo night without making it look like I planned the whole thing. I'd have been able to focus much better if my thought process didn't veer off every ten seconds and wander into sex-with-Peter territory, which was proving to be a much bigger issue than I'd anticipated.

God, did I just say "bigger"?

I didn't even realize that the phone rang till Mom barked at me. "Eric! Are you listening to me? It's Peter on the phone for you!"

"Oh. Sorry." I stood up and shuffled over to where Mom stood by the door, her arm extended as she held the phone for me, a really deep, dark frown on her face. Just as I reached for the phone, she snatched it back and covered the mouthpiece.

"Eric, is there something you need to talk to me about?"

"No. I'm fine, Mom. Thanks for asking." I made a grab for the phone, but Mom swatted my hand away. "Ow! Hey!"

She didn't budge. Covering the mouthpiece again, she said, "I'm not stupid."

"I'm not saying that you are!"

"No, but you're acting like I am."

"What, are you saying that you don't trust me?" Oh, that hurt. Well...yeah...

She cocked an eyebrow. "We've been through this before, mister, and the last time we had a talk like this, it was before you were forced to leave us to join the Trill. You can't blame me for overreacting when I smell something fishy."

I sighed, scratching my head impatiently. "Mom, if I want to talk, I'll talk, okay? Can I have some space, please? I mean, I know you worry a lot about me, even more than you worry about Liz, but I really want to be left alone." I paused when I saw that hurt look on her face. "I'm okay, really. I'm being very, very careful when I'm out there, and I've been doing exactly what you told me to do. I can't even hang out with my friends the way I used to ever since... you know...It really sucks being alone all the time." I shook my head, not knowing how else to say what I needed to say. "Mom, I'll be fine. All right? Don't baby me, please?"

Mom's look of hurt eased up, but I could still tell that she was affected by what I said. Nodding and taking a deep breath, she whispered, "Okay, honey. I'll step back a little. I'm sorry."

"It's okay." I took the phone from her. Then I

gave her a kiss and leaned against the wall, waiting for her to leave the kitchen before talking. "Hey," I said, lowering my voice in case of anxious maternal eavesdroppers. "You should've called and left a message on my machine."

"I tried," Peter replied. "You haven't cleared up your machine, you dill weed. It's full."

I loved it when he got all sappy. "Want to go out?" I toyed with the coiled phone cord thing, wrapping each coil around one finger till only the end of my finger poked out. I stared at it and pointedly ignored any Freudian reference the whole thing gave me. "Are you, uh, working today?"

"Not now, but I will soon. Tomorrow will be better."

We made arrangements to meet somewhere downtown because I told him about the retro arcade on Sycamore Lane. He agreed to meet there. Being the super-practical type that I am, I told him that we could just walk around and enjoy the time without having to drive all over the place and waste precious minutes.

Chapter 11

S o I asked Mom's permission after Peter's call. Naturally, she didn't like it. She was totally not into saying yes when I told her, even going so far as to argue, "Didn't you two just have a date recently?" But I was pushy, and she saw that I wasn't going to back down at all.

"Well, I guess it's okay, seeing as how it's daytime and all," she said, rubbing her temples and pinching her eyes shut. "Make sure to finish your homework and chores before leaving. Just be home by three, okay?" Three? *Three?* What kind of sorry date was that?

Peter and I agreed to meet at around noon, which didn't really give us much time together. "But that'll give us only three hours or something," I protested. "That includes all the time wasted, walking around and deciding where to eat and chill out."

"Eric, it's either three hours or nothing."

Damn.

I really hated being told to come home so early, especially since it was a stupid daytime date. It just plain sucked that Mom went to the other extreme on the maternal scale since my ordeal with the Trill.

I'd been following her orders, of course, of being with Peter only when he wasn't in superhero mode. That was cool. In fact, it gave Peter a good reason to strike a balance between normal teenage stuff and superhero work, and his parents turned out to be pretty cool about it. Even Trent, according to Peter, had to agree that his brother desperately needed to enjoy ordinary stuff, not just get all Type A over keeping Vintage City safe the way Magnifiman was being over-the-top Type A. He even went so far as to say that he could handle day-to-day crumminess on his own every once in a while, giving his little brother extra time for fun stuff. What a braggart. Sheesh.

Now it was like I couldn't do anything without Mom going all crazy over where I was going, whom I was going with, how long I expected to be out, etc. It was sort of like I might as well sign up for monk-hood or something. I didn't know how long this pressure cooker was going to last, but I figure that someday, something had to give. For now, all I could do was to grin and bear it because, well, I didn't want to upset Mom and Dad any more than I already had. Liz, I could still work on because, as you know, siblings were put on this earth to torment. Mom and Dad, no.

The other shoe just dropped! My date with Peter for later had just been rescheduled because there'd been an attack downtown. Guess who was the victim this time? Dog-in-a-Bun! It looked like one of my favorite junk food hangouts was jumped by an army of beagle-sized mechanical spiders. Yeah, exactly like the ones that attacked the mall last time.

Around noon, when the place was swarming with families all getting their dog fix, one of the employees said that she heard something scratching in the ceiling, like somewhere in the vents. She at first thought that it was nothing more than the air-conditioning doing weird things and rattling, but the sound grew louder and louder till everyone began to complain about the racket.

Bambi Bailey interviewed her for the news, and the poor girl looked about ready to throw up all over Ms. Bailey. She was so upset that she couldn't talk straight, but she said something like, "I called our manager and told him about the noise, and when he turned off the AC and brought out the ladder to check what was going on, white stuff started shooting out of the vents."

I was shocked. White webby stuff came flying out through the vents, covering people and trapping them where they sat or stood. Some tried to run out but were also caught in the web. Apparently the stuff sounded like a whoopee cushion on crack whenever it got spewed out. That sounded kind of gross and cool at the same time, I thought. People were stuck, with web solidifying around different body parts. Those who had the bad luck of sitting or standing directly under some of the vents were completely covered and nearly passed out from suffocation because of it.

Okay, this was the kicker. Apparently, things would've been way worse had it not been the fact that a force field—yes, a fucking *force field*—somehow got activated and encased the customer area with protective bubbles. So after the initial spewage, the force field suddenly materialized, and whatever else poured out of the ventilation systems afterward just sat on the bubbles till help came.

I couldn't believe it. A force field! Which meant that there'd been a superhero somewhere in the vicinity! I bet that he or she was one of the customers, and he or she just turned on the power and BLOOMP! There it was. I must admit that the thought got me all excited. Imagine, another superhero in our midst! I kind of expected Freddie to be the last one, but I guess not.

How did I know for sure if it was really a superhero and not a bad guy? Well, duh. Why would a bad guy have protected the customers and staff? If anything, he'd've cashed in on the incident and probably locked the doors to keep people inside.

"My goodness! Are you sure?" Ms. Bailey asked, and the girl she was interviewing nodded so hard that she almost tumbled down. Then again, she was also visibly shaking and really traumatized. Her clothes were a mess, her hair stood on end, and she had food splatters all over. I felt so bad. Why Ms. Bailey decided to single her out for an interview, I didn't know.

"Yeah. It was like giant bubbles...you know, the kind that you used to play with as a kid? You blow bubbles through a little loop and stuff? It was like that, but only way, way bigger, stronger, and there were so many of them popping up and closing around people."

"And no one knows who was responsible?"

"It all happened so fast, and it was so crazy..." The girl shook her head and then finally burst into tears and had to be led away. I should have written the local TV station and voiced a complaint about the way Ms. Bailey handled that one.

Spirit Wire responded to the emergency first, she reported. Made sense. I figured that it was easy for Althea to "reach the scene of the crime," so to speak, because her computer-possessing powers acted like range weapons.

"The cash registers first went crazy," said another girl who was being interviewed. "They kind of went off like those arcade games, the numbers moving real fast, the cash drawers opening and closing like when a UFO comes around, and they all made that clinking sound."

Apparently, the AC suddenly turned on by itself, freezing the webby stuff even as it was being puked out of the vents. Then it went off and the heater came on, raising the temps inside the place to pretty uncomfortable levels, but apparently it worked because the webby stuff started to soften up and melt a little. Then the force field bubbles vanished, and all the crap they'd collected just fell onto the floor in sticky puddles.

A few moments later, Calais and Miss Pyro appeared, while Magnifiman went about looking for the source, according to Ms. Bailey. People were freed. Those who nearly got done in by webby stuff had to be hauled off in emergency vehicles to the hospital. No one else who was interviewed could say where the force field bubbles came from.

Dog-in-a-Bun was owned by an Aaron Berkowitz, and he was also interviewed. Poor guy looked devastated. His business was temporarily shut down while police investigated, and there was also the damage situation on both the restaurant itself and the people, both staff and patrons alike.

"I don't understand," he said, shaking his head and looking really overwhelmed in a pretty bad way. "It's only a small business. What have I done wrong? I'm proud of our success, proud of my staff, and we've got so many repeat customers. I don't know. I don't know..."

Liz, who had today off from work, pulled me aside and talked to me about that weird feeling we both had when we were at the Dog-in-a-Bun.

"Isn't that crazy?" she asked. She looked really alarmed. "You know, we could've been there. It could've happened that day when we had lunch." I nodded. Yeah, it was best not to show our freaking out to Mom and Dad, or they'd just ground us both for life for our own safety. We both consoled ourselves with some cheesecake.

I talked to Peter on the phone later that evening, and he said that they'd found some bizarre-looking boxes sitting near each ventilation grate. There were no spiders anywhere, but those boxes were responsible for spewing out the white stuff.

"That's not even the half of it," Peter added, sounding pretty grim over the phone. "We also found timers on those boxes. They were supposed to explode at a certain time. It's a safe bet that it would be around the moment when the mutant web stuff was all emptied out and completely blanketing the restaurant."

"You're kidding. That's fucked up. You mean to say that this nutcase behind the spider attacks is actually bent on killing people?"

"Looks like it. But, Eric, a few people were pretty badly injured during the Puppet's attacks. Sucks to say this, but we've been kind of expecting something more drastic from this guy."

So now it looked as though we'd gone from robbing and terrorizing to attempted murder. I hoped like hell that this spider menace person was the last of the supervillains. From the Devil's Trill to the Shadow Puppet and then to the Deathtrap Debutantes, the craziness seemed to fly all over the place. This spider person freak was way, way more dangerous than the rest, and what worried me even more was that he might prove to be much, much harder to take down.

And the vents! All those accounts of noise rattling the ventilation systems of different businesses? This was the end result. Someone or something must've crawled through ventilation shafts to plant these time bombs, targeting different businesses. I hadn't heard from anyone, either the Sentries or the heroes, about the ventilation problems that had been happening at the same time. Then again, I never really bothered to pursue it.

"Oh, God, I'm an idiot," I hissed, slapping my forehead with my free hand.

"What's up?"

So I told him, which made him quiet. "Don't you think we should get those places emptied out or something, while the police search through their ventilation ducts?"

"I'll look into that," Peter replied. He sounded a little ticked off. "How come you never mentioned it to me or the others before?"

My blood froze. "I—I thought I did," I stammered. "I know that I told Brenda about them, and she said nothing."

"The Sentries and the heroes work together on a limited basis, remember? If you told Brenda, it's likely that she's pursuing that with the rest of the Sentries, while we're left in the dark."

I scratched my head, puzzled. "That's really messed up. Shouldn't you guys team up or something? I mean, your goals are pretty much the same. You want to keep Vintage City safe. So why aren't you getting together on this? I don't get it!"

Peter sighed heavily. When he spoke, he sounded a little tired. "They keep us at arm's length," he said. "It's their choice to do that. Hell, we're lucky that they're willing to help us with our training, antidotes, and spy work. Beyond that, we're two completely separate entities with the same goals. If the Sentries want us to work with them in investigating these ventilation problems, they'll let us know. In the meantime, we're talking to a brick wall."

"Man, that's messed up. It shouldn't be that way. I thought that all the good guys work together and stuff."

"Remember that they're a covert operation, and they're a little more vigilante-like than we want them to be. I wouldn't be surprised if they don't want the heroes' help in their investigation of these ventilation problems."

That was still messed up. "So what're you gonna do?" I prodded.

"I'll tell the others what you told me, of course, but you have to let me know exactly which businesses are affected. So far, only Dog-in-a-Bun got attacked, while the others aren't touched. But it's likely only a matter of time before they become victims. Do you remember who the others were?"

"Um..." I racked my brain. "Mel Bryant and Francisco Hernandez," I sputtered. "I'll have to get back to you on the others. Seriously, I'm kind of drawing a blank."

"That's cool. It's a start. If you can't reach me, just leave a message with the info. We really need to get to these people before anything else happens."

Oh, great. Now the safety of a few little businesses up and down Vintage depended on me. I think my heart momentarily stopped at the realization. "Okay," I said weakly. "I won't let you down." But what if I did? I didn't want to think about it. That was totally messed up. It wasn't until after I hung up the phone that I also realized that I'd forgotten to ask him about the strange force fields. I'd have to put a sticky note on my phone to remind me next time.

Chapter 12

Because of the Dog-in-a-Bun attack, Peter got himself swamped with superhero detective work. That meant our delayed date got delayed again, but that was cool with me. In the meantime, I figured I'd get in touch with Freddie Jameson and see if he'd agree to pretend to be someone who could give me an excuse not to go to bingo night. You know, I used to think of chameleon powers as cool enough, but never before did I even consider it to be absolutely, fantastically *awesome* when the threat of staring at a stack of bingo cards continued to hang over my head like a chemical cloud about ready to burst.

And then, as my way of paying him back, I planned to offer my services to him as a superhero sidekick. Like undercover work. I didn't see what Mom and Dad would object to, really. We'd only be spying or digging around for clues and stuff. It wasn't like I'd be in the middle of a fight or anything. Besides, they always told me that one good turn deserved another, and if Freddie agreed to work with me on Operation Blow Bingo Night, I'd work as his assistant for free. My backup plan to that was an all-out bribe, which meant coming up a way of scraping up enough cash to pay off a superhero, but I'd worry about that when the time came.

At any rate, I decided not to tell Mom and Dad what I had in mind. Best not to give them another reason to worry about me. Besides, I kind of lived with this perpetual threat of eternal grounding hanging over my head in this household. One false move, and BAM! I'd be turned into a monk for life. Mothers can be pretty crazy that way.

So I called him yesterday. I actually got him while he was in chameleon mode, and it took me a while to figure out that the grumpy old man mumbling on the phone was actually hyper, dorky, seventeen-year-old Freddie.

"Oh, sorry. Are you undercover or something?" I asked after I got my brain reset. It was a pretty common thing when it came to Freddie. If you want to go crazy in the shortest amount of time, lock yourself in a room with him and have him transform into one person or mythical beast or animal or whatever. I guarantee complete mental malfunction by the time he's done.

"Yeah, I am, thonny," he barked. I blinked. It sounded like Freddie's mask didn't wear false teeth, and he wasn't used to it, either, so he was having the worst time communicating with me. "I'm thitting at the park, watching the thtupid duckth thwim."

"That's undercover work? What're you after?

Rogue birds or something? I thought we're up against mechanical spiders."

"Dude, don't make me talk too long. Communicating without teeth ith hard. What do you want?"

I sighed. "You know, I'll just wait till tomorrow, when I go to Brenda's shop for my tutorials. I'll talk to you then."

"Hokay. Bah." I think he meant "bye," but I couldn't be so sure. It sounded like he had his mouth covered by something. "Oh. Damn. Thtupid minth. Jutht dropped five." Then the line went dead.

That was yesterday. Onward to today. Or, rather, this morning.

The upside to being tutored was that I didn't have to deal with other kids, who were annoying about 99.9999% of the time. Private tutorials were all about me, me, me, me, *me* in that little library-type room, with Dr. Dibbs coaching my skinny ass. Recess involved tea and treats from Brenda, and lunch was, well, whatever stuff Mom packed for me in the morning. School time varied quite a bit, too, depending on Dr. Dibbs' agenda for the day. Too bad it didn't vary according to my moods; if it did, I'd stop bitching about Geometry and Chemistry and consider those a fair swap for more flexible time.

I just hoped like hell that what we'd been doing would be recognized by the Board of Education or whoever was in charge of home schooling and private tutorials. Because I seriously wanted my diploma someday, and I sure didn't need my chances screwed by last minute deals made with Renaissance

High's school administration.

So that was the upside to my new educational situation. The downside was having Freddie come over every once in a while to harass me during my lessons. Though in this case, I blamed myself because I was the one who'd asked him to come over. A close second to that point was my having to wear a stupid tie. No, really. Dr. Dibbs took his role pretty seriously, but I could only account for that by saying that he was a scientist, and he was used to wearing a suit or something semi-formal under his lab coat.

So I was kind of sweet-talked into wearing a white dress shirt and a black tie to my tutorials. I resisted for a while, of course, but I gave in eventually. I was just happy that they let me wear jeans and my old blue Converse with those. Althea thought it was weird: "Okay, that's just *wrong.*" My parents thought it was cute: "Oh, my God, Frank, look at your Catholic school boy!" Liz thought...well, Liz was my sister: "Ha-ha-ha-ha-ha-ha!" Peter got horny: "That tie has a hundred and one uses, you know, and I'm not talking about playing dress-up, either." Oh, *baby.* Scanlon had yet to see me looking all geeky, and if he did, I'd be inclined to do something pretty drastic to him to make him forget.

When I went to "school" this morning, I was all dressed up, messenger bag stylishly slung across my body. No one was around when I entered, but I was used to that. Brenda spent half her time in the back, doing God knows what, whenever she didn't have customers around. So it was pretty weird when I started feeling as though I weren't alone. The feeling crept over me and made my skin prickle. I figured that I could never get used to Brenda's shop. It was really like stepping into some kind of time portal thing, and having the place packed with old things and smelling like old things while little light filtered through the windows only heightened the spooky feeling I got.

This time, though, I literally felt as though I were being watched. I tried to shrug it off as I picked my way through orphaned pieces of furniture and headless statues. Before I reached the counter, though, the feeling just got too much for me, so I turned around, a little freaked.

Then I saw *him*. OMFG. He sort of materialized from one of the darker corners of the shop, saying, "Oh, hi. I'm sorry. Looks like I surprised you."

Joshua Bell. In person. I just died and went to Buddhist heaven. He smiled and offered a hand. "Looks like you know me already." Lordy, he was *hot*.

I shook his hand. "Oh—yeah, kind of. I mean, I'm a big fan and so on. I've seen a lot of your performances on video, and I listen to your music and..." I stopped, and the world froze. Oh, *hell*. I narrowed my eyes at him. "Freddie?"

Like Cinderella's coach when midnight struck, Joshua Bell melted, and there stood Freddie, giving me that crap-eating grin. Since my hand still held in his, he decided to shake it, anyway. "Hey, how's it going, man?"

Nothing was going unless he was talking about his balls and what I was going to do with them, using Brenda's antique nutcracker. Apparently he was practicing quick change. "I can now transform in three-and-a-half seconds, not five. And the process doesn't blind anyone anymore like before. Did you see it?"

I glared at him. "I already know that, duh. God, don't you remember all those practice sessions we've had, with you guys morphing in front of me and giving me brain freeze?"

"Shut up," he said, grinning. What a dork. "Didn't you notice how cleanly I shapeshifted? No bizarre visual effects, man. Maybe you need a new eyeglass prescription or something. Oh, it doesn't even hurt you if I'm touching you while shapeshifting."

I told him that he was a lying sack of crapola, but he just gave me a bear hug and wouldn't let me go while saying, "No, really! Wait, wait..." Then I realized that it felt that he'd grown a few more pairs of arms.

"Check this out. I'm Kali. I'm working on Eastern religion and mythology now. Seriously, you should see me turn into a Chinese dragon. I can be my own Chinese New Year parade," he crowed in a weird woman's voice. More like a woman speaking through a long tunnel half-filled with water. Okay, an underground sewer maze sounded more like it. So I pushed against his shoulders and stared at what it was that was holding me.

It was Kali, all right. I only say this now because I had to consult Wikipedia after I got home afterward, but at that moment, all I could do was absorb the fact that this blue-skinned woman-thing with kind of wild, long afro-type hair stared at me with crazy eyes and a tongue hanging out and twitching. When I saw two of her hands appear, waving at me and then giving me a pair of thumbs up, and then felt myself still held tight by other arms, I did what every sane, level-headed boy would've done.

I totally lost it and screamed like a girl. Then gave a Hindu goddess a knee in the Cosmic Zone.

It also turned out to be a stupid thing to do because I'd just incapacitated my soon-to-be-undercover-partner and my ticket out of bingo night. I ask to meet him there, and I knee him in the 'nads. Go me. For the next several seconds, I cried out as I fell to the ground while Kali howled, her eyes widening, her tongue lolling, while a few of her hands went straight for her genitals. As she doubled over, still yelping, her figure melted and faded back into poor Freddie Jameson, who crumpled to the floor.

"Ohmigawd, I'm so sorry!" I cried, my hands plastered to each side of my head. I was majorly screwed. "Are you okay? Should I call a doctor? Freddie?"

He didn't answer. Well, he sort of did. "Goddamnit, sonofab—" he spluttered, rolling around on the floor in a tight fetal position. "That hurts, you crazy jerk!"

"Well, I—I can see that..."

Dr. Dibbs showed up with Brenda because of the noise we were making.

"What's happening?" he demanded. "What's all the racket out there?"

"Oh, my lord..." Brenda stammered. They stood

there, their jaws hanging low, while I bent over Freddie, pleading and apologizing while he writhed on the floor, all signs of a cosmic visit from a goddess completely gone. Just a seventeen-year-old black guy looking like an oversized fetus, swearing up a storm at me.

I also found out then that even though my education was really not much more than private tutorials, there was still such a thing as detention. Yeah, *detention*. I was dragged to the back room while Brenda looked after Freddie.

"Human genitalia are there for a purpose, Mr. Eric, and I'm not talking about soccer practice," Dr. Dibbs said when he filled out a detention slip. He was pissed. "But I'll also talk to Mr. Freddie about sneak attacks on people when he's practicing his masking powers. The ridiculous boy gets carried away sometimes, but that's no reason to assault him the way you did."

When I showed Mom my detention slip, she grounded me for a day. Fun times all around.

I told Peter what happened when I talked to him that evening, and he wasn't being very sympathetic. Okay, I deserved it, but shouldn't I be entitled to a little comfort from my own boyfriend? Sigh. I had a sinking feeling that all the superhero stuff was kind of reshaping Peter into being another Trent. I sure hoped not, but I wouldn't be surprised. Then again, he was upset because I screwed up. Again. I guess I shouldn't expect much.

"You know that we need Freddie for undercover work," he said a little testily. "Now that you just kneed him in the groin, I don't know how that'll affect him."

"I hope it doesn't," I said glumly. "I really didn't mean it, and you know that little accidents involving the 'nads don't leave permanent damage. Seriously, I didn't do it so hard that he passed out."

Peter didn't respond right away, but I heard some weird noises at the other end of the phone line, which made me wonder if he just squirmed in his chair or something. "God, I hate thinking about it," he eventually said. "I'm having sympathy pain right now."

"Okay, I won't talk about it anymore. I'm being punished by Dr. Dibbs and my parents, and now you're pissed. Let's move on before you all give me up for adoption or something." I thought it was best to wait till I got off the phone to feel sorry for myself.

I turned the conversation to what was going on in the city. I even remembered the other businesses that were most likely in danger of being attacked.

"Thanks," Peter said, sounding kind of business-like. "By the way, Althea's been to Mr. Bryant and Mr. Hernandez's businesses, and she checked out the ventilation system, with the cops' help."

"They found nothing?"

"Nope."

I frowned. "That doesn't make any sense. I wonder if the noise was caused by something that was, you know, staking out the place and stuff.

Maybe the mutant spider has little gremlin spider helpers it sends out to spy on places, like, scope out the general layout of the business and maybe even the customer traffic and so on."

"Yeah, that thought's crossed our minds, too, so we're not letting anything go yet. I'll tell the others about the gay bookstore and the international shop, but I won't be surprised if we don't see anything."

I took a deep breath. "Not yet, anyway," I said.

"Exactly."

So there we were, back to waiting for more shoes to drop.

Chapter 13

God, I was beginning to wish that I'd gone for a blog, anyway. All that handwriting stuff was starting to get really tedious. And my wrist hurt. I wondered if there were such a thing as carpal tunnel syndrome for those who did longhand.

Today I figured that I should come up with a Plan B. I thought that maybe Mrs. Zhang would be able to help me in my bingo night situation. I mean, she was pretty traditional, so I was sure that she knew a hell of a lot of herbal concoctions that I could use to make myself unavailable when the time came. Of course, they had to be safe. Duh. They also shouldn't make me come out weird in any way, and I wasn't talking about an extra arm suddenly sprouting from my navel and all that. I was pretty happy with the way I was, save for the virgin bit, so no tampering with what was already a good thing. Speaking of the virgin bit, I wondered if the Chinese also had herbs for, you know, horniness and all that. Like herbal

Viagra. I was thinking of sprinkling some of that stuff in Peter's coffee, so he could forget about all that lame "I'm waiting till the right moment" crap and just turn me inside out at the drop of a hat.

Anyway, if there were one thing I prided myself in, it'd be parental manipulation, but I needed to be a little more careful about that because Mom was starting to look at me funny right when I began to plan my next attack. Twice, I had to back off and pretend that I wasn't thinking anything nefarious, which kind of put a damper on things. Today, though, I wasn't going to back down.

Since I was grounded, I went straight home after my tutorials and waited till Mom arrived. By the way, Freddie was still kind of pissed at me, even when I asked Brenda to give him the box of lemon cookies I got for him. Mom looked tired, and she dragged her feet, so I planted myself between her and the stairs and asked if she wanted me to trot over to Mrs. Zhang's takeout joint for some Chinese food.

"I wish I could cook," I said with a shrug. "But my kitchen skills are less than zero, so if I want to help you around the house, the only thing I can do is run errands. So do you want to just kick back and let me to go to Mrs. Zhang's?" Please? Pretty please? *Remember, Mom, I'm the baby of the family and your only son. And I don't bully Liz; she bullies me. I'm totally, totally innocent. Unless you ask me about Peter—in which case, the deal's off.*

Mom just stared at me. I held my ground. Smiled ever so slightly so that only my dimples showed. Then she sighed and nodded. "Okay, honey. Go ahead.

My wallet's in my purse on the coffee table. Take what you need. You know what everyone wants." She even gave me a pat on the shoulder and a kiss on the cheek when I stepped aside, and she walked up the stairs.

God, I should have my dimples trademarked or patented or something. Supervillains' über-weapons ain't got nothing on these babies.

I was about three blocks away from Mrs. Zhang's place when I had to stop because of police activity. In fact, the whole three blocks, including the one where Uncle Chung's was located, were completely taped off. Squad cars were parked haphazardly up and down the street, and cops swarmed all over, some of them planting themselves midway through the block where I'd stopped, and telling people not to go near. I stared at the scene, heart thumping.

"Oh, my God, what's happened to Mrs. Zhang?" I called out, pushing my way past some gawkers. "What happened? Is she okay? Is Mr. Zhang okay?"

The cop I approached held up his hands and shook his head at me. "Sorry, son, but you have to stay back."

"What happened? I have to go get dinner for my family and stuff, and—"

"There's been an attack at the Yee Apartments."

Yee Apartments—an apartment building that catered to mostly Chinese immigrant families, and while I knew that Mr. and Mrs. Zhang didn't live there, it was still a pretty crazy thought. I walked past that building all the time, when I went to Uncle Chung's or to those shops at the other side of the main boulevard, which were only about two more blocks from Uncle Chung's. The Yee Apartments had always been a pretty cool housing block because of all the distinctive Chinese motifs that they used to celebrate their culture. Each floor had a decorative eave that you'd normally see in those old Chinese pagodas, but much smaller and less turned-up. I'd heard some people complain that it was an eyesore because it didn't blend in with the rest of Vintage City's faux nineteenth-century European architecture, but I always thought that with the grime and filth that covered every building up and down Vintage City, the Yee Apartments fit in really perfectly.

Since the cop wouldn't tell me anything more, I had to push my way back out of the crowd and run home. I immediately turned on the TV to the news before hurrying to the kitchen and digging around for whatever frozen food we might have lurking in the darkest corners of our freezer. I found a bag of chicken potstickers, ironically enough. That it was nearly cemented against the back wall of the freezer made me wonder how long that bag had been sitting there, completely forgotten, but beggars couldn't be choosers, so I just went on ahead and cooked them, which turned out to be a breeze. I seriously didn't realize how easy it was to cook potstickers. I needed to ask Mom to get more the next time she made up our grocery list.

After measuring rice into our rice cooker and pouring in some water, I checked the potstickers while they simmered in the bit of water I poured inside the pan before running back to the living room to see if the news was on. Nothing yet.

I went on ahead and took care of the rest of dinner—leftover tomato soup plus salad, which, if I were to add to the potstickers and rice, would make for a pretty mind-blowing time with the mega-sized bottle of antacids that Dad kept around.

I checked the news again once everything was cooked or heated up and the table was set, and Dad and Liz had gotten home from work and were both cooling off in their respective bedrooms. I sat glued in front of the TV, my mouth hanging open.

"Hundreds of mechanical spiders invaded the Yee Apartments this afternoon," Bambi Bailey announced. "They were smaller than those unleashed weeks ago at the Emporium Grande. While those spider robots were the size of beagles, those that attacked the Yee Apartments were more like beagle puppies. At twelve weeks old. Without their shots."

Most people had escaped harm because they were all at work. However, those who stayed behind, like little kids and grandparents, were victims. They'd been stung after being held down by the same webby stuff that was used at the Dog-in-a-Bun. Most of them had turned into fully-developed human arachnids by the time the superheroes arrived.

"What does that mean, 'fully-developed human arachnids'?" I demanded because Ms. Bailey, Sergeant Vitus Bone, witnesses, etc., wouldn't explain what that meant. How did they look? I kept thinking of Vincent Price in *The Fly* except that, in the movie, he had a teeny-tiny human head attached to a fly's body instead of a spider's body. Seriously, that was beyond mental.

I thought about the victims at the mall attack. I remembered that some of them were stung and were on their way to turning into human arachnids, according to reports, but that was way different from what I was hearing now. Intervention happened at the right time then. For today's attack, it was too late.

And why would the new supervillain want to turn them into half-human, half-spiders? Did he operate like the Shadow Puppet, trying to transform innocent people into an army of killer spiders with human heads?

"One final item," Ms. Bailey said, tossing her hair back, her earrings clicking from the dramatic flourish. Was there such a thing as a neck job in the creepy world of cosmetic surgery? Because Ms. Bailey's throat seemed longer than usual, but it could have been because her neckline was pretty low. She was seriously pushing the envelope there, and I was surprised that she still had a job. "Someone left a mark of identification on the wall of one of the victims' apartment units. It was sprayed-on greenish slime, from what's been described by police officers, and it said, 'No more. Arachnaman.'" She stared hard at the camera and gave a solemn nod. "Ladies and gentlemen, our new threat has a name."

After dinner, I waited by my phone in case Peter decided to call me, but he didn't. I figured that with this incident, he and the heroes were now up to their ears with work. I also tried calling Mrs. Zhang's takeout place repeatedly, but the line was busy each time. I really hoped that she and her husband were okay. I'd have to run over there the next day and see how things were with them.

By the way, Liz made a formal request with Mom and Dad to have me banned from the kitchen for the rest of my life.

I couldn't swing by Mrs. Zhang's on my way to Brenda's shop because Dad drove me to my tutorials on his way to work, the whole time nagging me about my detention.

"Just because you're being tutored, Eric, it doesn't mean special treatment," he huffed behind the wheel while I slumped in the passenger's seat, sulking. "What were you thinking, kicking that poor boy the way you did?"

"Dad, have you ever been given a bear hug by an Indian goddess with ten arms?"

There was a good-sized pause that followed my question. "Point taken, but did you have to kick him there? A yell would've been good enough."

"It was literally a knee-jerk reaction. I didn't have time to think. If that were the real goddess, I probably wouldn't be here with you right now. I'd be in the morgue, dead from fright and any kind of cosmic spell-thingie she might've cast on me. I might even be missing body parts, who knows?" Oh, that was a real beaut. Those words just rolled off my tongue like slippery jelly.

Dad sighed as he turned the car into the street where Brenda's shop was located. "I have to agree with your mother. You really *are* a drama queen, son."

"Don't blame me," I grumbled. "I was the one who inherited the gene pool." The car finally stopped in front of the antique shop, and I stared at it, wondering how many other kids were in bizarre schooling situations like me. Probably zero because I was totally made of fail. "Detention's after school," I said with a tired sigh. "I guess I won't be back home till five or something. Unless I run away and spare you all the trouble of having a boy who's probably too bright for his own good."

"Good grief, Eric, go to school."

Okay, that was worth a shot.

The buzzword of the day was Arachnaman. Everywhere I turned, I saw people talking nervously about this psycho. Local newspapers had that name splashed in ginormous letters across the front pages. I went inside the shop and found Brenda taking care of customers. I waved at her as I walked past the counter, and she nodded at me.

My "classroom" was the same back room that Brenda and Dr. Dibbs used after the Trill incident, where they checked me for abnormal readings and residual stuff from the Noxious Nocturne. They set it up for me, with an office desk for Dr. Dibbs and a separate study table and chair for me, which stood at the opposite end of the room. Dr. Dibbs wasn't there yet, so I just dropped my bag, took my seat, and pulled out my notes.

So I could, you know, pretend like I was really interested in my lessons and not show that I'd rather have my toenails ripped out with surgical tweezers than go over another craptastic social studies lesson. When Dr. Dibbs finally showed up, he looked really grim and distracted. He went over my lessons with me, but everything seemed mechanical and automatic, and he didn't appear to notice. He just rattled on and on about history and then literature and then gave me an hour to practice sketching, etc. I sure as hell noticed it, but I figured that it wouldn't be a good idea to say anything about it. Besides, I already knew what his response would be: "Keep your mind fixed on your lessons, young man, and ignore everything else. It's too dangerous. You know how it is." Yeah, I knew. Been there, done that.

But still! Couldn't an ex-supervillain sidekick-wannabe offer some help in dangerous cases like Arachnaman? I seriously could've worked like Freddie, doing undercover stuff though I don't have the advantage of masking powers. I mulled over that for some time, and before long it was my turn to be distracted. It was a good thing that my final lessons were Geometry and then Chemistry, so I didn't have any trouble having all that information fly over my head. I didn't even bother.

The clock struck 2:00, and I just watched Dr. Dibbs sift through his folder of handouts, which meant homework. Damn.

"So how are things with Sentry work, sir?" I piped up.

"The Sentries are alive and well and healthy, thank you, Mr. Eric. That's all you need to know."

I sighed, drumming my fingers on my study desk.

"So...is it possible for me to, you know, help out with undercover work? Since I've already seen how it is on the other side, don't you think that I might have something to offer the superheroes and the Sentries?"

He paused and stared at me, frowning through his glasses. "Young man, I do believe you've forgotten what we've told you about the Sentries."

"I know, I know, but I want to help!"

He kind of softened up and smiled at me. "I understand, but the Sentries work on their own, with no need for outside help. Stay away from trouble, sir, because that's the best thing you can do for your family's sake. And your friends'." He paused. "And Calais'."

By the way, detention involved getting my homework done while being spoiled with tea and scones from Brenda's pantry. I didn't expect that at all. I should've gotten into trouble more often, I guess.

I took a quick break from journal writing because I needed a snack. It was also kind of an awkward moment for me to cut out of my room like that, but I found out that Scanlon was due to stop by to take Liz out for a date, so I figured that I should get my ass downstairs real quick, gather my supplies, and barricade myself in my room before he showed up. I got back to find my window shut even with the relatively warm weather outside. My lamp was moved to my desk, and so were my journal and pen set. I thought at first that Peter somehow managed to sneak in and rearrange my private space, but he was nowhere to be seen, and when I went downstairs to get something to drink, I ran into Mom, who was walking out of Liz's room.

"I just closed your window, honey," she said.

"Why? It's not raining or cold."

"Safety. People are now being attacked in their own homes. Remember yesterday? I might have your window latch replaced, too. I checked it, and it felt a little loose and unsafe."

"But I don't have a ventilation system in my room! Remember? I'm always the one who's frozen solid in the winter and a soggy mess in the summer!"

"Do you need a ventilation system to be attacked?"

"Aww, Mom..."

"Eric..." I didn't have to say anything more. She gave me that look again. Major suckage. I'd have to come up with a backup plan that would keep both Mom and me happy. I should've consulted some online interior decorating sites for ideas. Anyway, maybe that was a good thing in the end. I guess it was time for my room to have a bit of a makeover.

Also, there was Freddie, and there was Mrs. Zhang. Apparently some cosmic conspiracy was working against me in my quest to ditch bingo night. I wondered if that was what people meant when they said that Mercury was in retrograde.

Chapter 14

Peter picked me up from "school" today. It was a total surprise, and it was because Renaissance High's faculty had a meeting. I was all resigned to another Peter-less day and another day completely isolated from my superhero friends, who'd be combing the streets of Vintage City for clues on Arachnaman. I stepped out of the back room, and Brenda yelled out from the shop area.

"Hey, Eric! Visitor!"

I thought at first that it was Liz. Didn't know why, but she crossed my mind first. Then I saw Peter sitting on the same bar stool I usually sat on, smiling and chatting up Brenda. I nearly did a swan dive on him. Seriously, I could've done it, too, based on my calculations regarding physical distance and hormone levels, but I played it cool and just held up a hand, saying, "Hey, how's it going?" Pretty suave, no?

He slid off the stool and gave me a kiss. I guess

he felt safe around Brenda, who pretended to be occupied by something on the ceiling the whole time we vacuumed each other's tonsils out, nearly tripping over some fancy coffee table and falling down, all tangled up. Too bad she couldn't stare at the ceiling for an hour straight because I wanted to do Peter right then and there. I guess I wouldn't have cared, regardless, had it not been for Brenda's warning: "Ahem! Water hose time! I've got a business to run, kids!" Of course, I was dazed and horny beyond words when Peter let me go, and I guess I wasn't very subtle about it, either, because when I turned to Brenda, she cocked an eyebrow and shook her head.

"Back room's off-limits, kiddo," she said and then jerked her head to the door. "Go on, horny toads. Enjoy the afternoon."

Peter thanked her, took my hand, and hurried out the door. "I really shouldn't get anywhere near you if I haven't seen you in a while," he panted when we stumbled out into the sunshine and warm air. I nearly did a cartwheel. Peter was feeling horny as hell? Like me? Score, baby! We paused after crossing the street, staring at the sky and calming ourselves down in the middle of pedestrian traffic. Nope. Didn't work for me. I still wanted to do him on the spot.

"Can we go home? My family's at work right now. They won't be back till around five," I offered. Okay, I pled. I was practically on my knees, begging him to go home with me, so I could, you know, do him.

He looked disappointed. I was torn between heartbreak and flattery. "I can't, Eric. I'm sorry. I only have less than an hour to be with you. We still have to go out on a real date, you know. Remember? I didn't even bring my car."

God, yeah, I remembered. That was a rain check that was just screaming to be honored. I had a pile of used towels and a set of crusty bed sheets to prove it. I grudgingly agreed to stay chaste, in the loosest possible sense, that afternoon and went to a small deli a few blocks down for afternoon sandwiches. There, in as quiet a voice as I could manage, I tried to quiz him about Arachnaman and the recent attacks.

"It's insane," I said, my voice nearly a whisper. "What does he want? Mr. Berkowitz wasn't doing anything. He was just trying to earn a living. And those people at the Yee Apartments...grandparents and kids? What the hell?"

Peter shook his head, looking angry and stricken at the same time. "There's a common thread in these attacks, Eric. We're still trying to piece things together..."

"And what about those human arachnids? No one's talking about what they look like and stuff. Do you know? They don't look like Vincent Price, do they?"

Peter looked a little confused for a moment. "Um, no. Are they supposed to? They look like—God, I can't describe it—just imagine a person who's got spider qualities mixed in with his DNA, like, in a pretty bad way. When I say 'bad,' I don't mean 'awful.'"

It was my turn to blink. "You're not helping."

"Think, um, cheese ball." He grimaced. "God, I

feel bad for saying that, but there it is."

"Uh-huh. Okay." I watched him intently, and he merely shrugged and muttered, "total cheese ball."

Apparently Peter really couldn't figure out a better way of conveying it. The cops and the mayor sure as hell didn't want anyone to know, but one thing was sure—those "human arachnids" couldn't do much but sit in one place and look around them blankly, according to Peter. I asked if it was like they were lobotomized, and he said that their behavior was sort of like that.

I was too grossed out and horrified for those poor victims to ask any more. I even forgot to ask about Mr. and Mrs. Zhang, being so caught up and practically gagging on what I was trying to picture in my mind.

"They're okay, though," Peter offered, after a long silence. "They're all kept in a holding-place, with the Sentries working on an antidote to get them back to normal. No one died, and it looks like no one's in any danger of dying because of the transformation. I guess we'll have to count that as a blessing. This Arachnaman jerk doesn't know much about full biological manipulation."

"What about their families?" That was a doozy. Most didn't want their loved ones separated from them. Who could blame them? Grandparents and children separated from the rest of the family over what? Some psycho's idea of fun and games? Unfortunately, they had to have a long talk with city officials and leaders of the Chinese community, and they all managed to agree on something because the victims currently are somewhere else, completely quarantined. I think one of the things they agreed on was that the family could arrange to see them during the healing process. Plus they weren't supposed to say a word about it, or at least there was some procedure that would be used to ensure that no one talked.

I thought about *Men in Black* and that memory-zapper thing they used on witnesses.

I still didn't know the details or whatever of the arrangement, but suffice it to say, everything seemed to be under control, and Peter made me swear never to speak a word of this to anyone.

"I'll keep quiet as long as no one uses a memory zapper thing on me," I replied, and he just grinned at me from across the table. "No, seriously. Do you have any idea what long-term damage the memory-erasing process can cause? I'm not even an adult yet, you know, and I want my brain intact when I reach eighteen." I considered for a moment. "But if you've got something that'll help me in school so that my grades would look like they're on 'roids...'"

"Okay, that's it. You're too cute. I gotta do you."

Oh, *baby*. "Seriously?" I said kind of lamely. More like stunned.

Prayer to great cosmic forces: whatever it was I said that turned him on, please make me say it again and again when he's around. Amen. Namaste. Hai. Whatever.

Then he ended our date by taking me back home, i.e., hyper speeding me home and setting us both down on the roof because my stupid window was locked, where we were able to enjoy several minutes of tongue gymnastics and hand-body-exploration. Screw broad daylight. Ours was one of the tallest houses in the neighborhood, which is a sad testament to the nature of the rest of them. It was easy to just lie flat (sort of) behind an old and no longer functioning chimney that was also pretty darned huge for what it was, ignore the roof debris, and just grapple lustfully with my boyfriend till, God...nirvana...

I just died and went to heaven. From the stunned and flushed face of Peter hovering above me, I can say that I didn't make the journey alone. After calming ourselves down, he left for "work," and I watched him vanish in a flash. He never transformed all that time, of course, but since he could move in hyper speed, he felt that he could get away with using his superpowers while in civilian clothes. Anyway, he told me in a phone call later that night that he was so drained and out of it that his usual path back to his home was like a drunken zigzag. He nearly flew smack against an old water tower, in fact, because his vision had grown a little fuzzy.

As for me, I almost tumbled off the roof after Peter left, trying to climb off it and onto the fire escape, so I could go back to my room via my bathroom window, which I remembered not to lock. It was a bad idea, maybe, but it did come in pretty darned handy during times like this. Now in addition to towels and bed sheets containing my gene pool, I had underwear to add to the pile. Seriously, I'd hate to come back in a future life as a washing machine owned by a family with teenage boys. That would seriously be gross.

"Took me a while to get my head straight and focus on superhero detective work tonight," Peter also said, chuckling, during that phone call afterward. "Wade literally knocked on my forehead and called out, 'Earth to Calais! Wake up, or I'll have to set fire to your tights!' Trent kept rolling his eyes at me. Imagine Magnifiman shaking his finger at me and looking dead serious the whole time. Althea—well, I'd rather not share what *she* had to say about my little lapse."

"I'll bet Trent gave you one hell of a sermon." Apparently Calais was *this* close to being grounded by Magnifiman, which would've been something I'd kill to see. "So is the next logical step for us to have phone sex?" I asked. Begged. On my knees. Forget the fact that I was on the damn phone the whole time, listening to him describe his foggy, post-not-quite-full-on-sex mental and physical state this afternoon.

"Don't encourage me," he said. "It's hard enough for me to be saddled with hero work on top of being deprived of time with you. Mom's already complaining about the amount of washing that the housekeeper does because of me."

I'd yet to wrap my mind around the thought of anyone living in this day and age whose idea of domestic life involved servants. But I guess if you had the money...

I tried to read for pleasure after I finished my homework, but I couldn't focus. Peter was still messing with my mind, and the only antidote to that was to gawk at my growing collection of hot studs from those gay ads I was collecting. I only had one clean towel left. Guess what I'd be doing tomorrow after school.

Things were still crazy at the Yee Apartments, and I hadn't received any word yet from Mr. and Mrs. Zhang, but I did learn that they didn't live in that area. I found out about that from an herbalist whose little shop I checked out this afternoon. She wasn't Chinese, no, but the lady definitely knew her traditional Asian medicine.

"I know them, actually," she said, smiling. "They live a couple of doors down from my apartment over on Myrtle Lane. They're both fine. They just can't operate their restaurant for a few days while police continue their investigation. Every building within a two-block distance from the Yee Apartments is being checked."

"You mean, like, to see if anything's been planted or something?" That made sense. The beagle-puppy spider robots were reported to be planted in the ventilation system, and they just spread out and did their thing when the moment came by melting the ventilation grates and then falling inside the rooms.

As I didn't want to take up too much of her time, after a quick update on the crime, I went straight to business. "By the way, do you have any herbs that induce diarrhea without, you know, killing me?" This was my backup plan, by the way.

"Are you constipated?" At that point I realized that my Plan B was really embarrassing in a Too Much Information sort of way, even though I didn't have constipation but wouldn't mind being a prisoner of the toilet when bingo night rolled around.

"Yeah. Sort of. It's been two months now of nothing." Was that about a good range for herbal laxatives to be called for? I just made that number up as I really didn't know how long that condition lasted for most of those who had it.

She just cocked an eyebrow. The jig was up. I guess I didn't look constipated enough or something, but she just said, "How interesting. I just had a couple of high school guys come around and ask for anti-constipation herbs, too. A few more questions later, they broke down and confessed to not wanting to go to some required field trip somewhere."

I gaped at her. "Damn. And I thought I had something pretty clever going here. I also just came up with it on my way home from school. It's all spur-of-the-moment. The constipation, I mean."

"So what are you trying to avoid, hon?" she asked, smiling, so I told her about bingo night. She looked sympathetic at first and then said, "Maybe you should just not think too much about hanging out with a bunch of old folks and their favorite game and just enjoy the moment. You might not know it yet, but bingo might actually be a pretty fun game in the end."

Hell, no! Never! I just thanked her and shuffled off, a bit pissed. What a waste of brain cells this afternoon had turned out to be. When I was about to step out the door, she called out, "Fresh persimmons! They work all the time!" Good thing she didn't charge for advice.

By the way, I saw that redheaded kid again. Yeah, the one who was being bullied by those punks some days ago. He was alone like before, which was really much better than being harassed by jackasses, chilling at the Jumping Bean. I went in there to get an iced mocha, and I saw him sitting by the window. He was reading and then looking at his watch and then looking out again, like he was waiting for someone or just plain waiting for the time.

I also noticed that a bunch of girls sitting at a table nearby were checking him out, but not in a good way. They kind of looked and then turned to each other to whisper and giggle a lot. A couple of them even made gestures that were obviously about the kid's weight. Arms held out on their sides and forming a large "O," cheeks puffed up like balloons—yeah, you get the picture.

I decided to go up to him and say hello, which he didn't seem to like very much. He just turned to me, surprised at first—like he never expected anyone to voluntarily talk to him or something—before frowning. "Oh, it's you again," he said.

"Uh, yup. How's it going?" I guess I should've turned tail and retreated, iced mocha in hand, the moment he looked at me. But then again, I'd always been a sucker for punishment.

"Nothing's going. Thanks for asking." He looked outside the window again. That was a pretty clear hint as far as I was concerned.

"Oh, sorry. I should've known you were waiting for someone."

He looked at me again. He frowned. Again. "Um, yeah, I am. Does it surprise you that someone actually wants to see me?"

I raised one hand and took a step back. "Okeedokee. I'm going. Jeebus." Shaking my head, I turned toward the door. "Oh, by the way, PMS pills are on sale at Baxter's Pharmacy. Buy one, get one free. It's always good to be well-stocked on that stuff."

Okay, so I never actually said the last bit, but I was pretty close to getting kind of bitchy on him. All I knew was that I'd have more luck holding a conversation with gum under my shoes than with that guy. I just went straight home, happily slurping my drink while wracking my brain for more ideas on getting out of bingo night.

I had to admit, though—there was something about that redheaded kid that stayed with me. I guess it was like there was something about him that bugged me but not in a bad way. Sure, he was obviously an easy target for bullies and for cheap shots from shallow types like those girls in the coffee shop, but there seemed to be something else about him that kind of nagged away at me, and I couldn't say what, why, and how. One part of me wanted to know him better, but that part happened to be a small portion of the Eric Plath pie. The rest of me would rather have my liver eaten out of my stomach by an eagle. Yeah, I'd been reading up on Greek myths.

OMFG, shoot me. Life couldn't be any more

boring than this. It was the afternoon, I had the house and the time to myself, and I did my laundry. I think I'd just scraped the bottom of the barrel.

Chapter 15

Holy crap! That Chinese herb shop I just visited? It was attacked by beagle-puppy spider robots! I saw it in the news while waiting for dinner to be cooked. Yeah, Liz got her way, and I was now forever banned from the kitchen.

"Dolores McBride, the owner of the Old Traditions herb shop, managed to escape, but her store's completely destroyed," Bambi Bailey declared. She was standing in front of the shop I'd been in only a few hours ago, and on camera, the place looked totally trashed. The display window and the front door were both shattered, glass shards littered all over the pavement. When the camera went inside to show the damage, I was stunned.

Everything was ruined. Glass jars filled with dry herbs, baskets, plastic bags packed with bulk items, Chinese knickknacks—nothing was spared. The shop's interior was covered with sticky white stuff, and anything that sat on shelves or tables had been swept off so that they all fell on the floor and got smashed into a gazillion tiny pieces.

"Damn," I breathed, staring in shock at the TV. "I was just there!" Yeah, I could even point out where I stood, exactly, a few hours ago.

I thought about the other two attacks before this one, and I also remembered what Peter told me about them. There was a common thread in all these attacks—hot dog diner, Chinese apartments, and herb store. Business, home, business. WTF?

Ms. McBride's words stayed with me because I had another bingo dream last night, and I rarely had recurring dreams. This time it was like Jabba had pretty much eaten about half of the bingo players, and I was left with the rest of them. I was still stuck where I sat, unable to move, my cards and marker thing both glued to my hands. I couldn't let go of them even though I could move my wrists. The game kept going, too, and no one seemed to care about the fact that their buddies were well on their way to being flushed down Jabba's toilet. Then again, if they were all zombies, they really wouldn't have cared at all. The fact that they kept shedding body parts without giving it a second thought as the game continued pretty much proved it.

What would I have against bingo night, anyway, besides the fact that it was boring and horrible? On my way to "school" today, I decided to take a quick detour and check out the old bingo hall about five or so blocks from Brenda's shop. I looked inside the window and saw the place empty, but it was easy to picture it completely packed with people, all armed with those big colorful marker things, hunched over a collection of bingo cards as the bingo ball caller guy talked into the microphone.

Consider this my way of figuring out my problem. Frankly, I saw nothing other than the fact that, yep, it was boring and horrible. What other reason did people expect from me, anyway? Everyone hated something, and everyone in his right mind would do anything and everything to avoid having to deal with it. Why couldn't I?

I certainly couldn't answer that, so I just sulked all the way to my tutorials. I made sure to bring Freddie a bag of jelly beans as a peace offering. I hadn't seen him since I kicked his balls, so I figured that it was enough time for him to stay mad at me. Besides, I was desperate. I really needed his help in getting me out of this without Althea, and especially Peter, knowing what I did. I was fast running out of ideas, and I was beginning to wonder now if every shop I went to or planned to go to would end up getting mowed down by bizarre beagle-puppy spider robots. At least Freddie was a superhero. If I got in touch with him and made him an easy target for those crazy spiders, he'd be able to defend himself. Plus the other heroes would come to help.

Brenda met me when I showed up, and she pulled me aside. "Freddie's here with Dr. Dibbs," she whispered, holding my gaze. "I asked him to come because I told him you've been wanting to apologize for nearly maiming him."

"Thanks," I said, relieved. "I brought him something, but I was going to hand it to Dr. Dibbs and ask him to give it to Freddie. I promise I won't kick his 'nads anymore. Ever." Unless he freaked me out again and made me do something I normally wouldn't have, of course, but you really couldn't tell with Freddie and his über-eagerness when it came to showing off his chameleon powers. I didn't tell Brenda that, no. I figured that Freddie had been given a talk about catching me by surprise with his masking abilities. Hopefully he listened.

Freddie was alone when I entered my "classroom." Dr. Dibbs had just stepped out, so I took advantage of that moment to fish out the bag of jelly beans and give it to him while he stared at them suspiciously.

"They're not tainted, I swear," I said in my humblest voice. "I'm really sorry I screwed up your masculinity. I promise I won't do it again."

"What flavors are in that bag?"

"Well, the store was out of the variety pack, so I just got a scoop each of watermelon, bubble gum, blueberry, and grape and mixed them all in here. Will that work?" I shrugged, embarrassed. "I'm a little biased toward blueberry, so hopefully you like it."

He took the bag. "It's cool, man. Thanks. For what it's worth, multi-armed gods are off-limits to me now unless I'm trapped and need to use that mask to freak opponents out. Or scare Brenda with when I'm bored."

"Hey, you can even use all ten arms to beat the

crap out of bad guys. Can you imagine the carnage? It'll be wicked!" When Freddie gave a big thumb's up and a hearty nod, I figured we were friends again. You really couldn't go wrong, urging a superhero to kick some thug's ass. They were kind of wired for justice and virtue and all that. So we shook hands, gave each other a slap in the back, and I was free to dump my stuff at my desk.

When I turned to look at Freddie, I saw that he'd taken to practicing his transformation powers when I had my back turned. He stood there—or, rather, a miniaturized monster did. Three heads, no arms, big bat wings, thick body and legs, scales all over...

What a show-off.

"What the..."

"I dig those old Japanese monster films. Don't you?" he said, swinging his massive tail and nearly swiping furniture off the floor.

I just stared at him. "Okay, I'm not even going to ask."

"I'm a miniaturized Gidrah! God, where've you been, dude? Hey, where's Calais? I can carry you off, and you can make like the damsel in distress, and he can swoop down, and we'll get some more search-and-rescue practice in..."

"He'll kick your scaly ass."

Gidrah snorted. Well, one of his heads did. I hoped. If that snorting sound didn't come from one of his monster mouths, I'd rather not have known what its other source might be. "It's good for my split-second transformation mode. If anything, his super-speed will be an awesome challenge. Think of it as friendly competition."

"I don't think so. Besides, how're you going to carry me? You don't even have any arms. Nice try turning me into a girl, bucko." An idea hit me, though, and I had to backtrack. "Actually, do you think you can be Gidrah and mess up my chances at bingo night? That looks like a pretty cool disguise. Do you breathe fire like Godzilla, too? Or do you spit snakes or something?"

"What the what?"

Another idea crossed my mind almost immediately after, and I wilted. "Oh, you can't. You'll probably scare all those senior players to death, including Grandma Horace. Do you have anything that you can use on Althea, so that she'll forget about my promise? Do you have a disguise that has corpse breath that you can use on her and mess with her brain without permanent damage?"

Gidrah just blinked all three pairs of eyes at me. I didn't think that communicating to a kinda-sorta monster with no arms would be so much hard work, especially since he had three pairs of ears. Dr. Dibbs showed up at that moment, so no scheming. He eyed us dubiously for a moment before grunting, "Mr. Freddie, enough with the horseplay. I know you're very proud of the advances you've made with your powers, but do leave Mr. Eric alone. It's class time for him, and you're giving him reasons to procrastinate. Besides, I'm out of detention slips and prefer not to be placed in another situation that calls for one."

Freddie shrugged. I think. I suppose that quick twitching of Gidrah's sides was the equivalent of a shrug. "Okay, fine."

I watched Gidrah melt into Freddie. I must say that I was pretty impressed with his new transformation process. I was sure it wouldn't be long before he'd be turning into one thing after another at lightning speed. I got so caught up with his improvement that I'd forgotten about my predicament. "You know, you can do a lot of fun things when you're bored. Hey, can you transform into a mutant snake that's rotting all over and then hide yourself in my sister's truck, like, under her seat? All you need to do is say 'boo,' and that's it." God, the possibilities...

"Uh, no. You're crazy. Good thing about being bored, though, is that I've been able to practice manipulating my powers some more. Real people, real animals, mythological things—you name it, I can be it," Freddie said with a broad grin. "And I don't need to sleep as much to regenerate."

"Furniture?" I prodded, plopping myself down on my chair because my tutor was already narrowing his eyes at me. "Or better yet, furniture that morphs into creepy crawlies, so you can freak out my sister? Have you ever seen *Beetlejuice?*"

"Nope, can't do inanimate objects. Made-up creatures, sure, but not inanimate objects."

"Same difference."

"No, actually."

I shook my head, my brain threatening to leak out of my ears. "Okay, whatever. I'm sure there's some kind of logic behind your power's limitations."

"Mr. Freddie," Dr. Dibbs said, jerking his thumb in the direction of the door. "Out."

"Okay, okay, I'm going. Hey, Eric, you need to tell me more about that bingo night thing. That sounds pretty cool."

I perked up. "Really? You'll help?"

"I've never been to one before. How much can I win? Is there a limit to raking in the cash?"

I withered. He wanted to *play?* Was he nuts? How screwed up was that? "I'll call you," I grumbled. He left the room, and Dr. Dibbs and I got down to business. It was pretty quiet for a moment while we sorted through our notes and stuff.

Then, from somewhere in the main store area, Brenda's scream sliced through the calm, and I jumped in my chair. Dr. Dibbs continued to do his work like he was deaf. I guess it was pretty obvious that he was used to this sort of thing. Go Freddie. Before I could say anything about it, though, the scream was followed by a hysterical "God *damn* it, Freddie! I *hate* zombies!"

When I got home after school, I discovered that the other places I knew were having problems with their vents were also attacked. Bam, bam, bam—one after the other. It was like Arachnaman finally went on a total rampage after all those days of silence. One after another, he claimed his victims. I didn't even know if anyone should speculate on whether or not today marked some kind of special anniversary because the destruction happened all at the same time.

I stared at the TV, wide-eyed and drop-jawed. "Jeebus, what the hell's wrong with this nutcase?" I cried as I watched Mr. Hernandez's Mexican grocery and Mr. Bryant's auto shop vanish in a thick spray of water. No one was injured, according to the cops, but there was extensive damage done inside.

And, yeah, even the gay bookstore was attacked. The news kind of did a whiplash thing, swinging from one crime scene to another, while Bambi Bailey and a guy reporter took turns talking to the camera. Both looked disheveled and smoke-stained. Behind them cops and firemen hurried back and forth, while three small businesses, all owned by decent people who'd done nothing to deserve this, went up in flames.

"Unlike the attack at the Dog-in-a-Bun and the Yee Apartments," Ms. Bailey said, her mascara slightly smeared around her eyes because of the tears that must've been pouring out of her eyes from all that smoke, "the simultaneous attacks today were all triggered by sabotage. Staff and customers weren't covered with web material; instead, there were reports of tiny bursts, like very small explosions, that were heard by witnesses. These noises were said to have come from somewhere in the back areas of each establishment. Police suspect that small spider bombs were planted, all timed to go off at the same time."

"Sick," I spat. Then I blinked. "Spider bombs?"

Ms. Bailey, who was probably psychic, nodded at the camera. "Yes, spider bombs. No one can say what the original devices looked like, but when they exploded, they unleashed a collection of small

181

mechanical spiders—much smaller than those in recent attacks—that spread out all over the shops, attached themselves to different merchandise and furniture, and then burst into flames."

"This Arachnaman psycho has quite a bit of an arsenal," I noted. Even though I was angry and upset, I couldn't help but be a little impressed by this nut-job's methods. He was definitely way more sophisticated than the Trill, the Debutantes, or the Puppet. If the Sentries could put together antidotes against his arachnid injections, I hoped that they had the resources to mix together a pretty potent bug spray in an aerosol can the size of a car.

"I'm glad no one got hurt," Liz said from the couch. "Dude, get out of the way. I can't see."

I walked away gladly. I was too disgusted and upset by the whole thing to want to hang around and learn more. I thought about Mr. Bryant and Mr. Hernandez and how long I'd known them. Since my childhood, in fact. Then I thought about that guy in the gay bookstore and how miserable he'd looked because his business was going down the drain.

I trudged up to my room, sickened. "I don't get it," I muttered. "What did they do to get this kind of crap done to them? Nothing! Like Mr. Berkowitz and Ms. McBride and all those families at the Yee Apartments..."

I shook my head and fired up my computer. Maybe a few online games would help. I didn't even worry about Althea, as I was sure that she already had her hands totally full with today's craziness.

Chapter 16

It had been three days since Arachnaman's last attack, and I hadn't seen or heard from Peter the whole time. A superhero's job is never done, anyway, so I'd been keeping myself busy with homework, chores, fending off the recurring presence of Scanlon Dorsey, and nighttime fantasies. I was cool.

He'd called me last night, though, sounding a little tired from all that superhero work, and we'd set a date for our date. Yeah, finally. How long did it take for us to get something set? Anyway, we'd talked about the retro arcade a while ago, and the time we made our original date, he agreed to meet me there. I mean, I figured that since we were stuck going out on a daytime date (thanks, Mom!), and I was expected back home by three p.m. (no, really, thank you—not!), we had to limit our movements to a small area downtown.

There was also a Mexican restaurant that we hadn't tried out yet that was also a block away.

The idea was to have fun at the arcade and then enjoy a steaming plate of Mexican goodness before separating and getting all angsty and heartbroken over an unfair curfew.

Considering all the bizarre genetic fallout of the recent months, one would think that Vintage City, for all its grimy, acid rain glamour, wouldn't exactly be a great place to start a business. With the recent attacks, who'd want to hang around here? Maybe there was something in the water that made us all major suckers for punishment. Well, the owner of the new retro arcade apparently saw something promising in our city, but as to what it might be, I'd no clue.

At any rate, Vintage City continued to live up to its name, and its new attraction was The Asteroid Belt, which boasted every classic arcade game that could be had. So that was where Peter found me, standing outside with my nose pressed against the glass, salivating over all those pinball machines and Pac-Man things.

I was so focused on what I was coveting that I didn't even hear him walk up to me—only felt a light brush of his hand against my waist as he took his place beside me.

"Now what?" he asked, sniggering. "Don't tell me..."

"Check it out!" I breathed, pointing at a machine that stood way, way in the back corner. "Look, it's Pong!"

"Holy cow. People still play that?" It was his turn to press his face against the glass. I swear, we looked like a couple of street urchins, yearning for some Christmas goose or something. "Wait, I didn't even know that Pong was, like, an arcade game. I remember my Aunt Sharon owning an old, old console for home playing, but I've never seen an actual arcade version. Wow."

"Do you think it'll explode or something after a few games? It looks pretty old. I mean, seriously."

"I'm surprised that it could still stay upright. Damn. Check out the fake wood paneling on that thing!"

"Come on, let's go in," I said, taking his hand and giving it a tug.

The spell had broken. Peter dug his heels into the pavement and looked at his watch. "Eric, we don't have much time. We can check this out another day. I'm hungry and want to spend more time with you."

"Well, nuts," I grumbled, staring longingly at the dusky interior.

Even the windows seemed to absorb light, so people could peer through the glass without being bothered by reflections or anything like those. The arcade's interior was dark and pretty grungy, the only lights inside coming from the different old-school machines that littered the place. Even the people inside looked as dreary and musty as the machines as they took turns, playing. For a few more seconds, I turned my attention to the kids inside, watching them shuffle from one machine to another, the only parts of their bodies I could see being their faces and hands. It must have been a trick of the light, or, in this case, the lack of, but it seemed that their complexions glowed softly. When a girl turned around after finishing a game, our gazes briefly met through the window, and I was startled by how zombie-like she looked. Skin abnormally white, eyes unseeing and sunken, a ring of dark shadows around them, mouth a little slack. I had to blink several times to make sure that I wasn't having some weird hallucination, but by the time I tried to figure out what it was that I'd just seen, the girl had already vanished in the shadows.

"Hey, Peter," I began, but he'd already looped an arm around my shoulders and was guiding me away. I tried to look back over my shoulder, but all I could see was a black window. There were no signs of life inside, let alone any faint lights flickering in the dusky interior. It was just—blank.

"No, no, no. We're not wasting time in junk crap like that."

I tried to draw his attention back to the arcade. "But..."

We'd already reached Peter's car, and before I knew what was happening, I was stuffed inside, and Peter was leaning in and kissing me hard. If he wanted me to shut up, he sure picked a damned good way of doing it.

He pulled away and, now leaning his head against the window, he raised his brows and gave a lopsided smile. "No buts. We're on a deadline. I'm also desperate for a stress-buster."

"I thought we were hanging out here." I kept staring at his mouth. I tried not to, believe me. Total fail.

"Nope. I decided to make it a little more special. That's why I brought the car." Then he closed the door and walked over to the driver's side.

"I think Trent's rubbing off on you."

"Okay, so we can go to Barron for lunch," he said as he hopped inside, fishing out his keys and quickly jamming them in the ignition. He glanced at his watch again. "That ought to take us, uh, about twenty minutes to get there, and then another hour to eat, and I think we should hang out there for another hour to save on driving time, and then..."

The car wouldn't start. Peter fell silent, blinked, and then turned the key again. The car made that wurr-wurr-wurr sound, and the more Peter turned the key, the slower it got till it just plain stopped.

"Uh-oh," I muttered.

"Fuck," Peter hissed, turning the key again and again and again, this time hearing nothing but clicks. "Damnit!" He slumped back in his seat, head thrown back, eyes pinched tightly shut. "And I left my cell phone at home."

I'd never seen Peter so upset. Even when he was pissed at me, he was never like this. It was all I could do to swallow and then gingerly rest a hand against his arm and give him a gentle squeeze.

"Um, hey, don't worry about the date," I said, hoping that my disappointment didn't show. "We gotta take care of your car first. Do you have the number for a tow truck? Oh. Sorry, I forgot about your cell phone." I winced.

Peter didn't answer right away. He merely knocked his head repeatedly against his headrest, hissing "Damnit!" again and again.

"Hey, quit that. You'll hurt yourself." I glanced around. We were parked on a side street, which was pretty deserted. Even with the tiny shops that were there, no one seemed to frequent this area, save for a random kid or two who gravitated toward the arcade. "If you don't, we can go to one of those stores and borrow their phone book."

"God, Eric," he finally said. He glanced at me, red-faced and helpless. "I'm so sorry. We just don't have any time, I really want to be with you, and I don't want to piss your mom off, and..."

"No, no, it's cool, really," I cut in, forcing a little smile. "We can go out another day. Maybe I'll be given more time then. Just take care of your car, okay?"

I think my voice shook a little. I was pissed—not at Peter, but at Mom for giving me such a stupid "curfew." I definitely shouldn't go home yet, or I'd barge into the living room and get myself in a full-blown fight with her. I figured that it would be better for me to hang out with Peter till the bitter end, let my mood lighten up, and enjoy what I could of his company with what pathetically little time was allowed us.

Then maybe I could go home, barge into the living room, and get myself in a full-blown fight with Mom.

"Okay," Peter said. He sounded much calmer now, thank God. "I'll go to that bead shop over there."

"I'll go with you."

"No, I need you to keep an eye on the car."

He opened his door and stumbled out. I followed suit, but stood next to the car, watching him jog down the street and then vanish inside the bead shop. I turned and stared at the arcade for a moment.

"I'll only be standing outside," I said, walking toward it. "I'm sure Peter won't mind."

I was soon standing by the window, peering inside like before. Nope, nothing seemed out of place. A few kids walked next to the window, but their faces were turned away from me, so I couldn't see what they looked like.

I glanced over my shoulder and saw that Peter's car was still there, looking all shiny and sexy amid the urban decay. Peter was still inside the bead shop, and I guessed that making arrangements for towing would take him some time. He might even be calling his parents in addition to the tow truck. That would definitely take him a while.

I shrugged. "Okay, I suppose it won't hurt to check things out for a few minutes." I walked over to the arcade's entrance and sauntered inside. From the gray light of Vintage City's dreary daytime landscape to the cheap, weathered darkness of a retro arcade, I was catapulted into a completely different world.

It was a world of flashing lights. Multi-colored spots of brilliance that pierced the gloom with brain-numbing frequency. Sounds of gunfire, laser beams, electronic chirps and carnival music, all melted into each other to create an endless stream of mechanized noise.

I paused in the middle of the arcade, looking

around me, my breath held. It was like sensory overload. Thank God the interior was kept plain— no paintings or decorations on the walls. All the machines along the perimeter were set against dull black.

"Not quite," I noted. The arcade's owner was probably a big Halloween fan or something because he'd festooned the ceiling with white web that looked pretty real. I glanced up. "Oh, he even has shadows of giant spiders crawling all over up there, and..." I froze. Oh, *crap*.

Chapter 17

Mechanical monsters come alive! Knowing that they've been spotted, they attack! BAM! Spewing innards-dissolving slime at helpless civilians, they move to consume thousands of innocents! SLURP! BURP! But wait—someone fights back! Look! In the middle of the green, gooey carnage, Starburst Boy rises, slippery slime falling off his broad, muscular shoulders! Eyes narrowing, he fixes his attention on the source: a gargantuan beast that looks like the love child of a Chihuahua and a minivan! His enemy spots him, and they lock angry gazes across the flailing mass of dissolving humanity! Starburst Boy launches himself in the air, shouting, fists ready! He meets his mechanical nemesis in the middle! POW! Slime and bits of metal rain on the fading citizens!

Okay, so things didn't happen exactly like that. It was more like...

"Oh, look. They've got some cool-looking spider effects on the ceiling."

"Those spiders look awfully big...and...realistic in that *Matrix* sort of way."

"Did that spider just look at me? Is it, like, independently thinking or something?"

"Gah!"

The long and short of it was that we were jumped by spiders—mechanical ones, by the way, that were the size of beagles. Not beagle puppies, but the real deal. I figured that I was the one who caused the whole mess because I was the only one who bothered to look around and then stare at the ceiling, while everyone else was sucked into one retro game after another.

White webby stuff rained on us, and we all ran around, screaming and flailing, while the door—there was only one door there, go figure—slammed shut and locked itself. I didn't know if the owner of the arcade was there, but his employees apparently hadn't expected this, either. Like the rest of us, they got attacked, though in their case, they were in the middle of sharing a joint when disaster struck. Frankly, I wondered how that might have enhanced their altered reality, but as I was about to be turned into lunch for a mechanical Shelob, I didn't stop to think.

Covered in white stuff, I looked around for something to throw against the windows, so we could get the hell out. Around me, a few kids collapsed, crying out, their bodies completely swathed in sticky web things, while robot spiders pounced on them.

I dove for one and yanked it away from a screaming girl even though I could feel the weight of the stuff increasing around my body. It grew thicker, I thought, and it slowly solidified so that I could barely move.

I tried to help another kid, but I fell over instead because my legs were completely encased. Stars exploded behind my eyelids when I hit the ground, my world spinning and filled with light and color while screams and sobs mingled with the clacking noise of spiders and the ongoing beeps and whatnot of the arcade machines. I tried to kick, roll, and punch my way out, gritting my teeth and feeling sweat trickle down my face and back. The more I struggled, the harder it got, and before long, I couldn't move an inch, though my head remained free.

I lay on the floor, staring helplessly at the ceiling and listening to the sickening sounds of bodies falling down and hitting concrete pretty hard.

"We're going to die," a girl sobbed beside me. "I don't wanna die."

I turned my head with some difficulty and looked at her. Red-faced and tear-streaked, she stared at me as though she were looking for some kind of comfort, but what could I say to her?

"Hey, listen," I said, my voice shaking, "we'll be fine. The heroes will come for us."

She only shook her head and broke out in a fresh wave of hysterical sobbing. Robotic spiders walked around us, crawling over bodies and so on, as though they were taking inventory or something. One stopped next to my head, fixing its eyes on me. I mustered enough courage to look back and try to take in what I could of its appearance. With the darkness in the arcade, though, I really couldn't see very well except for its eyes, which glowed a spectral white, but other than that, there was nothing else worth noting.

"Peter," I breathed. "Where are you?"

The spider robot thing raised itself up on its four rear legs, waved its forelegs menacingly at me, and then spat a healthy chunk of white webby stuff from its mouth or beak or whatever the hell it was that spiders ate out of. And it aimed at my face. The only thing that saved me was my glasses, which kept all that crap from blinding me. All the same, WTF?

"Bastard!" I cried, squirming in my cocoon, barely able to see through my covered glasses. "I'm going to get you for this!" Not that my threats made any difference, really, since my mouth was effectively muffled by robot vomit.

I suppose it could've been worse. It could've been pea soup, and that would've been just plain disgusting. I heard the spider move closer even as I cursed out a storm. I even felt it touch my neck with something pointy.

The arcade was a mess. Machines destroyed, smoke from those battered things as well as the twisted wreckage of what used to be mechanical spiders hovered above us like a nauseating cloud, which was pretty typical for Vintage City, really. Windows blown apart, the door nothing more than a gaping hole that opened up to a small side street that used to be empty but was now swarming with horrified gawkers.

Inside, the police were busy picking their way through the mess, and one by one, we were cut down from our prison to be carried off or led away for doctors to poke at. Everyone was talking at the same time, and my head throbbed. I *so* needed a soda. Good thing was that the stuff that was spat in my face earlier had fallen off in bits, so that I was able to see even though my glasses were dirty and partially blocked still. It didn't feel like the same stuff that was used on our bodies; it was definitely a lot less solid, and it was pretty ticklish, by the way. I kept making faces to alleviate the feeling since I couldn't move my arms to scratch away. Didn't work. I thought I was going to go crazy from that.

All of us, by the way, were strung up to the ceiling, dangling like spider food, and I suppose the only thing good about that was no one was hung upside-down. Oddly enough. Wrapped up from the shoulders down in white stuff, we hung face-down, our torsos secured to the ceiling by long, webby ropes, our legs hanging down.

It was just a *teeny* little bit awkward, to say the least. Thank heaven for Calais, who showed up first, and Miss Pyro, who followed a little after. Calais whooped some major ass while Miss Pyro helped out in the last couple of minutes. I guessed that Wade had happened to be out shopping when all hell broke loose, hence her appearance. Trent would've been doing something typically Type A too far away to respond quickly, and God knew where Althea and

Freddie were. To say that I was bursting with pride, watching my spandex-clad boyfriend smash one spider after another, would be an understatement. I was also glad to see Miss Pyro able to control her fire power much better, sending more muted fireballs and whatever in hell kind of flaming arsenal she had inside the arcade. We'd all be roasted alive if she didn't even try.

In a nutshell? The heroes saved the day.

The girl who'd fallen apart earlier dangled nearby, but she'd calmed down by now. All I could hear from her were a little bit of sniffling and coughing as she waited her turn to be released.

"Glad to see you're okay," I noted, offering her a smile, for what it was worth.

"I wanna go home," she croaked. "That's saying something, you know, 'cause I hate my parents. This sucks."

"Well—you kind of get used to this sort of thing after a while. Trust me."

She blinked. "You've been screwed up like this before?"

"More times than you can imagine. I look at this as character-building, sort of."

Calais had walked up to her by then. "Okay, don't move," he said as he grabbed hold of the white stuff that wrapped around her and tore it open with one powerful tug of his hands. The sound of ripping cloth followed, and with a little yelp, the girl fell straight into his arms.

The next few moments were like the longest ever in my short-yet-screwed-up life. Think of a really awful, sappy video of some really awful, sappy love song. Okay, imagine everything happening in super slow-motion, with the girl falling in Calais' arms. Then their eyes meet. He looks sympathetic yet remains professionally distant. She stares at him, stunned, her arms wrapped around his neck, her body easily held up because he's just oh-so-strong.

Oh, fucking *hell,* just think of the scene in *Sense and Sensibility* where Kate Winslet fell down and got swept up in Greg Wise's arms in the rain (thank you, Liz, for making me suffer through that movie). Are you with me yet? Yeah, that was it. That was bloody *it,* as the British would say.

"Easy, easy, I got you," he said, setting her back on the ground. It took her several more very annoying seconds before she let go because she clung like a leech to him even after he set her down. "You're safe now," he reassured her, prying her arms from his neck. "Okay, let me go, so I can take this guy down."

"Oh," she breathed, staring at him, wide-eyed. "Thank you."

God. I recognized that look.

"Wow, you're even better-looking in person," she added, tucking hair behind her ears.

Did she just giggle and blush? Calais smiled back and gave her a reassuring pat on the arm, and, encouraged, she stood on tiptoes and gave him a grateful peck on the cheek.

I sighed. "Hello, helpless victim over here. Very uncomfortable position. Probably damaged innards and ability to produce children."

"Thank you," she said, her voice taking on a little-girl-like tone. It took the appearance of a police officer to pull her away from Calais, and she trotted off, glancing over her shoulder for one final adoring look before vanishing in the confusion of activity.

"Well, will you look at that?" I said blandly. "I'm the last one to be saved. Yay me."

Calais stood before me, hands on his nicely narrow hips. "I leave you alone for three minutes, and all hell breaks loose."

"Hey, I didn't ask to be attacked! Are you blaming me?"

"I told you to wait by the car, didn't I?"

"Well, yeah, but..."

"Uh-huh..."

I sighed again, drooping. "I just wanted to check out the arcade," I said. "What's the harm in that?"

"Um..." Calais pointed at my web cocoon. "In case you haven't noticed."

"Look, I was born under a black sign. Can I come down now? This sucks. Oh, by the way, thanks for the Jane Austen moment back there."

"Huh?"

"Never mind." I frankly didn't know what was worse—seeing Peter/Calais with a girl or with another guy. Either way made me want to puke out all my innards.

Shaking his head, Calais tore at the stuff, and I fell into his arms, which was always a good thing, though it was too bad that he couldn't take me home like this. And there were way too many people around, so no huggy-kissy stuff and all the comfort-me-please things that happened when the hero saved the day.

"Thanks," I grumbled. Then I gave a start, stiffening. I looked behind me and then gaped at him. "What the...did you just goose me?"

He grinned. "The best thing about hyper speed. I can get away with so much crap with you." To prove his point further, he momentarily melted in a rush of color and then solidified a fraction of a second later. During that wee bit of time, I actually felt him kiss me, tongue and all. It was surreal. I thought I also felt pressure against my back, maybe from his arms as he kept me from toppling over because of his sudden movement. I was glad he didn't break my neck. "See?" he said. "I've been dying to try that for a while now."

"Whoa. Yeah, I felt that." I touched my mouth, half-wondering if it somehow got sucked into the vortex caused by hyper speed. Nope. Still there, and not to mention wanting more.

I got over my shock pretty quickly. On second thought, that was pretty damned cool. And sort of kinky. I was about to ask him to do it again, but Miss Pyro appeared, and I had to step away from him. There were definite drawbacks to being romantically involved with a superhero.

"The other stores are okay. Magnifiman's taking care of them right now. They suffered minor damage," she said. Then she saluted me. Literally. "Hey, how's it going?"

"My date with my boyfriend just went up in smoke, so I'm not exactly doing pretty good here," I said, picking residual webby stuff off me. My clothes, face, and hair were a mess, to say the least. I couldn't imagine what Mom would've said if she'd seen me like this. God. She'd've moved my curfew down to ten in the morning.

Miss Pyro blushed, glancing at Calais. "Oh, I'm so sorry. Maybe you can still pick up where you left off, later?"

"I'll explain everything another time," I said, dropping my voice. I sighed and turned to Calais. "I guess I'll just walk home. You guys have a lot of stuff on your plate now." *Besides,* I wanted to add, *Mom wouldn't want to see us together with you as Calais.*

"I'll call you," he whispered.

I guess I was supposed to be reassured by that, but I sure as hell didn't feel it. Every step taken in the direction of my home felt like I was dragging an elephant back with me, my head spinning with all kinds of things Mom was likely to say.

When I stepped out onto the street, I looked around and saw the general area not only swarming with gawkers and dizzy merchants, but also smoke-filled. A couple of stores had their windows smashed, and a car parked nearby also had its windows shattered. Plumes of black smoke rose from the stores' interiors, and I had to go to Peter's car to see if it was okay. Thank God it remained untouched, though I had to shoo away a couple of mangy kids who sat on the hood, gaping and picking their noses.

Since the arcade wasn't that far from home, I didn't have to suffer the embarrassment of people staring at my messy state or calling the cops on me or anything. I just made sure to hurry and pretend as though I were homeless and look like I'd just gone dumpster-diving. With the threat of Mom freaking out hovering above my head, it turned out to be one of those rare times when I actually prayed for acid rain to piss on the city and wash the webby stuff off me.

I turned the corner onto our street and saw that Dad's car and Liz's truck were still out. That was good—two less people to avoid. Of course, that also meant that the one person I wanted to avoid the most was at home somewhere.

The cosmos took pity on me because Mom wasn't anywhere when I entered, and tiptoeing past the master bedroom, I saw that the door was shut. I bounded up the last flight of stairs to my attic bedroom, taking two steps at a time.

I shed my clothes and jumped into the shower, heaving a sigh of relief.

By the way, the places that were targeted today were the arcade, the adult store, and the New Age bead store. From the looks of things, Arachnaman knew absolutely nothing about having fun. So now we had those to add to his list of victims, and I was still totally clueless about any kind of common thread linking them. Damn. I wasn't good in this analysis stuff. I wondered if it had something to do with my suckiness when it came to Geometry.

Chapter 18

As expected, I lost Peter again, with him throwing himself completely into detective work and stuff. I was once more a superhero's widower, which goes to show that I'm destined to live out a tragi-comedy type of existence. Althea continued to be low-key, which made me wonder what exactly kind of training she'd been going through with the Sentries' help. She hadn't harassed me about bingo night in a while, and she hadn't haunted my computer, either. Peter told me that she was up to her ears in training, superhero work, and school, which pretty much left her with absolutely no time beyond sleep and daily meals.

Of course, Peter just had to reassure me with this one time: "Don't worry. She knows you're still up for bingo night. In fact, whenever she remembers, she asks me if some blueberry jam from Mrs. Horace's kitchen, on top of the usual strawberry jam, would be enough to compensate you for the trouble."

Oh, damn it. Why did people always have to work

on my conscience like that? Why couldn't I be mean for once and get away with it? Sigh.

At any rate, I was boyfriend-less and friendless, with Freddie being my only lifeline to something that could pass for a social life. Even then, more often than not, he wasn't available to hang out with because of some undercover work he needed to do for the Sentries. I suppose the only good thing about all this was the fact that, with the heroes all up to their ears in Arachnaman terrorism, I didn't have to worry about playing innocent kidnap victim for their training sessions for a while. Score.

I took a quick break from journal writing and indulged in some leftover cheesecake. I didn't bother to check the expiration date on the box, but I figured that anything frozen had a better chance at longevity. I mean, I'd fed my family old frozen stuff before, and we were all okay. Except for Liz, but that had always been par for the course when it came to older siblings.

Since Althea wasn't about to cyber-haunt my ass, I spent my post-journal time surfing the 'net, and guess what I found.

The Unofficial Calais Fan Club, V.2. Yeah, no kidding. Since the Trill, I'd sworn off any involvement, even as a lurker totally engrossed in train wrecks, in RPG communities. Nope, no more role-playing creepiness for me. Stumbling across this fan club, though, was like experiencing inter-dimensional whiplash.

I gaped at the screen. How had that happened? No clue. A bunch of enterprising fans of my boyfriend in spandex just decided to whip up a website dedicated to him. They had the usual home page with the introductory welcome: "Thank you for stopping by the Unofficial Calais Fan Club! Here you'll find all kinds of goodies on our favorite Vintage City superhero, complete with a gallery of pictures of His Royal Hottie, accounts of real-life rescues, and fanfiction and fanart! Before leaving, please don't forget to leave a message for Super-Cool, Super-Hot, Super-Sexy Calais in the guestbook!"

I stared. And stared. And stared. And stared. I felt like Edward Gorey's Yawfle from his *Utter Zoo* book. All I needed to do was sprout long, shaggy hair all over till only my eyes showed, and then sit in a corner and stare. And stare. And stare. And stare.

I think my finger hovered above the left button of my mouse for ten eternities before I mustered up enough courage to click on the "merchandise" link.

"Oh, for the love of..." My jaw dropped lower. "They have an online store, too?" I cried. Then I backpedaled when a thought hit me. "An online store, huh? Is it part of a committed relationship to make money off one's boyfriend?" I had to remind myself never to breathe a word of that to Peter. I mean, I wasn't quite sure how he'd take to my entertaining the thought of whoring him out.

Further thought convinced me that he wasn't going to go for it. Bummer. There went all my plans for some serious cash earned and saved, which would lead to a nice happily-ever-after, running off into the sunset hand-in-hand, and shacking up in a little house somewhere near a national park. Fresh air, awesome views, with little-to-no noise and absolutely no neighbors within fifty miles of our little patch of paradise. Well, I suppose we'd have to deal with rampaging bears on occasion, but there was time enough to worry about that.

I shook my head and shuddered, clicking the "fanfiction" link. It took me all of five seconds before getting my ass out of that page faster than Calais' hyper speed. I let go of the mouse as though I'd just burned myself with it.

"Damn," I breathed, still staring at the screen. And staring some more. Okay, I really did *not* need to see that. What was wrong with fans these days? How stalkerish could they get? They actually wrote stories about my boyfriend! And they did art! If any of those crazies turned Calais into a furry, I'd sue! The site also had a guestbook, which I didn't check out. I had a pretty low tolerance level for psychological trauma as it was.

I sat back for a moment, waxing philosophical over the state of my generation. Fans. Jeebus. They were like a species unto themselves. I drummed my fingers against my desk and toyed around with another thought. Did Joshua Bell have a fan club? I was sure he did...more than one, definitely.

"Is there, like, fanfiction written about him?" Oh, the temptation was too great, but something smacked me upside the head and forced me to get over it. "Don't be gross, Plath," I said, shuddering. "That'd be no different from all the crazy crap being posted about Calais."

Fannishness should have certain limits. People should stop after the herd mentality and squeeing bit and then be normal beyond that.

Well, speak of the devil. Peter called me about an hour later, and after initial greetings and lovesick exchanges, I had to tell him about his unofficial fan club. He was quiet for a moment, and I kind of felt bad, embarrassing him like that.

"Eric, I've...uh...I've known about that site for a while now," he said. More like coughed. And mumbled. "And I've read the...uh...guestbook."

"You knew about it for a while? How?" I blinked. Oh, boy. "Did you set up a Google Alert on yourself? Did you, huh, did you?" I was *so* ready to mock him.

"What? No! Man, are you kidding? Only writers do that! No, no. I overheard it in English class sometime ago. Like...I don't know...sometime... ago..." Another series of low coughing followed.

I could barely stifle a grin. "Dude. You're checking up on your own fan site, aren't you? Come on, now, 'fess up." Well, I suppose I couldn't blame him. He was smart, hot, and hunky. He earned the right to have his ego stroked. I just wished that it was me exclusively stroking his ego. And more than his ego, anyway. I'd gotten pretty good at stroking.

"I, uh, well...yeah." Peter cleared his throat. I got him. "Sorry. Moment of weakness. Attention can be pretty addicting, but as far as the updated guestbook's concerned, it was Althea who alerted me to the messages."

"She knows?"

"Yeah, sure. She heard about the site the same time I did. In fact, she was the one who convinced me to check it out after she herself toured the place. Don't ask me what she thinks of it. Just...don't."

"Hey, you're too serious. You're sort of a local celebrity, and you've got fans. They're crazy about you. Okay, so some are crazier than others, but they love you, Peter. Shouldn't that account for something?" I grinned and toyed with the phone cord. "C'mon. Lighten up. This is a date-y kind of thing, even if it's only by phone. I'm not interested in sharing you with creepy fans when we're together, and our time's so short. Don't let them get to you."

He laughed, sounding relieved. "You'll have to get used to it, too, it looks like."

"What? I *am* used to it! And I feel pretty damned proud, watching everyone fall all over themselves for you, knowing that they don't stand a chance," I laughed. I also made a mental note to keep an eye on that site and the guestbook in case the creepiness factor got out of hand. I'd heard of stalker fans before. Crazy messages left online might be dismissed by everyone as nothing more than ramblings from lonely, insecure types, but I knew better. I figured that it would be the least I could do for Peter, considering how much he'd been doing to keep the city safe.

We talked shop for a while, with Peter filling me in on superhero work, at least those details that weren't confidential.

"The bastard's a ticking time bomb," he said. "He really laid things out pretty well."

"Yeah. It's, like, he's got specific methods for each group of businesses he's targeting. I don't know if there's a reason for that, but I'm guessing that he's doing that to throw you and the cops off his scent. You know, catch you by surprise, anyway, by switching tactics every time."

"He's clever, yeah. I hate him."

I smiled grimly as I glanced out my open window and took in the gray, overcast landscape outside. "I suppose you can channel all that negativity into some serious ass-kicking when the time comes."

"Trust me, I will. Even the others are pissed enough to want to destroy him the second we see him."

That was pretty unsettling, hearing him talk that way. I guess the incredible stress of being superheroes, especially when Peter had to see the wreckage and the victims every time, would have this kind of really scary effect on him. I thought about the others and realized that, while Wade was the mellowest and sweetest of the group, I shouldn't underestimate her ability to get as affected as Peter and possibly feeding her powers that way.

"Hey," I said after I got over the initial surprise. "No murders allowed. You're not the bad guy here."

Peter merely laughed, and I couldn't tell whether or not he meant it. I sure didn't sense any humor in that.

"Just be careful," I added. My voice sounded kind of weak and pleading, but I didn't care. I just wanted him to listen to me. "Please. I don't want any of you to get hurt."

He sighed. "I will. I promise," he said, his voice dropping. Like several other conversations I'd had with him, he once again sounded so tired and beaten. I wanted to reach out and hug him and file a vacation request with Magnfiman, so Calais could vanish for a little while and rest himself. Man, I could think of a thousand and one possible destinations for that. The stratosphere would be the common denominator, of course, and that wouldn't happen till *after* we reached those destinations. Hoo, boy.

"The businesses that've been attacked are closing, but there's a lot of talk about getting Mr. Bryant and the others back on their feet. I'm hoping that their insurance would help, but you know how screwed up insurance companies are."

I thought about things for a moment. "I wonder if people would help them out. You know, like put together some kind of fundraiser for them."

"It would be nice, but the real world doesn't always work that way, Eric."

"You're too young to be cynical," I chided. "Come on. Maybe I can look into that some more."

He laughed again. "Now look who's being the superhero." Ah, gosh. It'd be something worth doing, anyway. By the time I got off the phone with him, I was actually thinking more seriously about that, though I really didn't have a clue where to start. How did one go around, putting together a fundraiser for victims of attacks?

I wanted to raise the question over dinner, but

Scanlon was there, so I decided not to encourage him. Besides, he was in a pretty rare mood, all stern and anxious.

"If I had my way," he said, "I'd keep you all from stepping out-of-doors. Who knows what can happen out there, the way this city's falling apart? I say that we'll be doing the superheroes a big favor by taking care not to put ourselves in harm's way." He actually emphasized his point by pounding a fist on the table, making Dad choke on his soup.

Liz looked alarmingly starry-eyed as she listened. "You're absolutely right," she said. Or, rather, sighed. Dreamily. It was also a long, drawn-out one. My sister was gone, gone, gone.

Chapter 19

It was sort of like Minimum Day at my "school" because Dr. Dibbs said something came up in Freddie's undercover work, so I got booted out of Brenda's shop around lunchtime with a crazy pile of homework to occupy me for a couple of days or so. I'd had a few minimum days now, and on one hand, I wondered about the state of my education; on the other hand, who was I to complain? It was just too bad that I had to take the bitter with the sweet.

"It's your first set of take-home exams, Mr. Eric," Dr. Dibbs had said as he handed me about half a dozen stapled questionnaires that also ran about ten million pages long for each subject. "You need to stock up on those blue books, so you can use them for the essays."

"Essays?" I echoed helplessly, staring at each stapled test and feeling the blood drain away from me. "Seriously? Do I have to wait for college to do oral exams or something?" Boy, that was going to be a real pain in the ass to do.

He shook his head. "Essays, young man. Essays. You can't go through life without developing communication and critical thinking skills. Oh, and buy the large blue books, not the small ones. Your sister should be able to help. In the meantime, I won't be available, but you're welcome to contact Ms. Whitaker should you have any questions about your tests." He took a deep breath when he paused, as he'd been talking non-stop while stuffing my arms with that nightmare pile of his. "Do you have any question to ask me, by the way, before I let you go for the next two days?"

I scowled at the stack. "Am I eighteen yet?" Yeah, yeah, I know. I'd been going on and on about being eighteen, but what else was there to look forward to? Of course, if everything I'd heard about being eighteen turned out to be a total lie, there'd be some blood that'd be spilled.

"Last time I checked, no. Any more questions?"

"Can I come? I promise I won't get in the way. Can we just turn these essays into something like P.E. or hands-on stuff? I don't mind being graded for helping out in superhero work."

"Nope. Have a good day, Mr. Eric. And be sure to make good use of the dictionary. I assume that you know how."

I stared at him. "Of course I do! What's all *that* about?"

Dr. Dibbs didn't look ruffled at all. He merely cocked an eyebrow. "You'd be surprised, young man, at how many adults don't know jack about using the dictionary."

"Whoa. You said 'jack.' That's cool." I grinned. I couldn't help it. Dr. Dibbs said "jack."

He booted me out.

First contact with Mrs. Zhang made! With police activity spreading all over Vintage City, I figured it was safe for me to saunter on over to Uncle Chung's after "class," and sure enough, they were open. There are no words to describe the relief I felt at seeing the familiar neon sign and foggy interior through the windows.

"Hey, Mrs. Zhang!" I called out, and I saw her silhouette wave at me from behind the steam counter. "Good to see you again!"

"Yeah? Well, it's not good seeing you still skinny. What the hell's wrong with you? You not bulimic, are you?"

I just shrugged, totally relieved, and sat on a weathered stool while waiting for her to finish swapping a couple of empty food pans with new ones that were packed with freshly cooked stuff. Mrs. Zhang recently put the stools there, saying that they were for customers who had to wait for their food to be cooked. To be more competitive, she expanded their menu and added special dishes that her husband could whip up for anyone who might not care for the usual ready-to-go offerings, especially if they had health-related limitations. When Dad found out about it, he said it felt like he'd just died and gone to stir-fry heaven. Since Scanlon Frankie Avalon'd into our lives, we had to make good use of her new policy as well.

"So what happened to you guys?" I demanded. I slid off my stool when she waved at me to come close, and to my train wreck delight, she gave me a small bowl of hot and sour soup. "Wow, thanks!" Oh, I could feel my arteries constrict from all the grease I was set to ingest, but I loved her soup and its turn-your-ass-into-an-organic-flamethrower-when-you-fart spice levels.

"All trouble around here!" she cried, waving both hands above her. She scowled under her massive hairnet. "Innocent families attacked, and all buildings around them searched inch by inch! I'm glad they didn't rip up my kitchen, but they were close! I have pepper spray. I can use it on cops."

She'd've done it, too. I nodded, happily sipping my soup. "Any leads, though? Have they found anything yet?"

"If they did, they don't say anything. Not to me or other businesses around here." She paused and looked thoughtful. Sad and thoughtful, really, which I was never used to seeing from her. "Don't understand. Innocent families attacked. Why? They were minding their own business. Like hot dog restaurant. Good owner, I know him. Very nice and honest. Hard-working. Why make his life hell?"

I could only listen in sympathy. "You know, Mrs. Zhang, I'm gay. I've put up with so much crap from other kids before and after I came out. I've never done anything to piss them off. I guess simply existing is enough to offend some people, but my mom and dad have always told me that they're the ones with the problem. Not me. Sucks to be them, Dad used to say, with their heads stuck up their asses."

"Your dad said that? Cool dad!"

"Well, he made sure that Mom wasn't around when he made that point." My dad had his moments, yeah.

She grinned, nodding. "You're a good boy. Difficult sometimes, but good boy." She took my bowl when I was done and promptly filled it with rice and black bean chicken. "Now eat. Hunky boyfriend won't be too happy if you don't take care."

I went home all full and happy. I actually looked forward to doing my homework, which was kind of a sick sort of situation, but that was the magic of free Chinese food. Too bad that magic lasted as long as the food lasted in my digestive system. Eventually the charm wore off, and I was Cinderella, sleeping in soot. I actually took a nap and woke up in my bed, but the feeling of the remainder of the day being spent in academic drudgery latched on to me like brain-sucking leeches. I managed to do a little work before giving up and getting online for some Asteroids action.

Staying home and doing my homework bit hard. It was boring, and there were too many distractions. Yeah, Mom and Dad were all excited and tickled to see that Dr. Dibbs trusted me enough with a stack of take-home tests that required blue books, but once I was left alone the next day, I couldn't get myself to make some kind of dent. I was only able to work on one-and-a-half tests before I gave up, dug around for loose change hidden in the dustiest, grossest pockets under our sofa cushions, and ran off for some ice cream. I figured that I might have to go elsewhere to make sure that I'd be able to concentrate. Somewhere quiet and closed in, sort of, with nothing anywhere to distract me.

So I went to the public library after scarfing down my treat. And then promptly fell asleep on my notes. I must've drooled up Lake Loch Ness by the time a librarian shook me awake to let me know that it was time for me to go home.

"Your parents will be worried about you," she said while handing me a box of tissues. That was embarrassing. I had to wait till after she left before using the handful I pulled out. I went to the men's room before leaving to check out how I looked in the mirror.

Lopsided hair aside, my face looked as though someone just stamped a road map on it. Creases from my shirt- sleeves, my pens, and a crumpled ball of paper that happened to be in the way when I conked out, all made a pretty strong impression—literally.

"Damn," I groaned, running my fingers over the marks. Good thing I didn't have a date planned later that day.

It took me a few minutes to wash up, comb my hair, and restore my dignity before leaving the library. I still had a lot of time left before everyone came home from work. I was also not at all interested in catching up with schoolwork. Wandering on to the downtown area was more of an act of desperation than anything else. I hated having unfinished work hanging over me, and I hated feeling unmotivated.

I wandered kind of aimlessly for a while. Nothing seemed out of the ordinary in the downtown area. Then again, any Vintage City resident wouldn't think twice about all the construction work that now littered the area.

A visitor might ask, "Hey, what's with all the crappy traffic jams and the screwed-up buildings around here?" To which a resident would say, "Oh, those? They're nothing. Just good and evil going head to head. Same old, same old in Vintage City. You get used to living in a battleground between superheroes and supervillains after a while. Here, have a truffle."

In short, I totally ignored the damaged areas and wove my way through the crowd, sidestepping stray debris without even looking at it. Yeah, I was that used to the carnage. It wasn't unusual for me to stand in front of a store, ogling the merchandise, while swiping at bits of brick or plaster or even broken glass falling from a nearby casualty of a recent battle. Hell, I wasn't even surprised to see a number of folks, mostly seniors, walking around with umbrellas, rain or shine. There was a little group of old-timers, too, who wore hard hats, though I saw that one of them wore a brainsaver skateboard helmet. He must've borrowed it from his grandkid or something.

I just wandered around the main square, completely zoned out, I guess. Nothing registered in my mind, though I was pretty much aware that I stopped in front of a bunch of store windows, checking out stuff. I even stood in front of the founder's statue, which finally got itself a replacement head.

"Dude, that's lame," I muttered, frowning at the thing. Seriously, whoever the artist was, he didn't do a good job with keeping proportions consistent. His replacement head matched the rest of the statue in terms of color, texture, and amount of weathering, but size-wise? Yikes. Looking at the statue seriously made me think of the *Powerpuff Girls*, vintage-style, and in male drag. From where I stood, I figured that the new head was about three sizes too big. I didn't know how they'd managed to secure it to the statue, but I sure hoped that whatever stuff they'd used to glue the two separate parts together would hold for a long, long time unless the city was prepared for one lawsuit after another.

Imagine getting brained by the founder's new head in the middle of your lunch break. What a sad way to go.

Eventually I picked up where I left off, wandering around again without any purpose or direction and feeling more and more bored by the minute. I stopped in front of a small electronic store, blandly staring at their computer display. They had a little group of used computer monitors and keyboards sitting on a display table in front of the shop door, and for one crazy moment, I toyed around with the idea that I might need a new used computer for my room.

Then all the computer screens suddenly flared to life, flashing a bright white, pulsing a few times, before growing dark again. Then text appeared across them, marching from end to end. Oh, great.

Bingo night's upon us! they screamed at me in flashing colors. *I'll call you when Doomsday comes. Dude, I'm already breaking out in hives. Good to know that I get share the trauma with a buddy.*

I'd been so bored out of my mind that I'd lost track of time. Apparently school was done for the day. I rolled my eyes and gave the computers the middle finger.

I might not be able to see you, but I can feel your vibes. Because, you know, I'm just a really sensitive young lady.

I gave Althea a double middle finger dose with both hands.

Smartass.

Oh, this was getting way fun. I could just *feel* her working hard to break right through the screens and push out her electricity-lights-colors-digital-whatthehellever hands, and strangle me. Were the computer monitors actually shaking from her efforts? Ha-ha! But she had to behave herself, obviously, so no one would know she'd possessed those things.

"Shouldn't you be hunting criminals or something, not harassing best friends over bingo night?" I said, exaggerating the way my mouth moved in case she couldn't hear me from those old monitors. One can never tell with these superheroes. I was also in the mood to annoy the living daylights out of her.

Yanno, when I said I can sense your vibes, I wasn't messing around. Stop making all those faces when you talk. You're so weird. And you know I can hear you.

"Wow. Pot and kettle," I snorted.

A certain superhero wants me to tell you that if I catch you loitering around downtown at around this time, I have to play Mommy and tell you to haul your ass back home. It's too dangerous for you to be out here. So...haul your ass back home, mister. Or so help me, you're grounded for a month.

I made a face. "Quit babying me. God, you guys are worse than Mom."

Well, you're not supposed to go east of the main square. There's trouble brewing. That's why we're all out, and you really shouldn't be. Now scram. Or I'll have to use my power cables and play giant slingshot with you.

Aha—superhero action time. "I don't have plans of window-shopping in that direction. Lay off."

Dude. Watch your back.

"Oh, yeah, what're you gonna do? Take over someone's cell phone and ring me to death?" I snorted.

I said, watch your back!

I shook my head, chuckling. "Whatever, Horace," I said, waving a hand at the computers and turning away.

"Watch out!" someone yelled.

I barely noticed something large and flying—more like tumbling crazily through the air as it dropped from the sky. It wasn't coming in my direction, but it was about to crush the area where the founder's statue was, which also included a bunch of benches packed with people enjoying the sunny afternoon.

"Oh no! Look out!"

"Run!"

It was all I could do to gasp and reflexively dive for cover, though there wasn't any cover for me to dive to. I just rolled over the ground in front of the electronics store and then balled myself on the pavement as I pressed against a wall. Around me people yelped and ran, most diving for cover.

"Oh, my God!"

I pinched my eyes shut and waited for a loud thud or a sickening crunch, but nothing happened. People still yelled and ran, and I heard a few trip and stumble, but whatever had been falling a few seconds ago didn't make any noise.

"What happened? What's going on?"

"Did you see that?"

"What? What is it?"

"I don't know!"

I opened my eyes and turned in the direction of the main square. It was a small sports car that had flown down on us. It was obviously picked up and then thrown from another point, but I didn't know who did it or how. Actually, I didn't care. What mattered at that moment was the fact that the car hadn't crushed anyone in the square. How could it?

A force field had formed above the area, a giant bubble that I could barely make out. It was a massive dome that cocooned the people who hung around the founder's statue, and resting on its highest part was the car. It lay on its side, not moving.

"Look!" someone called out, and the familiar whooshing sound reached my ears.

Magnifiman swooped down and picked up the car, flying away with it. I was sure that he'd be back within a few seconds. In the meantime, everyone stood around and gaped at the force field, none daring to move forward and inspect it. Those who were inside eyed it in shock, and they looked just as frozen as everyone else outside.

A low series of firecracker-like sounds broke through the confusion, but there weren't any signs of the Puppet's mannequins anywhere. I looked around, poised for flight. No, no one was around, shooting at people in the square. It could only mean that the noise came from the eastern part of the city, where Althea warned me against.

Another sound grew louder, a familiar one that always made me catch my breath in anticipation. I looked up in time to catch Calais and Miss Pyro sailing above us, following Magnifiman's trail. I loved the little flame bits that Miss Pyro always left in her wake. They marked her progress with tiny dancing little fires that eventually faded and left nothing but faint black smoke.

Then the force field slowly vanished, its near-invisible domed silhouette fading gradually till nothing was left. Pretty soon people were moving again, walking cautiously forward and reaching out to feel around. Apparently the force field was completely gone by then. Everyone started talking at the same time, voices raised in shock and amazement.

I looked around me and found nothing out of the ordinary. No one looked as though he or she was responsible for either the car-throwing or the force field.

I hurried back to the electronics store display table

and knocked on one of the computer monitors. All the screens were black, occasionally crackling with white light.

"Althea!"

I told you to go home, didn't I? You're grounded for a month.

"Did you see that?" I asked.

No, but I knew what was coming. Why do you think I warned you? Heads up. I'm going offline—sort of. It's action time.

"I was talking about the force field, not the car, dummy!" I said, raising my voice and knocking on the computer monitor again. "Hey, are you still there? Can you hear me?" I kept knocking till my knuckles felt a little raw.

"Ahem."

I gave a start and looked around. A guy had walked up to me and probably heard me talking to a computer display. He stared at me with that familiar WTF look, his lower lip hanging open.

"What're you looking at?" I retorted, adjusting my bag and walking off. Man. Some people could be pretty weird.

Chapter 20

I think my whole family spent the rest of the day glued to the TV. Even Mom didn't pitch a fit when Dad said that he needed to watch the news. We ended up carrying dinner trays to the living room, finding our favorite spots, and watching Bambi Bailey tell us how much Vintage City sucked because of its out-of-control supervillain problems, while looking like a Hollywood star on the red carpet.

Ms. Bailey, bless her, must've gotten some kind of flack from her bosses or something over her TV reporter glam thing. She'd toned down her outfits and recently had taken to more sedate business suits, which impressed me at first till that fateful moment a couple of nights ago, when the camera made the mistake of including her in the shot when it panned out for a wide-angle type of view of the crime scene. We all saw her wearing the shortest, tightest little skirt that could ever be worn by a woman. You know, the kind of micro-mini power suits that only prime time lawyers on TV could wear and make everyone believe that *all* professionals looked like that. Yeah, right.

How she managed to move around without getting arrested or psychologically knocked up was beyond me. I was sure, though, that after the news report, all the straight men in the city had to lie back, light cigarettes, and drawl, "Baby, I hope that was as good for you as it was for me."

It was also pretty clear that she didn't like the idea of dumping her jewelry, but it did shrink. At least she stopped wearing those mini chandeliers on her ears. Her makeup also went a little more neutral, which bummed me out because Liz and I were deprived our "Where's Waldo" moment regarding her forever-moving fake beauty mark.

I could only conclude that since her obvious femme-fatale thing hadn't enticed Magnifiman, she probably thought that there was something to being a little more, you know, subtle about physical beauty in snagging a man. In addition to getting chewed out by her boss, I suppose. Okay, maybe that thing about her super-short, super-tight skirt was one of those "maybe he's a leg man" types of siren call; props to her for using every trick in the book. Too bad she just didn't seem to be willing to admit that maybe Magnifiman was plain not interested in mixing business with pleasure. Or that he was so seriously stuck to his job that any attachment he might have to a woman would go up in flames within half a day.

"Today's incident is a clear warning sign," she declared, looking all grim and subtly glam. She even furrowed her brows a little. "This new threat, this new supervillain, Arachnaman, is much more powerful than both the Shadow Puppet and the Deathtrap Debutantes combined. With an army of mechanical spiders he can unleash at any time, he can attack several locations at once, unlike the Shadow Puppet's killer mannequins, which are fewer, slower, and tend to move around in smaller groups."

Sergeant Vitus Bone of the Vintage City Police Department had been interviewed earlier, and the camera cut to that for a moment. "Our new threat so far—*cough!*—has attacked an arcade, an adult store—*hrrrum!*—a new age shop, and today, a German car dealer," he said, sagging, pouchy cheeks trembling from his perpetual coughing fit. "He'd also destroyed four other different businesses and a Chinese apartment building. We're working with the superheroes in piecing together—*hrrrum!*—this latest puzzle."

"So do you think that there's a method to his madness, sir?" Ms. Bailey prodded. I thought I saw the way she eyed the good sergeant, like she was all worried about whether or not she was going to catch his disease. In fact, now that I think about it, she tended to lean away whenever she had to interview him.

"Yes, yes, there is. *Cough!* There's always a purpose for these madmen's attacks, Ms. Bailey—*cough!*—even if it's as simple as mindless vanity and an abnormal appetite for bling, like you see from the Deathtrap Debutantes."

Ms. Bailey leaned away a little more till it looked

like she was suffering from some horribly debilitating back pain. I wanted to give her a cane for Christmas. "And what do you think is this new villain's purpose, sir?" She was beginning to grimace from the effort, too.

"Ah—*hrrrum!*—that's all classified information, Ms. Bailey. *Cough!*"

"Oh. And you don't think it's simply because this new threat is hopelessly repressed?"

The interview was terminated when Sergeant Bone gave Ms. Bailey this look, one that I frankly couldn't describe other than "Lay off the bong, lady."

The news then returned to the present live reporting. "We haven't had an opportunity to interview any of the superheroes..."

"Especially Magnifiman," I muttered, stuffing my mouth with a roll.

"...especially Magnifiman," Ms. Bailey reported, pausing for the smallest fraction of a second to steal a glance at the sky. "We've yet to find out what they've learned about—"

Ms. Bailey paused when a voice, most likely from the news crew, interrupted her reporting. She turned in surprise when a hand appeared from behind the camera. It held up a scrap of paper. She took it and read its contents, blinking and looking a little confused. But she was a seasoned professional and was able to compose herself in another second.

Looking straight at the camera, she said, "Apparently, we've just received a response via Twitter. This is regarding our earlier interview of Sergeant Bone." She cleared her throat and read.

"'We're like kicking your ass when we come back, bitches.' That was, uh, @DeathDebs. You know who they are."

Another hand, or maybe the same one, appeared with another scrap of paper. Ms. Bailey sighed, tossed aside the Debutantes' threatening tweet, and plucked out the new message. "This one says, 'Ur hairstyle is like *so* 2008.'" Ms. Bailey rolled her eyes and crumpled the note into a ball. "For Channel 3 News, this is Bambi Bailey reporting."

Even with school still in session and Peter being stuck doing superhero work part-time, I considered myself pretty damned lucky to be going steady with him. He didn't have to work-work, that is, because his parents wanted him to focus on school. Well, not until he turned eighteen, he told me, because he was determined to strike out on his own, though he was still tied to Vintage City as a superhero.

"I had all these plans for college and stuff, but I don't know," he said one time, shrugging. "When life throws you a curveball..."

"Maybe your powers have an expiration date, and when that comes, we can just pack up and move away from this dump," I offered, but he only laughed and then distracted me by unzipping my jeans.

I told him that I'd take any opportunity that came my way, so long as we were able to spend as much time together as possible. I also dug the fact that his future plans helped shape mine. I didn't want to think about how my parents would react to "I decided to stay put, and I'll think about college later on." A PhD was too abstract a goal, anyway, for someone my age. I figured Mom and Dad would eventually come around to it, but in the meantime, best to just shut up and wait and hope that a local junior college would suffice. Okay, it seemed to work for Liz, so I didn't see anything wrong about my following in her footsteps.

At any rate, it was still school time, neither of us worked, and our time apart was largely spent planning the best way to make use of the little time that Mom allowed me before "curfew" hit. After the phone calls, we'd meet somewhere, or he'd pick me up. Sometimes I just invited him over and dragged him upstairs to my room. Weekdays, when everyone was at work, were the best times to do that.

I got home at around three, which gave me a little time to prepare for my planned after-school mini-date with Peter, who was expected to stop by a couple of hours later.

I'd just set the pizza down on the table when the doorbell rang. "It's just us two," I panted, stepping back from the door and letting him in.

"Okay, cool," he said vaguely.

I kept my eyes on him as I closed the door. "What's up? You look a little out of it."

"Hmm? What?"

I chuckled and locked the door. Walking up to him, I leaned closer and gave him a loud, sloppy kiss. "You're distracted. Anything wrong? Things a little crazy at the office?"

Peter blinked, and I swore I saw fog dissipating in his eyes. He looked back at me and finally grinned, eyes clear and mischievous. "Things are always crazy at the office," he replied, returning my kiss, his hands wandering over familiar territory. "But I—"

"You can't tell me, I know. Classified information, yadda, yadda, yadda," I said. Funny how my body parts tended to develop their own consciousness, completely separate from my brain. Then I figured that it was just as well that they did because once hormones kicked in, my brain was useless. "That's cool. Don't let the husband in on it..."

One unique talent we'd both developed was to hold a conversation while making out pretty heavily. I'd no idea how we managed it, but we did, and who the hell was I to complain? It didn't matter where we were and whether or not we were upright. We were both knotted, sweaty messes, clothes partly undone, hands and lips navigating through more areas than all Portuguese explorers did combined.

I had him pressed against the wall this time. Wasn't aware of that till we nearly lost our footing and slid down to the floor.

"No, I'm just not sure if I should tell you," he breathed against my cheek.

"I'm not twisting your arm or anything..."

"You're doing something much, much better than that..."

Yeah, I was. Jeebus. I needed to stop before we had major accidents in the hallway. I forced myself to pull away and nearly passed out from the effort.

Seriously, once horny levels had shot well past the stratosphere, making myself rational again was like worse than spiritual death. I'd say "hell on earth," but that distinction was already reserved for bingo night. Besides, throwing cold water on myself felt like dying a hundred times over with nothing to show for it.

Perfect subject for haiku, no?

"Thanks," Peter whispered, pressing a kiss against my forehead once we calmed down. "You know, if this were the kind of welcome I'd get after a hard day's work, I'm not going to think twice about dropping to my knees and proposing to you right now."

"Funny you should mention that. I've got dozens of ideas where we can elope." Were those little hearts fluttering before my eyes? Ew. God, when I got schmoopy, I sure got *schmoopy*. I pulled away and buttoned up. Once my breathing had gone down, I readjusted my glasses, which I discovered were slightly smudged, and gave Peter a loopy smile. "There's time enough for that. Let's eat." I took his hand and led him to the dining-room. "I got us the thick-crust garlic-bread-type pizza with your favorite toppings. Do you want some soda? Dad stocked up on the stuff..."

"Eric?"

We'd reached the dining room door by then. Residual adrenaline kept my mouth moving. My brain stayed behind in the hallway. "I forgot to ask you about the salad, so I hope you're okay with the spring salad mix that Mom's so crazy about..."

Peter gave my hand a gentle tug. "Eric, I think Calais has a stalker."

Oh, *great*. One more item to add to the running list of The Heartbreaks of Being a Superhero's Boyfriend. I just stared at him. "Are you kidding me?"

Guess not. "You can check out the guestbook of the fan club if you don't believe me." Oh, I sure as hell believed him. In fact, I believed him so much that I almost carried him, our pizza, drinks, and salad upstairs to my room in one fell swoop. Apparently my jealousy-induced adrenaline-attack wasn't strong enough, and I ended up recruiting Peter into helping me haul our meal upstairs.

I turned my computer on and immediately went for the fan site. Peter sat on the floor, leaning against my bed, while eating pizza. "I don't know if the message is still there, but it was in the guestbook. I wouldn't be surprised if the site owner deleted it by now," he said in between bites. So I checked the guestbook, but I saw nothing other than gooey, misspelled messages from starry-eyed fans. For one insane moment, I wondered how much Althea would charge me if I hired her to hack into the damn place and destroy it completely, but logic took over pretty quickly. I supposed others could swoon over Peter as long as they didn't do anything more.

"There's nothing there," I said as I took my place in front of him, crossing my legs under me and taking up my plate and unfinished pizza. "What did it say?"

"Well, it was a flame, really, but on the surface, you kind of expect that from fans who blur the line between reality and fantasy."

"I've seen stuff like that before, yeah. But what makes you think this is a stalker?"

Peter thought for a moment, slowly chewing. He swallowed and then took a sip of his drink. "I don't know, to be honest. The message went something like 'You're a bunch of bitches and whores, yadda, yadda, yadda...fuck your stupid site and stupid wank stories because you'll never have him!' That's most of what I can remember, anyway. And I've seen the same message pop up in the guestbook at random times. Whenever it showed up, it got deleted."

I decided not to tease him any more and then frowned. I've never dealt with anything like this before. Then again, I'd never had a boyfriend before, let alone a boyfriend who also happened to be a superhero. "Hmm. The internet's full of creepy jerks like that." I paused when Peter's gaze finally settled on mine. "Are you actually nervous?"

"No, not really," he said. "I can take care of myself. I do wonder about that person, though."

"But what if it was just a lame joke? I mean, people post crazy stuff like that all the time."

"What about copycats or that message actually being read by the wrong person, who really *is* a stalker type? Would she be incited to freak out and do something?"

I sighed and scratched my head, glancing back at my computer. The site was still up as I'd never clicked out of it. "I don't know," I confessed. "Seriously, what can we do in a situation like this? You really can't call someone a stalker unless you're literally hounded everywhere you go, right? Or find, like, decapitated horses' heads in your bed or something?"

Peter raised an eyebrow at me. One more sexy move of his, I might add. "Hopefully things won't go that far." Our conversation pretty much mellowed out after that, and we were soon talking about everything else *but* superhero-related things. The time came as well when we pretty much stopped talking altogether.

And so the Afternoon Weekday Date Scorecard went like this: gay boys, 3. Bedsheets, below zero. Vatican-enforced check on virginity, 10. Sometimes life just plain sucked beyond the suckiest of suckage. And I was out of clean bedsheets, too.

Chapter 21

Okay, so one drawback to being good friends with superheroes was that I walked around with a bull's eye on my forehead for Freddie's chameleon practice. The wily bastard. There were several others, not the least of which was the cyber-harassment I got from Althea over stupid bingo night.

The good thing was being able to sit in on their superhero powwow, which happened every once in a rare while, though Trent was never around. Whenever I asked Peter where his brother was, he'd tell me that Trent was at a meeting at work or doing some covert investigation sort of thing and stuff.

"Does he ever go on vacation?" I asked once.

"Vacation from what?" Peter replied, looking a little sheepish. "Vacation from superhero work or work-work? Either way, the answer's no."

I grimaced. "Damn. I guess it's good that he's single. I can't imagine any girl putting up with that."

"Oh, several have tried. All have failed. It's actually Trent's motto."

"Hmm. I can say the same about your fangirls." Oh, yeah, I just had to throw that one in. I loved saying it, too. Many had tried, all had failed. Hell, yeah. Though that also reminded me to check up on Calais' fan site and see what had been going on there. Maybe see if I could muster enough courage to read a fanfic from start to finish or check out some fanart. Maybe keeping an illegal bottle of whiskey around might not have been a bad idea, after all. Other people's fantasies about one's boyfriend were the stuff of nightmares, but they did have that certain train wreck appeal that kept calling to me. I was sure that it wouldn't be long before my defenses were breached, and I'd be subjecting myself to all kinds of lurid artwork and stories about Calais.

Superhero Powwows sometimes took place in a restaurant, where we'd all gather and "talk shop," sometimes in code, depending on how busy it was around us. Well, *they* did, anyway. I was just there for the ride, and at least I was useful as an outsider whose opinion they wanted every once in a while. Okay, so not everything I said carried any weight to them, but I guess it helped, anyway, sharing my thoughts about things, being a regular person and all. Besides, after going through what I went through with the Trill, I guess that I pretty much earned my way into their select little group. I just wasn't sure whether or not I should be flattered by that, considering that how I earned my way into their clique involved a few weeks spent neck-deep in

Satan's cesspit, fighting against my own friends.

For this particular "business meeting," Wade decided to take us to some posh restaurant she really loved.

"I've got Dad's card," she confessed, grinning and looking a little embarrassed, which she always did as an apology for being born into money. Sometimes I wondered if she was switched at birth, and some high maintenance Prada-obsessed type was whining her way through middle-class existence. "He told me to use it for work, and he'll get tax write-offs from them—or something like that. He's good friends with the restaurant owner, and he made sure to let the other guy know that I'm using his card." She turned to Althea. "Pretend that it's your birthday because that's the excuse Dad gave his buddy."

"You mean I'll be getting froufrou cake and dessert?" Althea said, wide-eyed. "Girl, if I could have a birthday every day at that restaurant, I'd be all for it!"

Wade made a face. "Yeah, but the portions tend to be small. You know how it is in these places."

"Shoot, that never stopped me before," Althea said, all sparkly-eyed behind her glasses, as she linked arms with Wade.

I hadn't met Wade's parents or the rest of her family. I was frankly afraid to; if meeting Peter's filthy-rich folks was enough to make me break out in anxiety-caused hives, the mere thought of being introduced to Wade's millionaire parents made me want to get bricked up alive. Going to a posh restaurant that required us to dress up a little proved to be the farthest I was willing to go in rubbing shoulders with anyone who earned at least a six-figure yearly income.

So I had to shower and then throw on a dressy ensemble, which included a tie. I stared at my reflection once I was done, my shoulders drooping.

"This is depressing," I muttered, looking at myself up and down. Oxford shirt, slacks, slightly scuffed-up leather shoes, and a tie—I seriously missed my second-hand wardrobe. The outfit was *not* me. Sure, it made my parents stop dead in their tracks and stare in shock, with my dad narrowing his eyes and looking suspiciously at me and asking, "Eric? Is that you?" Mom, in the meantime, looked as though she were about to burst into tears. And Liz, bless her, pulled me aside and whispered, "You'd better use protection. I refuse to be an aunt at nineteen." On the whole? Being dressed up made me itch. Literally. I considered bringing a small tube of anti-itch cream in case the allergic reaction I had to looking uptown turned into a problem.

Even in the restaurant—called Flambeau, by the way—and safely tucked away in a private booth that Wade had reserved for us, I couldn't get myself to relax and feel comfortable. Peter's admiring stare when he picked me up earlier didn't do much to calm me down. Seeing Althea and Freddie all dressed up as well helped a little, but not by much. Though I must admit, I almost laughed in Freddie's face because he looked just as uncomfortable in his shirt and slacks as I was in mine. In fact, he kept tugging at his collar as though it were choking him. At any rate, itching and all, I tried my best to suck it up and enjoy the company.

The next time the heroes decide to have a powwow in public, I'll have to dare Freddie into showing up in drag or something.

"No manifesto published yet," Althea said as we worked through appetizers. "And so far, my examination of the spider bots didn't show anything weird or unique. They were all just regular robots, I guess, with each group designed for specific methods of destruction."

"So no real clue as to what this new guy really wants from all this, huh?" Freddie asked in between nibbles, which was a pretty funny sight in and of itself, considering how beefy he was and how delicate the appetizers were. He just couldn't toss one down without looking like some crude frat boy.

"No, so far, nothing's come up. Not that he needs a manifesto, anyway. The graffiti he left at the Yee Apartments was enough for us to go by."

Peter nodded. "Yeah, I think you're right. He doesn't need to advertise anything. He just comes and destroys."

I stared at my plate of shiitake mushrooms all stuffed with chestnut and apple chutney. I'd already soiled my shirt with some of the stuffing that popped out when I took a bite, and I was a little too self-conscious to carry on with it.

"Just think about his targets," Peter added, mercifully clueless about my embarrassing situation. I stole a glance at him, and he popped those mushrooms into his mouth without an accident or two. In fact, everyone seemed to be having a way better time of it than I was. "It'll be easy for us to figure out what the common denominator is."

"An arcade, an adult store, a New Age shop, and a foreign car dealer," Althea piped up. "A gay bookstore, a mechanic's shop, a Mexican grocery, and an herbal shop. Sounds like he doesn't know how to have any fun."

"I think at this point the whole city knows that," Peter said with an emphatic nod.

My gaze drifted to the silverware flanking my plate in clean, precise lines. Were dinner settings in froufrou restaurants always made for people with more than two arms? Why were there more than one fork and more than one spoon lying next to my plate? Was there a difference between them? I couldn't tell beyond the sizes. The middle fork was larger than the others flanking it. So what?

"So—we might be looking at someone who's got problems with..." Wade's words faltered. She grinned at everyone. "Oh. Sorry. I lost my train of thought. These mushrooms are totally to die for."

I turned my attention to the two spoons that were on the right side of my plate, but those were way easier to figure out. I recognized the teaspoon. What the hell was up with the forks? Did I really need three of them for one meal? What a waste! Even the wine glasses were totally mental. There were three of them standing where glasses normally stand, but I didn't get it. Not only were there three glasses, they were also different sizes. Should I empty out each one and move on to the next when I was done? Couldn't I just reuse the glass like, you know, normal people did? It was also good for the environment, or didn't the restaurant know that?

Did rich people fuck around with each others' minds when they ate? I just sat there, frowning and counting silverware and glasses. It sure as hell would've helped if dinner at Flambeau came with a set of instructions for us non-hoity-toity types. I could imagine Dad spluttering something indistinguishable before pushing all the excess stuff aside and diving into his meal with a fork and a knife.

"There's a list of other businesses that Trent and I drew up," Peter said, his voice dropping a little. "I'll fire them off to you guys tonight."

"What's up?" Althea prodded.

I sighed, resolved to pretend as though I knew how to eat something French. I picked up a stuffed mushroom and bit into it, taking care to lean farther forward and make sure that any drippings or loose stuffing would fall on the plate, not on my shirt.

"I have a hunch, and I want to test it out," Peter replied, now talking in almost a whisper. Everyone but me had to lean forward a little to catch his words. "We all need to keep an eye on those places. In fact, we need to search each of them. I have to talk to the powers that be into giving us permission before the next round of attacks."

Freddie blinked. "Do you think they're gonna be targets?"

I chewed my appetizer slowly, deliberately, while staring down in horror at my shirt. I didn't know how it happened, considering all the precautions I'd

241

taken, but there they were—a couple of large marks on my shirt, with bits of stuffing still clinging to the greasy fabric. No, those didn't include the first stain I'd made.

"Yeah. I hope I'm wrong, but you can never tell." Peter fell silent for a moment as he drank some water. "Actually, I know I'm right. That's the kicker. We've got to act fast."

Wade piped up. "We'll all have to be assigned an area to watch. I don't know how many you have on the list, Peter, but hopefully we won't have to spread ourselves out too much."

I took my glass, pretending to drink water. While no one was looking, I pulled up my napkin from my lap, tilted the glass to soak it a little with my drink, and then gently dabbed the wet napkin against my shirt. I grimaced when I saw that while the grease was picked up, the spot grew because of the moisture in the napkin. Within seconds I was stuck with three gigantic spots on my shirt, which I couldn't hide behind my tie.

"We'll cover what we can, but we have to move fast since we're such a dinky group," Peter said, and everyone murmured their agreement. He sat back with a satisfied little sigh. So did the others. When they started talking about other things, Peter turned to look at me. The smile on his face froze, and I could only sink in my seat, my face burning.

"Um, you don't happen to have a blow dryer on you, do you?" I asked, my voice tiny. "I kind of had a little accident with the mushrooms. Sorry. I've never eaten French food before."

By the way, Althea got her froufrou cake and dessert. She almost refused to share.

When Peter dropped me off at home, he gave me a watch. "Don't lose it," he said as I buckled it around my left wrist. It looked pretty standard, all black and very swanky, but knowing Peter, it was some kind of tricked-out gadget that he'd made just for me.

I looked at him and pointed at the watch. "Is this sort of like the friendship bracelet you gave me a while ago?"

"Yup. I'm getting better with the special gadgetry skills," he replied, grinning proudly. "Can't you tell?" Then he blushed. "Actually, I had a lot of help from the Sentries. They're seriously good at this sort of thing, even though they're not all that cooperative half the time."

"So what's it supposed to do?"

"It's a communication device. It goes both ways, so if you need to get a hold of me during an emergency, just press the upper-right button. Yeah, that one." He paused, hesitating a little. "I hope you don't think that I'm trying to control you with this, Eric. I'm only trying to keep you safe. If it's any comfort, I gave Mom and Dad their watches, too. Well, Mom's is way fancier than that, of course, and..." He looked a little puzzled now. "What? What's so funny?"

I shook my head. I'd been snickering the whole time he talked, and I couldn't stop. "Nothing," I said, pulling him close for a kiss. "Thank you." I didn't stumble out of his car for another ten minutes, my slacks tenting.

As much as I hated to admit it, that French restaurant thing stayed with me for a while, and I went to bed that night sulking a little and mulling over how things would be if, say, Peter and I were to hook up forever, and I'd have to face his family, like, *forever*. I never asked Peter how Mrs. Barlow liked me. I figured that she did, even with my obvious lack of social graces and stuff, but a part of me kept saying that what she showed me could very well be different from how she really felt.

I mean, seriously, I was a guest. I was her youngest son's boyfriend. She was rich, well-educated, successful, and very classy. It made sense that she'd behave in a very classy sort of way even if she couldn't deal with my existence. I also expected Peter to be just classy enough to keep all bad vibes from me because, well, he was just too damned cool that way.

At any rate, I couldn't help but apologize over and over to Peter that night even though he looked like he didn't care but was still concerned about the crappy state of my clothes.

"I'm sorry I embarrassed you," I kept whispering to him.

"Eric, there's nothing to be sorry about," he whispered back, over and over. "Really. Accidents happen. And you were with friends."

Accidents happen, but not like that, I was going to say. I decided to just shut the hell up and figure out how to avoid putting him in a similar situation in the future.

"Oh, God," I muttered, staring at my bedroom

ceiling in the dark as I lay in bed. "Does that mean that I have to enroll in some kind of stupid charm school?"

I desperately wanted to make an effort to be on par with Peter and his family. He was pretty down-to-earth, yeah, but as they say, relationships go both ways. In our case, Peter was already meeting me on my turf day after day; it was only right for me to work hard to raise myself up from slightly-lower-middle-class crudeness to upper-class refinement.

"Great. How would I do that?"

Yeah, that was the question of the century as far as I was concerned. Who'd teach me without laughing in my face? I didn't want to Google references. I could only stay glued to the computer for a limited amount of time before my head and my eyes melted.

I told myself that I should go to the library and dig around there for books that I could use. That should be private enough. I only hoped that the librarian wouldn't give me a hard time.

Of course, I could always have just asked my family, but I figured being laughed at by them would be way too harsh to deal with. It was bad enough that I had to go through with this, but I wanted to do it for Peter.

Incidentally, I went online first before hitting the sack, and checked out Calais' fan site. I couldn't find the courage to read fanfiction or look at fanart about my spandex-clad boyfriend, but I did look through the guestbook. Nope, nothing unusual had been posted since I last visited the site, but I figured that anything bad would've been deleted by the site owner by then.

I went to bed easy in my mind and certainly not as inclined to worry about freaky fans. They were a dime a dozen, and as long as Peter remained safe, that was all I cared about. Besides, like he'd said before, he could take care of himself, and to that I'd add, "He's also got a gaggle of superhero friends to protect him and not to mention a boyfriend who's more than willing to break the law if it means keeping psychos from touching him."

I grinned in the darkness, my earlier doubts gone. Yeah, I kind of liked that thought. I might not be anyone special, but I'd go to jail for Peter. Now *that* was what I'd call teen romance. Have I ever mentioned how schmoopy I could get?

Chapter 22

B eing a man of action, I went to the library the next day. Being a clueless man of action, I pretty much clung to the librarian's apron strings the whole time, shadowing her while she marched to the aisle where I could find the books I needed. If I could, I'd have shrunk myself to about two feet high. It was embarrassing, asking for books on proper manners and stuff. What was more embarrassing was having to put up with the librarian going all gooey on me, saying stuff like, "Awww... you're going to make your girl *so* proud!"

I figured it was bad manners to counter that with "I'm gay! Quit shoving the status quo down my friggin' throat, lady!" So I just bit my tongue. Literally.

Then again, I was too busy dying of shame the whole time, so I wasn't exactly in the right frame of mind to get all snarky on her. I gave her my library card. She scanned all three books and handed them back to me with another goofy little grin and a "This is too cute for words."

"You're not helping, you know," I grumbled, practically crawling on the floor by now and making sure that the books were buried at the bottom of my messenger bag.

Once I stepped outside to breathe in a few lungfuls of classic Vintage City urban oxygen, my watch beeped a couple of times. I raised my hand and saw *Stay close to home today. Love you.* It was black text sharply contrasted against a light grayish-silver background.

Peter had shown me how to use my watch to communicate with him, which wasn't any different from the tricked-out watch that the Trill had given me. I just held my wrist close to my face and, pressing the upper-right button, talked into it.

"Got your message. I was just at the library and on my way home."

I looked at the watch face, waiting for whatever was going to happen next after I spoke. Apparently it picked up my voice and turned it into text, or at least that was how I guessed it worked. At any rate, it took a few seconds before I received a response from Peter.

Very studious. Stay safe.

I made a face as I adjusted my bag and pulled up my hood after inspecting the overcast sky. If only Peter knew why I was there. Ha. I still hadn't replaced my old bike, so I was stuck walking home at a pretty fast pace to avoid the coming rain. I could've taken the bus, but I wanted to save money because that was the only way I could afford to partially pay for my dates with Peter. Begging for date money from Mom or negotiating terms with her was turning into a major psychic vampire ordeal as far as I was concerned.

It started to shower a little when I was around halfway home. Then I heard distant gunshots, more like a machine gun going off, and some crashing noises. I paused and looked around, but the street I was on remained quiet. The pedestrians, though, did the same thing I was doing, and before long, the whole area was at a standstill, save for the cars that continued to drive through.

"Did you hear that?" a lady asked her friend. They stood around ten feet away from me, their arms loaded with grocery bags.

"Yeah, I did. Where did it come from?"

Another round of gunfire silenced her. Then came another crash.

Standing there, being nothing more than an ordinary guy with nothing to protect myself with, listening to those sounds made my skin crawl. I was just glad that the crashes, whatever they were really all about, didn't come closer to where we stood.

"We'd better hurry," the first lady said, her voice shaking now. The two of them walked away at a pretty fast pace.

Looking around, I saw that the rest of the pedestrians were doing the same, with a few actually breaking out in a run. It was pretty nerve-wracking, having to weave my way through a half-panicked crowd, especially with the showers pelting us.

I turned a few more corners and soon spotted my house. That whole time, I kind of wished that I still had my energy power if only to help out the superheroes with. Hell, it didn't even have to be as strong as it had been when the Trill first manipulated me. Just enough to throw some kind of protective cloak over the people of Vintage City would be nice. Sort of like a force field.

I blinked, pausing in front of the door. Force field. The one in the recent attack downtown. I just realized that no one in the group had said anything about it over dinner. How weird. Did it mean that they didn't know? I'd completely forgotten about it, and I guess with no sign of who might've done that, it seemed to just fade from everyone's memory. Then again, Trent would've said something about it, since he'd plucked that car off the top of the force field and flown away with it.

Okay, this was getting way complicated. Why was I worrying about what the heroes knew, anyway? They had their own method of tackling stuff.

Another crashing sound broke through my thoughts. I fumbled for my keys and went inside. I didn't know where the trouble was, but I hoped that it wasn't in the same general area as Dad and Mom's work. Oh, and Liz's, too, I supposed.

Even inside the house, I could hear the same sounds, but muffled. So I hurried up the stairs and nearly fell on my face when I ran into my attic room and tripped on the old rug just inside my door. I figured that I could probably spot what was happening from my bedroom window, considering where it was, and if that didn't work, I could always climb up to the roof and get a bird's eye view of the area.

"Damn," I sighed when I threw my window open and got pelted by raindrops. It wasn't a downpour, but it had gotten a little stronger. I had to shield my eyes with both hands and squint through the rain and gray air to see what was going on.

Nothing.

I guess common sense would've told me to just quit while I was ahead, and not risk my health and safety by climbing up to the roof in acid rain, but I'd never really listened to common sense. Just ask my parents. I went to my bathroom, climbed out of the window there, and used the rusty, rickety fire escape to get to the roof.

I stood there for a while, eagerly searching the area for signs of trouble. The crashing and gunshots came from somewhere to the left of my house, and when I looked in that direction, my jaw dropped.

Something moved from building to building. I had to blink a dozen times before I could be sure of what it was...or, rather, before my brain could finally accept what I was looking at.

I was right. It was the same thing that I'd seen creeping from one warehouse rooftop to another. This time, I could see it more clearly. When before I thought I'd seen a giant mutant spider, I realized now that I was wrong. Sort of.

It was a giant spider-like thing. No, not a spider-spider, but a spider-like thing because the robot had a pilot. It looked more like it had eight gigantic legs sprouting from a small body, and that body was like a little capsule that encased a person. From where I stood, I couldn't really tell what that person looked like, but I did see that his upper-body poked out of the robot spider-thing's thorax, completely protected inside a clear bubble, and with the legs being so long and large, my view of the pilot continued to be blocked. All I could enjoy were split-second glimpses. The spider-robot's mouth, or fangs, snapped open and shut. Then from the space between them, something came out. It was a cloud of greenish smoke getting blown out and at the heroes.

Miss Pyro yelled something, and everyone flew up in a second. Freddie—I guessed it was Freddie behind the *Terminator*-like cyborg mask—narrowly missed getting hit with green gas. I was amazed that even as a robot, he moved like a human, and he could punch, kick, and use his weapons. It looked like the only thing he couldn't do was fly, so I guessed that he depended on the transportation ability that came with his masks to help him move from place to place.

Someone else yelled. I think it was Magnifiman. He swooped down and gave the spider's thorax a massive blow with his fist, making it rock and nearly tip over. Its legs stiffened, though, as though they were digging into the rooftop to keep the rest of the mechanical body from tumbling.

Then it was Calais' turn. He vanished or went into hyper speed, delivering another massive blow against the spider's thorax. I didn't even see him do it. I just watched him disappear where he was hovering, then the spider's body snapped to the side as though something just hit it, but it stabilized itself. Within seconds, Calais reappeared at another spot, well beyond reach of the spider's legs, while Miss Pyro took her turn trying to take the monster down with her arsenal. BAM! BAM! BAM! One after another, like a fireworks display, white and red fire shot out of her glowing fists, hitting the spider at different parts of its body. The mechanical body shuddered, a couple of its legs raising themselves up and waving, like, reaching out to get her, but Miss Pyro flew off to another point without letting up on her attack. Before long I spotted trails of steam rising up, most likely because of the showers mixing it up with her fire balls.

"Get him!" I yelled, balling my fists and pounding on the ledge I leaned against. "Get the bastard!"

Terminator-like-Freddie turned one arm into a machine gun type of thing. I couldn't tell for sure how futuristic it was because of the distance, but I sure as hell saw the lower arm reshape itself and then a spray of bullets come pouring out of it. Smoke rose from different points of the transformed arm. Magnifiman had to swoop down and pluck him off the ledge where he stood before one of Arachnaman's swinging legs knocked him off and sent him falling to the street.

He set Freddie down on another rooftop, where Freddie immediately transformed into an army soldier, complete with fatigues. He was also heavily armed, judging from the pretty crazy stuff hanging off his belt and draped down his back. I wouldn't be surprised if he had some huge hunting knife or two hidden in his combat boots. He raised something that I thought was a massive, massive gun that looked bigger than his arms, and aimed. He didn't shoot yet. Maybe he was waiting for the green light from someone. It was Magnifiman's turn to pummel Arachnaman, whose robotic body was beginning to show signs of damage and fatigue.

Its black thorax shuddered and jerked. Arachnaman frantically turned knobs and pulled levers around him. The clear bubble that protected him from the attacks looked pretty stable, but the rest of the body was slowly losing control. On occasion, it would hoist itself up on its four rear legs, its four front ones flailing and stabbing at whichever hero hovered nearby.

Magnifiman, Miss Pyro, and Calais flew around the thing like little flies, taking turns attacking it. But the giant spider's legs would try to bat them away whenever they got too close, and I saw Calais get knocked away at one point. It looked like it just swatted a bug.

"Oh, crap," I breathed. "Peter!"

Calais vanished in the rain, but he was back in seconds, this time keeping his distance while Miss Pyro took full advantage of her range weapons, and Magnifiman tried to grab hold of a leg and tear it off. Well, at least from where I stood, it seemed that he was doing that.

Someone yelled again. I guessed it was Calais, who swooped down and got as close as he could. I realized that he was trying to distract Arachnaman by placing himself within shooting distance of the spider's mouth. Another green cloud exploded, nearly enveloping him. Magnifiman managed to wrap both arms around one of the spider's legs at that moment and held on even while the leg waved crazily around to dislodge him. Calais yelled again and then vanished as he went into hyper speed.

The spider rocked violently from what I figured was Calais' kick or punch against its thorax. That gave Magnifiman the leverage he needed. As the spider moved from side to side, Magnifiman gave the leg he held a massive pull, breaking it at one of its joints in an explosion of colorful sparks.

Calais appeared at another area, completely safe.

I didn't know till then that spiders screamed, but this one did. It was horrible. Like an eagle's cry, but more shrill and hollow. With one leg amputated at the joint, Arachnaman's spider tried to retreat, but it was obviously too damaged to manage more than a jump to another rooftop, one that was only about two rooftops away from my home. I instinctively fell back and ran for safety toward the unused chimney, where Peter and I had tangled recently. Shaking from the cold and excitement, I hid behind the chimney and peered out. With the fight so close now, it was easy for me to catch details from where I stood. Or crouched.

The spider landed on the roof with a loud crash, damaging the weathered ledge were some of its hind legs attached themselves. A little smoke rose from where it landed. Several broken bits of cement also flew up. The body shook, and Arachnaman continued to work his control panel. Around him the heroes hovered. The downside to manning such a big and clumsy (but powerful) machine was that it was pretty damned awkward to control it once it was damaged. The "injured" leg just hung limp, with sparks shooting out of its joint. The rest of the legs moved jerkily now. They still waved and tried to attack any hero who came too close, though, but they sure made for a pretty difficult escape.

The screaming sound that came from the monster had turned into a long wail that was like a creepy mixture of an eagle's cry and creaking steel. From above, Miss Pyro let loose a volley of small but super-fast fire blades. From where I was, they looked like boomerangs on fire. One after another, they hit the spider at random points, but a few struck another leg, and they finally found their target. One of the joints burst into flames, with sparks flying all over. The leg didn't lose its movement, though, but it shook pretty badly every few seconds.

Freddie, who had to be carried by Calais in order to follow Arachnaman, had scrambled over to a pile of crates, and from there, he started shooting at the robot. Many bullets hit the thorax in a bizarre light display where they made contact, but it was soon clear to me that he was aiming for another leg, trying to incapacitate it.

A sudden flash of light from my right broke through the rain, and I turned to find Spirit Wire flying down and landing on another rooftop. She stood there, rigid. One would have thought that she wasn't alive at all.

Then something weird happened. The spider froze

in mid-action. For a few seconds, it did nothing, while Arachnaman began pounding the control panel with his fists. I wouldn't have been surprised if he was yelling and cursing the whole time. Then he visibly jumped, waving his hands like they just got burned.

"What the hell..." I blinked several times and squinted, even with my hands shielding my eyes.

Something glowed. It was his control panel. Buttons, knobs, levers—whatever thingamajigs made up his machine, they all lit up real brightly. Then the spider's remaining legs started moving again, but instead of reaching out for the heroes, they curled back, contortionist-like, and started clawing at the pilot's protective bubble. It was insane. Like something from a nightmare or a really freaky sci-fi movie. The spider collapsed on its belly, while six legs twisted and snapped, their pointed ends pounding and scraping at the bubble till I could hear it break. The leg that Miss Pyro damaged had finally gone limp, and there it lay, useless, twitching and on fire.

I stood there, horrified, wondering if the legs would continue their attack even after the bubble broke. If so, they'd be tearing the pilot to pieces. Magnifiman and Calais had stopped their power punches and waited. Miss Pyro had a massive fire blade in her hand, ready to let it loose. Freddie kept his humungous gun aimed.

It was surreal. All I could hear were the rhythmic bashing of some super strong material, the small sounds of cracking glass or plastic or whatever it was, the rain, and traffic below. Police sirens wailed here and there. I stood and watched, completely immobilized.

"Finish it!" someone yelled. I think it was Magnifiman.

Two of the spider's legs whipped back and came back down on the bubble, and it exploded in a million bits, shards of the material flying all over. When the legs pulled out, the protective bubble was gone, and Arachnaman was curled up in his cockpit, his head bowed, his arms covering it defensively. He was screaming, but not in fear or anything. Even from where I stood, I knew that it was anger. Possibly pure hate. It made my skin crawl.

Around him, the battered spider collapsed, its legs spread out, lifeless, pillars of smoke rising from all over. The heroes just waited for a moment, and then the control panels turned dark. It was over. The thorax sagged for the last time, resting at a bit of an angle.

"Way to go, Althea," I breathed, my heart pounding. Just as I spoke, Spirit Wire staggered back and collapsed. I thought she was hurt, but she waved a hand and yelled something. Calais yelled back and turned his attention to Arachnaman. I figured then that Spirit Wire was just totally spent. Eventually she stumbled back to her feet.

Magnifiman made the first move. He flew down, grabbed Arachnaman under his arms, and yanked him up. I was glad that he wasn't strapped in, or Magnifiman would've torn him, literally, into two pieces. Vintage City's main hero flew off, followed by Calais and Spirit Wire. Arachnaman continued to scream. I shivered from the noise he was making. Yeah, he was screaming in rage and pure hate. I could tell. He sounded worse than an animal.

Miss Pyro and Freddie stayed behind, no doubt waiting for cops to get there. I heard a whirring sound from somewhere growing louder, and I turned to see a helicopter fly toward them. Miss Pyro signaled with her arms, guiding the helicopter pilot. Meanwhile, what was left of Arachnaman's robot lay in a nightmarish pile of smoldering metal, plastic, and whatever else was used. The rooftops where the battle took place were a mess. I hoped that the people who lived in those buildings had been able to get the hell out when the signs of trouble first came.

I had to get out of there. Soaked to the bone, I ran back to the fire escape, praying to every cosmic force out there to keep the heroes safe in whatever else they needed to do still. Before long I was back in my bathroom, securing the window and peeling off my wet clothes. I turned on the shower and jumped in for a quick cleaning, my mind still on the fight I saw.

When I got out, I ran back to my bedroom window to see if I could spot something. The rooftop where the action took place was now crawling with cops. Other buildings across the street from that area also had police officers moving around. Below, traffic was snarled as a couple of blocks, or maybe three, were shut off from the public. Lights from police cars and fire trucks broke up the drabness of the scene. I finally closed my window and went downstairs to recover from the shock of watching the heroes take Arachnaman down. I pulled out a mug and made myself some tea, which helped, but I knew it wouldn't be as effective if I didn't have a few slices of toast spread with Mrs. Horace's jam. For the next half hour, I sat alone in the dining room, eating, while listening to the rain and the occasional police siren outside.

It was a totally miserable time. No one else was at home with me, the rain got heavier and heavier till it drowned out all sound and light, and I told myself to wait for a reasonable length of time before it was okay for me to call Peter and see if he was safe. Now that they'd nabbed Arachnaman, I was sure that he'd be out all night. In the end, I decided that it would be best to wait for him to call instead.

Sitting in the kitchen, alone and nervous, was just plain hell.

I was quiet when everyone came home, all excited and horrified about the big spider monster appearance. Once Dad saw that we were safe, with all body parts accounted for, he dove right into a non-stop monologue about Arachnaman. Liz got into it, too, as did Mom. They were crammed in the kitchen, helping Mom prepare dinner, so I decided to sneak out and creep back to my room and hover over my phone in case Peter called.

Nope, no messages left. Yeah, it was way too early, but I didn't care. It was still raining pretty hard outside, the books I checked out from the library continued to look boring as hell, the computer threatened to give me a non-stop migraine, so I just plopped down on my bed, listening to the rain, and waited.

Okay, I fell asleep. The rain tended to work on me like that.

I also woke up because Liz was kicking my bed. I'd like to say that the rain tended to work on her like that, too, but she always kicked my bed to get me up. It goes to show that older siblings, whether or not they were on a PMS rampage, were all descended from Mr. Hyde.

"Dinner time, Briar Rose," she said, standing by my bed with her hands on her hips.

"Look, if you're going to spend the rest of your life kicking my bed, how about rotating your attacks on the legs?" I snarled groggily. I refused to sit up on her account, so I just glared at her from where I lay. I must've looked pretty intimidating. "That leg you keep victimizing is on its way to collapsing on me. How about kicking the others next time, fer chrissakes?"

"I really don't want to waste any more time trying to get you to wake up, hot pants. Come on before Mom goes on a rampage."

"You're just cranky because it's your turn to wash the dishes."

I sighed and dragged myself out of bed, Liz marching behind me in case I decided to turn tail and run back to my room. You know, the way ordinary teenagers usually avoided their families. The kind of thing that adults tended to forget.

When we reached the top of the stairs, I caught sight of my special communicator watch because of the way it reflected the light. I stared at it for a few seconds, my heart dropping.

Peter hurt. Not too serious. Althea will contact you with more info. Wade.

Chapter 23

Peter didn't get hurt from the attack. It happened immediately after, when they were flying Arachnaman away from his machine. Apparently someone decided to watch the action up close by climbing onto the topmost part of an old fire escape at a nearby tenement. It looked like the fire escape had given way under her, and she'd fallen, just as the heroes were flying in her direction. Althea said that Peter caught her, but somehow his body had twisted itself when he got the girl (most likely because she was falling head first), and he didn't have much time to turn himself over and land the way cats landed on their feet. He basically hit the roof of a parked truck and used his body to cushion the impact for the girl, who suffered a few not-too-serious injuries but was mostly in shock.

I read Althea's message on my computer, my hands tearing clumps of hair off my head while my stomach knotted itself.

"So what's the damage?" I asked.

Back pain, she said. *But here's the kicker—he's almost fully healed now. Is that crazy or what?*

"What do you mean?"

Genetics, dude. His healing has sped up. Maybe it's like this when he's in superhero mode, but it's something that never even crossed my mind till now.

I sank in my chair, heaving a sigh of relief. "It makes sense," I replied. "Maybe the injury wasn't too bad to begin with. I just...I just hope that he'll never be messed up so bad that his system won't be able to heal itself quickly...or at all."

No kidding. I hope no one gets hurt bad, period. In Peter's case, I hope he doesn't get hurt again.

"I have to see him. I have to."

Aww, how sweet. Sorry, Eric, can't do. He's at the police station with Trent and Wade, interrogating the suspect. Okay, I'm with them, too, but I'm supposed to be taking a quick break and getting myself some coffee and a doughnut. I just had to touch base with you. I need to head back in a bit.

My eyes widened. "He's still alive?" I spluttered. "Are you serious? Arachnaman? You should've just offed the bastard!"

Hey, hey, hey, hombre. Calm down. No vigilante crap allowed here.

"But he—"

Eric. Calm down. We all know what he did. But we can't do him in like that. Things just don't work the way you want them to, you know? Besides, wouldn't that make us just as bad as him?

I sighed, raking my hands through my hair. "Yeah, I know. I'm sorry. I'm just really upset over everything. Hearing about Peter getting hurt didn't help."

I know. Don't worry. We've got everything under control.

"Okay. Hey, what about the girl? The one Peter rescued? Is she with you guys?"

No. She was taken to the hospital, but she's out now. Peter sustained more damage, but you know how that went.

I nodded. "Thanks, Althea. I guess I'll have to sit around and wait for an update from you." I paused when a thought crossed my mind. "Hey, can you use the communicator watch thing when you get back to me instead? I'm getting off the computer and won't be available."

No prob. TTYL.

Damn. I wished that they still had the girl. It was pretty easy to put two and two together, at least from where I was sitting. I'd bet that she was Peter's stalker. I wouldn't be surprised if she happened to be the same girl who was hanging next to me in the arcade when it was attacked. I remembered the way she looked at Peter. If there were such a thing as absolute, total love at first sight, that definitely was it.

It was just too bad that I didn't have a way of knowing for sure unless she happened to place herself in danger's way on purpose just to be rescued by Peter. Oh, did I mention that part of my hunch? Yeah, I suspected that she went to watch the fight and actually placed herself in a dangerous position just so she could be saved by her idol.

If I were right, I seriously didn't know what to say to her if ever we'd cross paths again. That was some pretty messed up thinking, and to endanger Peter's safety because of a totally skewed perception of her "romance" with a superhero wasn't getting any sympathy points from me. God, that pissed me off. Come to think of it, I'd been pretty high-strung lately. Was I going through some form of gay boy PMS and stuff? Because it sucked.

It was almost eight o'clock when Althea "logged out." I was also feeling pretty restless and under the effects of residual annoyance, excitement, and horror. Eventually I forced myself to go downstairs and relax with everyone else. I kind of eased up pretty quickly. Even though I didn't want to be with anyone at first, I found that just hanging with Dad while he watched TV—Mom was on the phone, and Liz was in her room—helped a lot. I guess it was plain familiarity that made things better. Besides, Dad being a huge cheese ball movie buff, it was always an experience watching his entertainment choices. He was lucky that we lived in Vintage City, where reruns and old movies of every quality enjoyed their second, third, or even fourth lives.

"Dad, is that another one of those hokey horror movies from the '60s or something?" I asked once I'd gotten comfortable on the couch, sitting with my legs crossed under me and hugging a big, plump throw pillow against my chest. Even the smell of old fabric with a bit of dust made me feel better.

Dad scratched his head while aiming the controls at the TV to adjust its volume. "This one's a real gem from the late '50s, actually. Haven't you seen this one?"

I shook my head. "Nope. Unless it freaked me out so much when I was a little kid and made me pass out."

"Oh, gosh, I wouldn't go that far."

"It's *that* hokey, huh? What's it called?"

"*Attack of the Giant Leeches.*"

I grinned. "I like it already."

Dad shifted and sat back, sighing contentedly. "I thought you would. Just wait till you see the leeches."

"Eric, wake up."

I said something. Most likely cussed out whoever was trying to mess up my sleep.

"I'm going to ignore what you just said to me, mister," Mom said, her voice getting clearer by the second. "Come on, get up. You need to sleep in your bed, not down here."

"Wh...huh?" I mumbled, rubbing my eyes as I struggled to get up from the couch. "Whrum I?" God, I hated waking up when my brain wasn't ready for consciousness. I finally sat up and realized that I still held on to the throw pillow. Blinking the fog from my eyes, I groped around for my glasses and found them on my lap. "Sorry, Mom."

Mom just ruffled my hair and sat down next to me. "The late news is on. Honey, turn up the volume, please."

"They probably have that crazy spider guy in the

headlines," Liz said. She'd taken her place on the floor, while my parents and I shared the couch.

"I slept through your movie, Dad," I said, running a hand through my hair. I glanced at him and smiled sheepishly. "Sorry. Did the leeches die?"

"I don't like giving out spoilers, son. You'll have to watch it all over again to find out," Dad replied. He actually sounded kind of smug about that.

"Shhh! Here it is!" Liz said. We all fell silent as the news began.

After the initial introductions, yadda, yadda, Bambi Bailey finally came on. Her segment was recorded after the battle, obviously, because it was still light, though the rain kept everything pretty gray. She reported under an umbrella, and behind her was a mess of police activity. I wouldn't be exaggerating to say that it was the busiest I'd seen of a crime area that had been captured on camera. Cop cars packed the street behind her. There was at least one fire truck nearby, and amid the gray wetness were the disco-ish flashes of red and yellow lights from all emergency and police vehicles.

Ms. Bailey pretty much summed up what I'd seen that afternoon, though at times I wanted to butt in and tell her how much worse things really were. My parents were around, though, and I didn't want them to know that I stood on the roof in the rain, risking my health and my safety by watching Arachnaman get taken down by the heroes.

Sergeant Bone was interviewed, as were a couple of other officers and some regular Joe Blows who witnessed the fight from their apartments.

"While it's true that Arachnaman is now in police custody, Vintage City's still not free of his plan to take down what he considers to be undesirable elements," Ms. Bailey said, a slight crease forming between her brows. She paused, and the camera switched over to another scene, this time the police station, where Arachnaman was being held.

I stared at the TV, wide-eyed. The camera focused on Arachnaman, himself. He was in costume, just like every other supervillain. His bodysuit was in a really bright red shade that shimmered a little in the light. His face gave me the creeps. He didn't wear a mask, but that part of his costume was just this oval nothingness. It was black, but it didn't shimmer or give off any indication as to its material, no matter how the light hit it. It looked as though it absorbed all light. There were no eyes, nose, or mouth anywhere. It was like staring at a void in the middle of his head. When he raised his hands, I saw that they were in chains, and they were also covered in black gloves of probably the same material as the mask, and the fingers were shaped like spider legs.

"You might all think that you've got the better of me," he said, his voice sounding pretty young and also robotic. I felt my skin prickle. He couldn't be older than any of my friends. All that destruction done by a teenager? I couldn't wrap my mind around it. "But you haven't. You never will."

He chuckled when he paused, shifting on his chair to make himself more comfortable. I heard the clanking of chains when he did. It was so surreal. "Don't bet on it. For now, I'm here, but you can't hide from me. I'm around you still. I *am* you, you know. I'm that tiny part of you that you don't want to acknowledge because you just can't face up to that small but important fact about yourself." He laughed this time. "Now...as far as what that small but important fact is, I'll leave it to you to figure out. Vintage City people aren't stupid."

The camera shifted back to Ms. Bailey, who prattled on about the fight between Arachnaman and the heroes. I glanced at Mom and Dad, both of whom looked puzzled and nervous.

"He's psychotic," I offered, which earned me some vague shaking of their heads, but they still didn't seem to really hear me. With that, I got up and said goodnight to everyone. I hoped to check up on Peter the next day.

Chapter 24

I couldn't talk to Peter long. He was fine, he said, and had to tell me about a gazillion times not to mess around with that girl if we ever crossed paths again. Somehow I felt that we would, but I supposed I should show a lot more restraint than she had.

"She might be having some major problems at home," Peter said. "If anything, I feel kind of sorry for her."

I sighed. "Yeah, I guess you're right. I promise I'll be more understanding if we ever see each other. But if she tries to pull something like that again just to get your attention and then hurts you in the process? Hell, no, I—"

"Eric?" Peter cut in. "Do it for me, please?"

Damn! I had to take a few breaths before I could speak again. "Okay, okay. Just remember, though, if the tables were turned, and I was hurt by someone stalking me, I'm sure you wouldn't think twice about raising all kinds of hell. And you've got the superpowers to do it, too."

"I know," he said, laughing. "That's why I'm glad it's happening to me instead."

I shook my head, grinning. He got me, as usual. "So what's gonna happen to Arachnaman?" I asked.

"He's going to be locked away, but I'm not going to be so confident yet. He's incredibly smart and much more dangerous than everyone else. I wouldn't be surprised if he manages to escape even with all the security measures we used on him."

"You're too cynical!"

"I'd rather be cynical and prepared for the worst, than walk into things with my eyes shut. We'll be busy for the next few days, by the way. I won't be able to talk to you at all. We'll be combing the city for devices he might've planted in different shops and residences."

"You know which ones to go to then?" I asked, amazed. "You figured out the common denominator?"

"It was so obvious, we didn't see it," he replied, his voice hard. "He's a flaming bigot, Eric."

With the Sentries still busy working with the heroes and their workload doubling now that they had Arachnaman in custody, I was given one more day off from school. I spent my time really hunkering down and working on my take-home essays. I finally got into the swing of things after a few moments of struggling with inspiration, so that by the time everyone started coming home, I only had about one left to do. I just did everything in the dining room, so I could drink a soda and munch away at stale tortilla chips without having to go anywhere for sustenance. Of course, I felt a little bloated once I was finished, but beggars couldn't be choosers, and if the combination of carbonated sugar and stale tortilla chips helped with my inspiration, I'd take it, gas and all.

I went to Olivier's with Liz after dinner, who was feeling kind of restless. She also called Scanlon to meet us there and hang out because, well, she was totally into him, yanno? I said nothing. Just listened to her chatter away like a prepubescent girl who was on the phone with the hottest boy in school. Yikes.

The rain had stopped, but the sky remained overcast. It was also a little on the warm side, which was weird, but I figured that the greenhouse effect simply did that after the rain sometimes. For that night, the shopping strip enjoyed larger than normal pedestrian traffic. Maybe people needed to get out and expend all that nervous energy from so many days of waiting and then getting attacked by Arachnaman. With his mocking "confession," or whatever it was called, last night, I wouldn't be surprised if people just wanted to forget that we had a psychopathic bigot in our midst. Hey, whatever worked, right?

My sister and I spent a good bit of time browsing for books, but we ended up with nothing because we're just too high-maintenance that way. Scanlon eventually materialized from somewhere, actually tiptoeing up to Liz, whose back was turned to him, while signaling me to keep quiet, and then covering her eyes with his hands.

"Guess who?" he chirped.

"Hmm," Liz said, grinning behind his fingers. "Is it Christian Bale?"

OMFG.

"I can be!"

Commence loud giggling and lots of tickling between a couple of lovebirds. I just stared at them blandly and waited for the Hallmark moment to pass, hoping that it'd pass real soon before I puked my dinner all over them.

"Hiya, Tiger!" Scanlon said, reaching out to tug at my cap. Good thing he didn't do it too hard so that the visor came down to my nose. He'd done that before, and I could've kicked him for almost tearing the visor off my favorite flat cap. Besides, it was embarrassing. Then again, when was I not embarrassed by Scanlon Dorsey?

"Yeah, yeah, hi," I grumbled, pulling off my cap and setting it back on my head after inspecting the visor. "Looks like you survived yesterday's drama."

"I did, yeah! Wasn't it crazy? I couldn't believe it!" Scanlon shook his head, speechless shock on his face. "I'm just glad that you guys didn't get hurt, considering how close it was to where you live."

Liz looped an arm around his and gave him a quick tug. "I'm not in the mood to go over crazy stuff like that," she said. "Come on, let's just hang out somewhere." She looped her other arm around mine so that we wandered downtown arm-in-arm, looking like Dorothy, the Scarecrow, and the Tin Man. I'd rather not guess who was whom in that scenario. All we needed to do was sing and skip around like the total dorks that we were.

"Man, I'm bored," I whined after about half an hour later as we window shopped, taking our damned sweet time the whole way. "I'd go for some big-ass ice cream right now, but I'm not hungry for dessert or anything edible." Okay, that sounded pretty mental.

"Want some?" Scanlon asked, looking a little too eager. I narrowed my eyes at him.

"I'm not going to that kiddie ice cream place, bucko," I said. "I'm all about adult stuff now, in case you haven't heard."

"Sure thing! Tell you both what. I'll go to that gelato place a block down and get us all something. What flavors would you like?"

Okay, so I wasn't about to bite the hand that fed me, so I told him that I wanted a two-scoop deal with half dark chocolate and half espresso. I hoped I didn't salivate too much when I gave him my preference. Scanlon listened, that loopy grin on his face the whole time, and then bounded away with a "Be right back, yo!"

I blinked as he vanished in the crowd. "Man, Liz, you sure know how to pick 'em."

"What now?" Liz demanded. "Are you going to go off about him again? Christ, Eric! What's wrong with you?"

"What do you mean, what? You've seen how he works! You've seen how he treats me like some kind of ten-year-old!"

Liz stared me down, her hands on her hips. It was a little bizarre, getting yelled at by someone who stood a good eight inches shorter than me, but she was my older sister, so...

"You know, I've always been down with your boyfriend, Eric. I've never said anything bad about him even though I think he's a little too serious and nerdy for you..."

I raised a hand. "Whoa, whoa! Hey, you don't even know Peter!"

She raised her brows in answer. "Have you ever listened to yourself?"

"What're you talking about?"

Liz rolled her eyes but didn't budge. We were in the middle of a busy sidewalk, yelling at each other while people had to bump into us to get by. We acted like the rest of the world didn't even exist. "Are you really that dense? Man! I don't know enough about your boyfriend, and you sure as hell don't know mine! Who do you think you are, going around and judging him the way you've been, making all those faces at the dinner table and giving me all kinds of sarcastic crap about knowing how to pick 'em? You know jack about Scanlon, Eric, and it's no one's problem but yours! Yeah, you know, he's been doing everything he can to try to bond with you. I don't give a flying rat's ass if you get embarrassed by what he does because as far as I'm concerned, he's got bigger balls than you do, risking your attitude and emo snarky bull just to be friends."

I looked around. People were staring when they

walked past us. "Okay, okay, point taken. Time to end the conversation."

"No, it's not time, you big diva! It's not! I'm not done with you yet!" Liz retorted. "You're so selfish, you know that? Everything revolves around you and what you want! You think you've got the perfect boyfriend who shouldn't be criticized or whatever, and everyone else is fair game if they don't happen to fit your standards. Well, guess what! I happen to like Scanlon, and he happens to make me feel special, and I happen to like making him feel good about himself. Wow, what a concept, huh? Suddenly, it's not about Eric Plath! Whoa! How'd that happen? In short, little bro, I don't care what you think! Lay off Scanlon, deal with the fact that we like each other, and get snuggly with your boyfriend. If I lose Scanlon, it's because of us, not you. Got it?"

I just stared at her. Jeebus, what the hell was that? Talk about taking things a little too extreme! Liz must've read my mind because she calmed down with a long sigh. She continued to scowl at me, but when she talked, her voice was quieter and more even.

"You know, when I told Scanlon that you're gay, he didn't even bat an eyelash. In fact, he told me that he'd like to get to know you more because he's never had a younger brother before." She looked away, finally, shaking her head. "Just think about that the next time you decide to make fun of him."

Liz walked off to check out a display window, leaving me to squirm and look stupid in the middle of pedestrian traffic. I looked around and didn't see Scanlon, so I figured that he must be in line or something. I adjusted my cap again and walked up to Liz, hovering behind her as she gaped at shoes.

"Are you kidding me?" she presently blurted out, pointing at a pair of painful-looking high-heel shoes. You know, the ones with the toes that sharply converged to form this super-dangerous-looking point, with heels that rose high enough to make the woman move on tiptoes? Yeah, that kind. "That's about three days' worth of work for me!"

"I guess some women don't mind paying for torture," I noted, appalled. I felt my toes curl in empathic pain. I followed her to another display window, hoping that we were friends again. The display was on novelty toys. For a moment, we fell silent and watched a group of fake puppies sleep in their beds. "Man, this is consumerism for you." I sighed and stifled a yawn. "I'm getting tired, too. There's really not much to see out here, is there? Same old stores, same old stuff."

"Yeah, I know what you mean. Looks like we won't be having much drama around here, though, with Arachnaman in custody."

I chuckled. "Dude, I'd rather be bored than terrorized by a crazy freakish spider type." I glanced across the street and spotted a shop that looked new. "Hey, is that an African store?" It was, judging from the really awesome wooden masks that were on display behind the main windows. "Come on, let's check it out."

"What about Scanlon?"

"I'll keep an eye out for him. I mean, look—the

gelato place is just right there. He can see us." Sure enough, when the crowds momentarily thinned, I spotted Scanlon standing in line, craning his neck as he searched for us. I took care to make eye contact with him and then wave, pointing at the store across the street. He got it and smiled, nodding and waving back.

"Okay, cool. He'll follow us," I said.

Liz didn't seem too keen on it, but she let me drag her across the street. We stared inside the window for a few minutes, with me salivating over the masks. They sat on their stands, some long and narrow, some round, all of them distinctive with their painted accents and details. Each piece had a little card that explained what the mask was made for. When I looked up to scan the store's interior, I saw that it was an African home décor shop. The place was nearly packed with all kinds of furniture and statuary, shields and wall art, among others. They were all beautifully painted with some pretty cool patterns and colors against dark wood. If this had been a second-hand shop, I'd have blown every penny I had, and my sad little attic room would be this fantastic African oasis sort of thing.

"Hey, I want to check out that shadowbox over there," Liz said, pointing at something inside. "It's got daggers or something in it."

"Yeah, sure. I'll be there." I was actually half-listening to her the whole time because my attention had been diverted completely. I'd just turned around to scan the area for our next window-shopping stop, when I spotted that redheaded kid again, moving through the crowd. He looked a little nervous or on edge, like he was waiting for something or looking for something. He was alone like before, and the longer I observed him, the more I grew aware of something unusual about that kid. He seemed to thrum with a nervous energy, like all tightly-coiled inside him and about ready to be let loose. Something in my gut told me that he could be dangerous, even though he looked like the least dangerous person on the planet.

He stopped several feet away, staring and frowning, his head bowed. He was in the middle of the sidewalk, blocking people's way, but he didn't seem to care. In fact, he didn't seem to be aware of anything else but what it was he was thinking about. Was he concentrating? He glanced up and tipped his head back a little. I could see his nose crinkle, so I guessed that he was sniffing the air. For what, though?

Then he froze—or stiffened. The look on his face changed from cautious alertness to wide-eyed fear.

"They're here!" he suddenly cried.

Chapter 25

S ure enough, just as he spoke, the lights went out inside the African store and a few other shops up and down the street. No one outside noticed right away, but they did a fraction of a second later. The doors to those shops—those that stood open— slammed shut.

I realized then that Liz wasn't with me. The African store was pitch-black, and from inside, cries of panic started to rise.

"Oh, my God! Liz!" I yelled, lunging for the door and yanking at it. It was locked. I banged at the glass, hoping to break it, but it was too thick. "Liz! Help! My sister's in there! Someone help!"

It was useless. Up and down the street, panic rippled through the crowds as they responded to screams for help from inside those shops. People pounded on glass doors and windows.

"No! It's too late!" someone cried out. It was the redheaded kid. "Get away from those doors! Get away!" He started running toward me, waving his arms frantically.

As he ran, a kind of white aura appeared around him, like a silhouette of hazy light. People who saw it fell back, all freaking out. He raised one arm and pointed at me, yelling something. There was a quick, sharp flash of light, and all of a sudden, I felt myself and a couple of other people standing next to me encased in something.

It was a bubble. No, a force field. A quick scan confirmed it. I could barely see the faint silhouette of a gigantic bubble that surrounded me and the others. I was stunned. I could still breathe and move around, but the sounds outside were a little more muffled.

Just as I was about to reach out and touch the force field, the door to the African store exploded, sending glass shards and bits of metal flying all over. I dove to the floor, crying out and covering my head, but I felt nothing. The force field saved me and the other two guys, both of whom had thrown themselves onto the pavement as well.

"Holy crap," I breathed, exchanging shocked looks with them.

"Look out!" one of them shouted, pointing. I turned in the direction of the hole where the shop door used to be.

Human arachnids emerged. It was like being in a Halloween movie—like, a really bad B movie. I mean, really *bad*. Talk about a major letdown. All this time, I'd been imagining all kinds of gross cross-breeding looks. I'd come up with spiders with human heads, or human bodies with spider heads, or something that looked like a monster from John Carpenter's *The Thing*. That movie rocks, by the way. I expected bits of human flesh fused with bits of insect armor or whatever they were called. I thought they'd be covered in thick, pus-colored slime from head to foot, and that when they moved, you could hear the stuff squish in a way that'd make your stomach turn. You know how it is in movie special effects.

Instead, I saw people looking like people, only with spider legs sprouting on each side of them. They were all gray-skinned, too, as if they'd just gotten off a pretty crazy roller-coaster ride, and they were ready to hurl. Their eyes were sunken, their pupils gone, so they were just white eyeballs looking out... do white eyeballs actually *look* at things? They had fang-things jutting out from their mouths, and they looked so out of proportion that their mouths just hung open to accommodate those spider fangs, with strings of drool hanging off their chins. It was like one of those fake vampire fangs that you'd stuff inside your mouth. Then you'd walk around, looking like a vampire-wannabe with a major bucktooth problem.

Seriously, WTF? I suddenly remembered what Peter told me a while back about what human arachnids looked like. He'd said "cheese ball." Boy, he sure wasn't messing around.

I just stared at them as they staggered out, walking like zombies. I recognized them as customers and the shop clerk, but I didn't see Liz anywhere.

They staggered and stumbled past my bubble, and when I looked around, I found that pretty much everyone else who wasn't turned into B-movie rejects within the vicinity was safely inside a force field. Individually or in small groups, they were safe. The redheaded kid saved everyone.

He stood there, glowing and grim, taking a step back each time the human arachnids edged closer. He held his arms a little higher at his sides, and his hands were nothing more than a pair of glowing white orbs. From the other shops, those that were also attacked like the African store, customers and shop employees who'd become lobotomized half-monsters ignored everyone else and went after him in their slow, zombie-like way.

"What's happening? They're not coming after us," asked one of the guys I was trapped in the bubble with. We were all frozen inside our force field, pretty much helpless the whole time.

"Run!" I yelled at the redheaded kid. I tried to pound on the bubble, but it just yielded against my fists like thin rubber. "What're you doing? If you can fly, get the hell out of here, you idiot!"

He didn't hear me. I didn't think that he would've given a rat's ass, anyway, if he did. He had ideas of his own, but whatever they might be, I guess that it included getting pounced on by lobotomized human-spiders and probably eaten alive. Instead of running or flying, he just kept stepping back…and back… and back, drawing the half-monsters away from the area. And away from us.

Pretty soon, everyone trapped inside the force field bubbles was shouting at him. Run! Go! Save yourself! He didn't. He just kept moving slowly away till he was practically standing in the middle of the street. From up and down the block, I saw other human arachnids stumbling out.

"I got 'im!" someone shouted.

The redheaded kid paused, blinking, and just when he turned to look up, something swooped down on him. He vanished in a flash, leaving a fading trail of what sounded like "Gwarrgh!" in his wake as Calais carried him off and into safety.

The human arachnids stopped for a moment and then turned their attention to Miss Pyro, who'd just taken her position atop a parked truck across the road. I wasn't sure if it was me or a trick of the street and shop lights, but Miss Pyro looked a little different from when I'd last seen her. She seemed more streamlined, in a way. Her costume was brighter in color, and her hands and feet had some kind of fiery, pulsing halo around them. She also carried herself differently. She was a lot more confident and aggressive, no longer this stumbling newbie who was prone to crashing into something. She stood there, assessing the scene with a grim smile.

"Hmm. How to take care of you guys..." she quipped. Just as the first few arachnid-types touched the sides of the truck and made like they wanted to claw their way up to her, Miss Pyro's hands vanished in a burst of white fire, and she flew up, throwing a stream of flames around her. Those she hit dropped to the ground, screeching and hissing, but they didn't look burned at all. Maybe stunned or something.

Police sirens broke through the noise, and Magnifiman appeared, drawing some of the arachnids to him. Within seconds, Calais took his position a little farther away, and soon the street was a confusion of light, fire, speed, power punches, and drool, as the superheroes took the human arachnids down. I saw that they didn't hurt anyone, only knocked them down to stun them or something. The cops swarmed the area within moments, all of them masked. They took their positions behind parked cars and stuff, waiting.

Magnifiman, who'd just tackled a couple of elderly arachnid-types to the ground, glanced up and nodded. "Yours, gentlemen," he said in that sexy, authoritative voice of his. He released the two poor seniors, who flailed on the street, gurgling, their bizarre fangs snapping at Magnifiman. Just as he flew off and hovered above the scene, the cops tossed a bunch of canisters in the middle of the squirming, drooling group. The canisters released a burst of pale gas that quickly spread over the human arachnids, who hissed, screeched, flailed, snapped, and made all kinds of gross sounds till they gradually passed out from the gas. The stuff blanketed them and swelled, sort of, till I saw that it took on the form of thick ground mist that rose to only a few feet above the street. It was creepy and awesome at the same time.

Around me, people still trapped in bubbles cried out for their loved ones, and many cheered on the superheroes. I just gaped the whole time, my heart thundering. The gas eventually dissipated, and the mass of inert bodies lying on the street looked normal. No more fangs, no more stupid B-movie-grade spider limbs sticking out from their sides. They were a total mess, though, as they were all covered in dirt and slimed with their own drool. But they were normal. And passed out.

The bubble around me faded at around the same time, and I had to reach out and test it to make sure. "Yes!" I breathed, turning and grinning to the other guys with me. "We're free!"

We all sprang up with a loud whoop, and everywhere, people began to run around, many of them going for the poor victims of the spider attack. Police came forward and tried to hold everyone off, while the superheroes investigated. More sirens wailed, and ambulances appeared at one end of the street.

I had to find Liz. I took one last look at the scene and saw, to my surprise, Dr. Dibbs and Freddie, along with a handful of other people I didn't recognize, mingling with the superheroes and kneeling over victims. I figured that the Sentries were there, doing their own investigation, too, and probably even injecting the victims with antidotes and stuff. I wouldn't have been surprised if they were the ones who'd put together the formula for the gas that the cops threw at the human arachnids.

I quickly ran inside the African shop. "Liz!" I yelled, groping around and straining my eyes. The lights were still out, and illumination from the street barely made a dent inside. "Liz! Where are you?"

I stopped when I heard a muffled shout from somewhere. Then a series of pounding sounds followed. "Liz! Keep yelling! I'll find you!" I continued to grope my way farther inside the store and then stopped next to a chest. The yelling and pounding was pretty frantic then. Thank heaven the chest, which was large enough to fit a body, didn't require a key to open it. A hook had swung down and secured the lid, most likely when Liz had thrown herself inside and slammed the chest shut.

"Oh, my God!" she cried as she pulled herself up to a sitting position. Even in the dark, I could see her hair all wild, her eyes nearly popping out of their sockets. I sighed in relief as I helped her up, giving her a hug once I saw that she was okay. "God, what a nightmare!"

"What happened?"

She leaned against me the whole time, and I led her out of the shop. "It happened so fast. The lights went out, and I heard scratching noises everywhere. I figured that the shop was being attacked, so I just jumped inside that chest without even thinking about what I was doing. I could hear everything, Eric. It was awful. A lot of screaming and crashing..."

She rambled on and on. I felt her trembling against me, and it was all I could do to wrap an arm around her and maneuver us both through the crowds once we were outside. We stopped when we heard Scanlon yelling our names.

I turned and found him pushing his way to us, looking frantic and disheveled. He saw Liz and bounded toward us, nearly running over people. "Are you two okay? Liz?" he cried, catching my sister when she pushed me away and stumbled toward her boyfriend.

"I am, yeah. How about you?"

They talked for a while, kind of lost in their usual little world. With all the noise around us, I couldn't make out their conversation, but I didn't think it'd matter. I just watched them interact with each other and wondered if that was how other people saw me and Peter when we were together. Well, not that we could behave the way straight couples behaved in public, anyway, so forget I even wondered about it.

I had to look away when Scanlon kissed Liz. I must admit that I still had some hang-ups about him, but I figured that after spending more time with Scanlon, I should be able to deal with them properly. I hoped so, anyway.

"Come on, scamp, we'd better get you two safely home," Scanlon said, breaking my thoughts.

I turned to him and grinned. "Sure. Thanks, Scanlon." He tugged at my cap's visor, and I just tried to pretend he didn't touch it.

We made it home, somehow. I can't remember how we managed that, but we did. Mom was freaking out, and I expected her to ground Liz the way she grounded me, but she didn't. She just, well, freaked out and gave my sister a hug. Then she gave me a hug. Then she gave Scanlon a hug. Dad was furious and immediately turned on the TV for late-breaking news.

Eventually it came on. Bambi Bailey appeared, and declared, "Even with Arachnaman in custody, the danger isn't over yet. Tonight's attack is only the first, he says, of a series of planned attacks on the city. Ladies and gentlemen, Arachnaman has planted dozens of robot spiders at different strategic locations.

All are timed to attack—to terrorize the citizens of Vintage City and to disable the superheroes." She paused to take a breath. "With the bad news comes the good, however. Vintage City now has a new ally—a defense hero, a young man who possesses the powers to protect innocent civilians with force fields. For those who were saved tonight by Quickshield, you owe your lives to that remarkable young man…" And she went on and on and on.

I winced. Poor Quickshield. See, this was the reason why I preferred that the superheroes came out with their own aliases before Bambi Bailey got to them and destroyed their reputations forever.

Chapter 26

The following days were crazy. I stayed away from all my friends because they were now, literally, zipping up and down Vintage, following leads that they managed to squeeze out of Arachnaman. The crazy jerk had planted different kinds of robotic things that were all timed to go off, with about half being set to detonate, or whatever that might be called, at the same time, and the other half set to go off in a more staggered schedule.

I sure would've hated to be a fly on the wall when Trent asked to be left alone with Arachnaman. Peter said that the Sentries had provided him with something like a truth serum that he managed to inject into Arachnaman's arm...well, after he wrestled Arachnaman to the ground and pinned him there. It took a couple of minutes for the formula to work, and before long, Arachnaman was this sweating, shaking tattletale who couldn't have shut up if his life had depended on it.

So, in brief, Arachnaman got outwitted, and he spilled his own beans. You know what I mean. After the serum's effects wore off, he got all crazy and started hollering all kinds of obscene things at everyone, threatening to destroy all the heroes once he freed himself. I wouldn't doubt that he'd end up free someday. Supervillains did that a lot. For the time being, I guessed Arachnaman was whisked away to an "undisclosed location" for safekeeping. I wouldn't have been surprised if people were to swarm the police station and try to tear him to pieces after everything that had happened.

"Peter, you guys really need to up your defense and offense," I said, chewing on a cuticle nervously as I listened to Peter over the phone. It was the only phone call I enjoyed with him during the week of The Great Purge, as local papers were apt to call it, and he sounded so, so tired. I really wished that I could stay with him and comfort him in some way, but he specifically told me to stay home when I wasn't in school.

"We will. Don't worry about us," he said, yawning. "We'll just have to put in more practice hours. You up for it?"

I grinned. "Sure. Why not? Just don't tie me up."

"Man, you sure know how to rain on my parade."

For the whole week, several businesses and apartment complexes were purged of Arachnaman's planted robots. Even my old church was a target! One by one, they were cleaned up. There were a few messy accidents involving robot spiders self-destructing once they got cut off from their main connection, but they caused minimal damage. At least no one got hurt even though some merchandise went up in flames. In a couple of cases, the shops' back doors got blown apart when Spirit Wire threw the robot spiders just as they self-destructed. It could've been worse. I knew that superheroes could heal themselves, so long as the injuries weren't too severe, but all the same, I'd hate to have Spirit Wire temporarily out of commission because the robot spiders she held went haywire and tried to off themselves.

By the end of the week, Vintage City was declared safe from Arachnaman. At least for the time being. We knew that it was only a matter of time before he'd strike again. For now, it was best to pick up the pieces, brush ourselves off, and move forward.

I also managed to finish all the take-home work that Dr. Dibbs gave me, and it was sort of good that he was so distracted by all the cleaning-up happening around the city that he'd forgotten to ask me for my work.

I just played coy when he finally remembered. It was Thursday, and we were in the middle of Chemistry lab. Yeah, I know. It sucked.

"Oh," I said, flashing him my sweetest, most innocent smile. *Ever.* "I didn't think to bother you with them, seeing as how you've been so busy with out-of-school stuff." That was the truth. I just didn't admit to procrastinating on my last essay all that time as opposed to getting everything done before the week started. Then again, he never asked, and I wasn't about to encourage him.

"Why, thank you, Mr. Eric," he said, blinking and scratching his head. "I really appreciate your consideration. But work is work, as they say, and I'd like to have your essays back tomorrow, please."

"Okeedokee." I watched him turn his attention back to his notes, mumbling to himself as he rifled through them. I pursed my lips and tapped my pen against my lab notes. "Uh, can I ask you a question?"

"Hmm?" He continued to search for something.

"Are all the human arachnids okay now? I mean, those kids and grandparents at the Yee Apartments, are they normal again?"

Dr. Dibbs sighed and sat back, regarding me with a look of mild surprise and amusement. "They are, thank you for your concern. Arachnaman might be a genius in causing physical damage, but his biological attacks? In a word, Mr. Eric, he sucks."

I chuckled. "Those are two words."

"Ah. So they are. The progression of their development into so-called human arachnids was severely lacking, and rather than terrorizing us with completely transformed monsters, he gave us a gaggle of half-breeds, you can say, all of whom appeared to be suffering from a transformation process that got cut short."

"Yeah, but they still ended up like monsters in some way. Pretty cheesy-looking, sure, but they were like zombies, almost. Like, they were lobotomized or something."

He nodded, pushing his glasses up his nose. "It was to our advantage that those poor folks didn't change all the way. I had doubts about our antidote, you know. The formula was created under such enormous time pressure from the heroes that we didn't have time to test it. Had the transformations been more complete, I don't think we would've saved any of them."

I listened to him, horrified. "Does that mean Arachnaman's going to try to up the ante next time? I mean, we all know that supervillains find themselves back on the streets even after they get put away. And we all know that he's going to be pissed as hell. No one's going to keep him from mixing up something even worse than what we've seen here."

"You're a very astute young man, Mr. Eric," Dr. Dibbs said, smiling. "I like that. You'll go a long way, for sure. But to answer your question, yes. We anticipate that, and while he's locked away, we'll continue to work with the heroes in developing stronger protection as well as antidotes."

"Can I help?"

He laughed, his belly shaking. "Thank you, thank you, but no. We're fine as we are right now, but I'm sure that you'll prove to be one of our most significant allies down the road."

I perked up. "Really? Even without any special powers?"

"What, should you have special powers for you to be an asset to Vintage City?"

I shrugged. "Just wondering. That's all. Well, at least you have one more good guy joining your ranks. Quickshield's with you now, eh?"

"Ah, yes. Him. We're about to get him started on his superhero training. He's a little shy and defensive, but we're trying to get to know him better, and he seems keen on being a part of the group. I doubt if we'll have too many problems with him."

"Yeah. Hope to meet him soon. I mean, formally, that is. He didn't seem to like me the last couple of times we talked, but then again, he was being bullied one time and being laughed at the other time."

"I certainly hope to see you two become good friends soon. Now, let's get on with our Chemistry lessons..."

"I haven't seen or heard from that girl since the accident," Peter said. "The one I saved, that is."

"I guess that's good," I said, sighing, as I drew up my knees to my chest and watched the sun sink a little more. "I have a feeling, though, that we'll still hear from her later on. It's not the end of it."

"I'm sure you're right." Peter draped an arm around my shoulder and fell silent. We sat on an old, tattered blanket, which we'd laid out on my house's rooftop. We'd kind of decided to have a spur-of-the-moment picnic, but since Peter was set to turn into Calais soon and continue to watch over Vintage City, we didn't really have much time to pack something big and special and then drive off somewhere that was more romantic. For the time being, chowing down on tortilla chips and salsa and chasing all those down with sodas right on the rooftop was the best that we could do. At least the rains had stopped, and we'd been enjoying a week of uninterrupted sunshine.

"Well, I suppose if I can't be with you all the time, helping you out in protecting the city, the least I can do is keep an eye out for you online." I grinned, turning and leaning closer to kiss him. "See? I'm not all that useless."

He kissed me back. A couple of times. Three times, really. "I never said you were, but I want you to stay safe. Being my online guardian angel is good." He kissed me again. "You know, my birthday's coming up. We should do something."

Oh, God, yeah. "You'll end up filling your day. I'm guessing that you'll have at least half a dozen celebrations. You've got your family, then the superheroes, then my family, then Althea's family, then me. That's what happens when you turn into a superhero and go steady with me."

"I don't mind being spoiled," he said, dropping his voice to that hot little drawl of his. He knew how it affected me, too, the sneak. Not that I was complaining or anything...

I shifted and moved to straddle his lap. He laughed while I slowly pushed him down on his back while stretching myself out over him. "I feel like spoiling you right now, actually," I murmured against his mouth. I felt his fingers weave through my hair as he pulled me close. I think we didn't resurface for air or whatever for a good long while. Before he left for "work," he made me promise not to ditch Grandma Horace and bingo night. Phooey.

Before I went to bed that night, I decided to go online and check his fan site, immediately clicking on the link to the guestbook.

I hate you all. You stupid hacks and wannabe artists. Calais is way better than all that crap you've been vomiting all over this phony site.

I quickly did a screencap of the message and saved it. "Over my dead body, girlfriend," I muttered. When I refreshed the page, the message was gone. I wondered why the guestbook owner didn't bother to ban her ass. Then again, maybe she'd figured out a way around that.

The day of reckoning finally came, a month and a half after Althea's first bingo hint email. Sucked to be me. I stared at my cards. My vision had gone quadruple at that point. I'd already refilled my coffee, and judging from the fact that I was slowly slipping away from the moment, I couldn't help but suspect that they served decaf at the church's community hall.

OMFG. "Wha...huh?" I spluttered, blinking. "Did they just call out a number?"

"Yeah. He said G 60." Freddie glanced at my cards. "You've got nothing. Man, did they give you dud cards? I'm rolling in cash, and the night's just started!"

Go Freddie. "I don't care," I grumbled, yawning for the tenth time in one minute. "I just want to lie on the floor and die."

"Ssshh!" Althea nudged me. She sat on my left, and Freddie sat on my right. Grandma Horace happily played beside Althea, even though she could barely hear a thing and had to depend on her granddaughter to yell the numbers in her ear. "Dude, come on. Don't make it worse on anyone. Shut up."

Across from me, on the wall, hung a pretty large close-up picture of the Pope. I'd say that there was some kind of conspiracy involving seating placement because my chair happened to be directly in his line of sight, so the whole time I languished, I was also being given a major stare-down by the guy who was supposed to be St. Peter's successor or something. If I'd had my way, I'd've sabotaged the lights so that they'd all turn off, and during the confusion, I'd drag a ladder to the wall, climb up it, and turn the stupid picture around. I'd rather look at dead insects getting fossilized on the back paper of a frame than be subjected to the Pope's hollow-eyed glare.

"I can see you, Eric Steven Plath," he seemed to say to me from across the room. "You don't fool me."

I jerked in my seat. "What? Number?"

"Hey—bingo!" Freddie yelled, jumping up and pumping a fist in the air. I felt myself shrink.

"Oh, look, that's another ten bucks," I sniffed as one of the bingo officials, or whatever they were called, walked toward Freddie and inspected his card.

"It's fifty, dude," Freddie crowed, elbowing me. "I'm seriously rolling here!" He paused and looked around before leaning close and whispering, "And I'm not even twenty yet!"

"Better watch it," I whispered back. "Karma's got a pretty funny way of working sometimes."

He ignored me and got his next card ready. The announcer dude then said, "Oh. I almost forgot to give you guys a break." He laughed, and the microphone he was talking into shrieked. Around me, poor senior citizens cowered and covered their ears. Beside me, Althea sighed, pointed a finger at the clunky old console that operated the microphone and the big screen that flashed the numbers, and shut it down.

"I hate microphones," she said, glancing at me. We both looked like hell. Eyes bloodshot and rimmed with shadow, posture drooping and ugly—we were totally Freddie's opposite. We just sat there, drool practically hanging down from our mouths, while he stood up, stretched and cracked a few joints, before hurrying off to get himself a soda.

"I'll treat you to a hot dog, Eric," he said, slapping my back and nearly sending me toppling forward. Great.

Althea kept Grandma Horace company, holding a conversation with her by yelling in her ear. I watched everyone else move around, refilling their cups or plates and chatting happily. I sighed for the gazillionth time. I don't know. I guess bingo night wasn't too bad. Those folks were having fun, so there must've been something to it. Too bad I just didn't get it at all. Ahead of me, the Pope continued to pin me down with his stare.

"I'm turning Buddhist," I said, glaring back at him. "And you can't stop me."

"Okay, here you go," Freddie piped up. A paper plate containing a pretty hefty-looking hot dog cradled in a bun appeared on the table in front of me. "And since you can't really eat that without choking, I decided to treat you to a drink, too."

A cup of soda appeared next to the hot dog. I nodded. "Thanks, Freddie. I owe you a rubbery hot dog and a soda."

"No problem, man. I'm really enjoying this. Thanks for bringing me here." He took his place next to me, even rubbing his hands as he marveled at the hot dog he got himself. It was covered completely with all kinds of condiments. Judging from the pile, I figured that he loved relish. I mean, *loved* it. Like, he'd probably have sex with it if it weren't illegal. I couldn't even see the hot dog at all. It was just the bun with a pile of relish, onion slices, tomatoes, mustard, and catsup. It was gross.

"And I'm loaded." His eyes sparkled as he grinned. "Althea, how many times do they have these bingo night things?"

"Um, too often," Althea grumbled.

"What was that, dear?" Grandma Horace asked.

"Nothing, Grandma!" she yelled back. Althea turned to us. "Ohmigawd, I'm going crazy."

"Don't look at me," I hissed, staring at my food. "I never said that suffering with you was going to keep you from going insane. Come to think of it, you're already insane. Being here's just redundant."

"Okay, let's go!" Freddie said after taking a gulp of his drink. He pushed his food aside just as the microphone came to life. I turned and glowered at Althea, who shrugged.

"Hey, I can't just take away everyone's fun," she

said, taking up her super bright pink pen. "I don't abuse my powers that way."

I continued to glower at her. "Boy, if your mom could hear you now..."

"All right, ladies and gentlemen," the bingo announcer guy said after gingerly blowing into the microphone. "I apologize for the sudden equipment malfunction, but it looks like we're back in business. Everyone settle down, and we can move on with the next game."

I took a bite of my hot dog. Beside me, Grandma Horace asked, "What did he say? What?" I stared, glassy-eyed, at my food. I hated to admit this, but rubbery hot dogs weren't too bad.

Hayden Thorne

About the Author

Hayden Thorne is a self-professed Anglophile who finds inspiration from classic literature and often sets her historical fiction in 19th century England. Partly balancing this near-idolatrous passion is an equally-gosh-darned-near-idolatrous passion for satire, surrealism, and just plain quirky stuff that makes what she's had for breakfast highly suspect. A former (penniless) college lecturer who taught Freshman English Composition, she's now a (penniless) worker in the fine art industry with a fetish for coming-of-age stories in silk waistcoats and frock coats. She lives in the San Francisco Bay Area with her husband and three cats (all of whom are non-Anglophiles, but she's working on them). For more information on her novels, short stories, and whatnots, visit her website at http://www.haydenthorne.net/.